MADONNA

on the

BRIDGE

A Historical Novel of Courage
by a Circassian Family in World War II

BERT C. WOUTERS

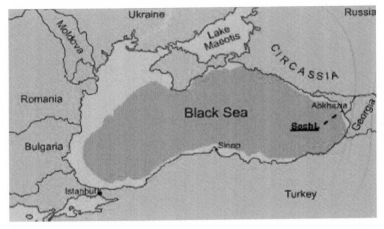

Map of Circassia, Sochi Capital

PRAISE FOR MADONNA ON THE BRIDGE

This story was borne out of the author's own family history, resulting in a passionate personal connection to the storyline. The character descriptions for Danya, Manus and Arie, along with the supporting cast were so visual, so descriptive and by book's end they were like an older relative from 70 years ago. The 10-year story against the backdrop of World War II was suspenseful and captivating. The story plays out in the European countries of Belgium and the Netherlands (Holland), unfamiliar to most Americans. The history of the Circassian heritage was prideful and inspiring. The narrative delivery felt like a documentary account that anchored the story and gave it a deep realism. In a few spots the family sub-plot context vs. geographic location and timeframe in the chronological sequencing was unclear. All taken together, it was a great read and the highlight of this year's holiday inspirations.

—Andy Wilrodt, Moorpark, California

Bert Wouters is a masterful writer! Madonna on the Bridge was a splendid read that will tug at one's emotion by giving a clear and entertaining account of Circassian history, courage and romance all while describing what it was like living under the terror of a world war. The characters were real; the description of places and people clearly written and the drama of individual's struggle for freedom during time of war riveting. This book is a must for those interested in historical fiction, intense drama and personal struggle in times of adversity.

—Dave McCormick, Saint Padre Serra Writers Club, Camarillo, California

Madonna on the Bridge is an unforgettable masterwork of love, espionage and survival, all woven into a very dangerous time in history during WWII. A gripping, historical novel depicting not-so-common personalities in their desperate struggle against a force bigger than themselves. Bert Wouters' novel is a Five Star read, a classic page turner, and a true keeper.

—Georgette Hadvina, Author of By Dawn We'll Be Free.

MADONNA

on the

BRIDGE

A Historical Novel of Courage
by a Circassian Family in World War II

BERT C. WOUTERS

Bert C. Wouters, Publisher

DEDICATED TO THE PEOPLE OF CIRCASSIA WHO LIVE IN THE DIASPORA

Driven from their homeland in 1860 by Russia, the Circassian people in the diaspora remain determined to regain their sovereign right to re-settle in the beautiful region of their ancient ancestors on the Black Sea. The story underlying this work underscores the resiliency of the Circassians to endure hardship, deeply engrained in their fighting spirit for freedom and independence. The novel is dedicated to the unwavering courage of the Circassians to regain their homeland on the Black Sea.

In Madonna on the Bridge, the author portrays a remarkable people, the Circassians, their customs and traditions. In the history books Circassians rarely make it beyond a footnote, despite the critical role they played in the early migrations into the European continent.

Madonna on the Bridge sketches a portrait of a Circassian family in Belgium and the Netherlands (Holland). Chosen by the Allied to play a vital role in the resistance movement of the German occupying forces in Holland during WWII, they succeeded beyond the ordinary in courage. The Allied understood that their courage ran deep in their DNA.

Today, as a people living far from their homeland they have become a mere member of the Unrepresented Nations and Peoples Organization. They hold their spirit of Adighe (Circassian) high in the hope that someday they can go home to the land where their ancestors played a critical role on the old Silk Road. While reading the novel, one will hear the unique Demoiselle cranes beckon the people to return home.

Madonna on the Bridge

Published 2018 by Bert C. Wouters

Camarillo, California

A catalogue record for this book is available from the Library of Congress. Cataloging-in-Publication has been applied for by publisher.

Date of publication: July 1, 2018

Copyright Registration Number TXu 2-038-075 – Effective Date January 08, 2017 – Year of Completion 2016 - Title of Work: Madonna on the Bridge

ISBN: 978-1-54393-849-4 (print)

ISBN: 978-1-54393-850-0 (ebook)

Tracy Marcynzsyn, editor

IN MEMORIAM

Dedicated to Amjad Jaimoukha

Author and publicist Amjad Jaimoukha (Jordan), a prominent specialist on the Circassians, passed away in October at the age of 53. Madonna on the Bridge could not have been created if it was not for the encouragement by Amjad Jaimoukha, who inspired me to write this novel.

Passed away in October 2017.

Dedicated to Harold, veteran of WWII

He fought in the Battle of the Bulge in Belgium. When Harold met the author before he wrote the first lines of this book, he urged: "You must write your remembrance of the war. Soon there will be few left of us … to tell our story." Harold passed away three weeks after he spoke these words.

ACKNOWLEDGMENTS

Estelle, for her patience and unwavering support; Tania, for her encouragement and technical advice on social media; Ton Pelkmans, family archivist for providing details about the characters; Amjad Jaimoukha, who offered insights into the fascinating world of the ancient Circassian beliefs, traditions and customs; Tracy Marcynzsyn, who provided superb editing service, transforming the manuscript into a novel. K. Van Loon, author of Verzet In En Om Dordt (Dutch), who provided in-depth information on the role of double agent Arie; Roger LaManna, for his continuing support as a fellow artist; Writers Group at Padre Serra Parish in Camarillo, for their weekly meetings with messages of inspiration; Dudley Jacobs, who inspired the author from day one to go forward with this project; the Men's Club at Padre Serra for their individual as well as organizational support for this writing; Knights of Columbus, Moorpark Council for their pledge to help promote Madonna on the Bridge.

MADONNA

~ *on the* ~

BRIDGE

A Historical Novel of Courage
by a Circassian Family in World War II

BERT C. WOUTERS

CONTENTS

PROLOGUE

Early in the morning, Kadir walked along the bridle path through a forest of Linden trees. He lived in the mansion located on a vast domain in an upscale suburb near Antwerp, Belgium. The surrounding woods, a large lily pond, manicured lawns, and flowerbeds blooming with roses and tulips reflected the social status of the Mandraskit family.

Every day, rain or shine, Kadir took a walk to meet with the owl, his friend, who was waiting for his step. When the wood owl swooped down in a full circle Kadir raised his ornate cane and tipped his bowler hat, greeting his friend. Making a large loop, the bird returned to the same branch where he had started and let out a loud hoot, his sign of acknowledgment. His big eyes fixated on Kadir, following his every move. The beginning of another day.

For some reason, this day was going to be different. There was no mistaking it; there was no hoot. Instead, it was a gibber sound as if the bird was speaking directly to Kadir. Halting his walk and standing still, Kadir trained his gaze on the owl perched high in the tree. Did he hear the voice of Sergey, his little boy who had died in a terrible accident when he was only five months old? Suddenly, the owl took off, as he heard the name of his young daughter in the distance: "Danya ... Danya."

Kadir's ancestors were from the ancient Circassian tribes, who lived on the shores of the Black Sea. They are the oldest people in the world and called themselves "Adyghas." For millennia, history ignored these primordial inhabitants from the crossing of the European and Asian continents. They played a crucial role as the "nexus people" in the Caucasus Mountains, where civilizations of the Eastern and Western continents intersected, exchanged ideas, and traded products.

In the homeland of Circassia, these unique people developed an elaborate social structure. For thousands of years, they were known for their fierce courage on the battlefield, where women were often the leaders in the battle charges and excelled in heroic feats, as described in the writings of the *Book of Sagas*.

Circassian people are strikingly handsome, and historians often portray the women as exquisitely beautiful and elegant, in the likeness of Queen Nefertiti and Cleopatra.

As the patriarch of the Mandraskit family, Kadir followed the guiding principles and customs of his people, the Circassians, detailed in the *Book of Sagas*. The scribes created the characters with so much detail, they spring to life, despite being incredibly archaic. They embody a treasure trove of ancient mythology, little known by the literary community. Most revered are the sagas of heroes who shared a single mother, the ageless and beautiful Queen Satanaya.

For years, Kadir and his wife, Fatima, grieved over the death of their baby son. With their hopes of passing on their heritage to a son long gone, the couple sought consolation in the famous writings of their ancestors highlighting their heroic feats in the *Book of Sagas*.

One of the sagas gives an account of a mythological bird, an owl, described as the messenger between a dead child and the parents. A small child wandered unattended to a deep ravine and stumbled over the edge to his death in the Kuban River. At the funeral ceremony, people shouted in chorus: "If our lives are short, let our fame be great!" Every time they read this, Sergey's parents paused to think about the broader significance of this mantra.

On the morning that he heard the owl speak to him during his walk, he recalled the sacred writings: "Your boy lived a short life without knowing battle or glory. Remember: 'Let your fame be great.' You are Circassian, and you are endowed with the courage to be the patriarch of a particular family."

Parents continuously instilled courage in their children as part of the core values of the ancestors, to be a warrior to the death in defense of the homeland.

After a long walk in the woods, Kadir concluded that he needed to visit his homeland. He had never traveled to the Black Sea and planned to meet someone he could trust with his feelings, the Circassian way. He resolved to undertake his trip with a mission.

"I will visit Colonel Voroshilov, a relative in Sochi, capital of Circassia. There, in the shadow of the Caucasus Mountains, I will find my calling," Kadir decided. A calm came over him, and he hoped to discuss his destiny soon. He looked forward to being in the forests of the Northern Caucasus, where the ancient people of Circassia held council thousands of years ago.

Commissar Boris Voroshilov was a high-ranking official of the former Circassia Nation, now part of the Soviet Union. He lived on the Black Sea in a dacha. The moss-covered wooden structure looked immense, with huge windows giving a spectacular view of the Northern Caucasus Mountains and the Black Sea.

On the day Kadir left his home in Belgium, he hugged Fatima with a sparkle of hope in his eyes. For him, visiting the land of his ancestors was a lifetime dream coming true. When he looked over Fatima's shoulder, he saw his beautiful girl, his only child and wondered if he would learn about her destiny as a Circassian beauty.

When he arrived in Sochi, the weather was cloudy and drizzling. With its Black Sea location, Kadir had expected sunny weather. It was their first meeting. Voroshilov, dressed in military uniform, proudly displayed two rows of service ribbons on his chest. Heavyset, with dark hair and a Stalin-like mustache and bushy eyebrows, Voroshilov greeted him coolly.

"Welcome. Come in. Finally, I get to meet family from Belgium," Voroshilov began. "In the Circassian tradition, there is nothing more important than to receive a member of the family, even though it has been decades since our families had contact with each other." Kadir's grandfather had escaped with his family to Belgium in 1860, at the height of the Russo-Circassian War. The Russians had systematically exterminated high-ranking aristocracy through execution or expulsion from the homeland.

Kadir, disappointed by his relative's cold demeanor, reminded himself that he was in the presence of a Soviet Union state employee. What Kadir did not know about was Voroshilov's strong allegiance to Circassia. In his heart, he remained a pure-blooded Circassian, despite the Russian occupation. Although he lived in the shadow world of Stalin's Communists, he will always be a descendant of an aristocratic family who had resided in the region for hundreds of years.

Reaching for a bottle of vodka, the host filled two glasses to the rim. As they warmed up to one another, they raised their glasses.

"When Circassians get together it symbolizes the renewal of our bond of loyalty to our people. How is the family?" Voroshilov suddenly changed the conversation. Kadir gave him a brief account of Fatima and Danya.

"Fatima is always busy decorating the mansion with remembrances of the past. She convinced a local sculptor to create a statuette of Satanaya, which sits on the dresser in the foyer. As for myself, the king of Belgium has granted special status as a purveyor of fine jewelry to the royal court. In the process, I have gotten to know King Leopold III and Queen Astrid. They enjoy the elegance of the jewelry produced in Antwerp. My daughter, Danya, is turning sixteen, growing up to be a beautiful Circassian girl. She reminds me of the time when our son Sergey was born." Voroshilov had not learned of the accident.

"What do you mean 'back to when' you had your son? What happened?" Kadir took out his handkerchief, wiping away a tear.

"We lost him in a terrible accident sixteen years ago. It has been hard on us." Voroshilov expressed his condolences. Then, after a pause, he shifted the subject.

"We have some important matters to discuss. Do not let this dacha on the Black Sea mislead you. I live here, thanks to the Soviets. However, I could not care less. It does not belong to me. It is the property of the Soviets. Let us discuss matters of importance to both of us. You must keep our discussion top secret," Voroshilov advised. Kadir reassured the Soviet:

"You have my word of total secrecy, as long as no harm comes to my family. How did you stay out of prison? Was your family also in danger?"

"Fifteen years ago, during a raid, the Soviets imprisoned me. However, something most fortunate happened." He now had Kadir's complete attention.

Leaning back in his chair, he created a big frown between his bushy eyebrows, clenched his fists, and looked Kadir straight in the eyes.

"Let me start from the beginning," Voroshilov began. "Stalin was born and raised in Georgia, a neighboring state to the south of Circassia. One of Stalin's nieces in Tbilisi married my uncle, Nathir. That night a state vehicle called a 'Black

Raven' quietly rolled up the driveway of where my home stood. Dressed in dark trench coats, two men rushed to the front door. They were staff members of the Comintern, the inner circle of Stalin's regime. When I opened the door, they signaled for me to come outside and follow them to the automobile. Ordering me to get in, they drove directly to the federal jail facility.

"When Nathir found out that the Russians had thrown me in jail, he took it upon himself to contact Stalin. Within days, Stalin had issued an order to release me. The agent present immediately came to the point. Comrade Stalin had hand-picked a few local aristocrats as trusted individuals, to become leaders of the new regime in this region. They announced: 'You happen to be one of them,' they informed me." As his anger grew, Voroshilov took another swig of vodka. "Of course, I realized quickly that my family relation with Stalin had played a key role, but the agent did not mention this. He made it clear that I was to become Commissar of the Adyghe Autonomous Region," Voroshilov revealed, looking worried about what he had said and staring at Kadir to see his reaction. Kadir just sat there listening with intense interest, waiting to find out how the story unfolded. Voroshilov needed to make sure that Kadir understood how devoted he was to the Circassian cause.

"Please understand I never renounced being a true full-blooded Circassian. It runs in our genes. Every day I live in fear that the Soviets will find out what I am telling you next. No matter where we make our home, Circassians never surrender their identity to any foreign government. Immediately after my appointment, I started to hate my responsibilities. However, it occurred to me that in my role of Commissar, I had a chance to advance the cause of Circassia becoming an independent nation. In secrecy, I decided to start an underground intelligence network as a countermeasure against future aggression from Germany. I have in mind to deal with the Russians after we settle our account with the hated Germans. Under no circumstances can we allow Hitler to invade and conquer Circassia. The German threat is real, and for now we need the Russians to stand with us in defending our homeland, but just for now. I know that Germany and Russia are in a political game of creating a Non-Aggression Pact, but Germany is our arch enemy." Kadir straightened up and looked at Voroshilov.

"How do you see me being a player in this dangerous world?" Kadir asked. "Belgium has remained neutral for now, not alienating the Germans. Our royal family is of German origin, descendants of the princes of Saxon-Cobourg. I know they have maintained their ties with the aristocracy in Germany since the first King Leopold I ascended the throne in 1830. Some of the aristocrats in Europe are sympathetic to Hitler's policies."

Voroshilov was quite excited to hear Kadir's information, wanting to know more about his royal connection. "My friend, this information is of great importance to me. As you can see, my housekeeper has set the dinner table." Kadir wondered what he had up his sleeve, knowing as he did that Russians prefer to have serious discussions over a glass of vodka. After consuming several drinks, Voroshilov loosened up.

"Look, to show you how confusing the situation has become, two months ago, four Germans paid me an unexpected visit. They made no bones about the intent of the visit. They informed me that they had determined that the Aryan Race had originated here in the Northern Caucasus. I thought it was utter nonsense until they told me about their intent to conduct excavations at our dolmen, our ancestral gravesites. I became outright angry. I have no idea where they came up with the historical evidence showing that there were Aryan settlements in Circassia dating back thousands of years."

Kadir shared his anger. "Are the dolmen sites not considered sacred, as is written in the *Book of Sagas*?" Kadir asked.

Voroshilov, with rage in his face, growled like a bear and pounded his fist on the table. "Of course they are! I objected to any digging around the gravesites of our ancestors, however, to no avail. They threw their official papers on my desk and commanded that I sign them. I looked at the signature on the bottom of the document and was appalled to see Himmler's handwriting. To me, it was an unbelievable sight to see a letter from the head of the SS on my desk. The letterhead showed the swastika and skull and detailed the official authorization order to research evidence of the Aryan Race in the Northern Caucasus, by any means. When they produced another document with the sickle and hammer symbol on the letterhead, it became clear that someone in the Kremlin had authorized a permit to start digging immediately. I was appalled at this turn of events and felt defeated. After two weeks, they returned jubilantly to my office, announcing the results of their digs. They displayed pieces of pottery bearing the swastika symbol. I was about to belittle their finds. Any pottery with swastika symbols found here originated in India and was transported on the Silk Route from Asia. Hitler made the swastika the symbol of German Nationalism. The visiting German researchers seemed desperate to come up with proof of the origin of Aryanism. They aren't aware that Indians used the swastika to signify only 'goodness,'" Voroshilov explained.

"Soon we will find out how truthful they plan to be to this mantra. The use of the swastika is nothing more than a ruse to convince the conquered people that Germany has come as a savior." Voroshilov was anxious to address the true reason for meeting with Kadir. "One year ago, I founded the Adygha Intelligence Organization, headquartered here in my office. Our secret organization consists of a network of intelligence units established in Germany, Italy, France, and Holland. Belgium is particularly important because of its neutrality status in Europe. Collecting intelligence for the Allied is a lot safer than working for the 'Axis Alliance' countries. Kadir, you are uniquely positioned to be our Belgian liaison officer for Adyghe. We know of your unique position with the royals in Brussels. The ties of the Belgian Royal Family with the Germans are well known and are a critical liaison to our intelligence organization," he said, relishing over the possibilities that Kadir presented.

At this point, Kadir was not sure whether he should be worried or flattered by the mention of the royals. He started to sweat heavily, partially from drinking too much vodka, but also out of fear of what he might learn in his role with the intelligence organization. He decided to ask for an explanation of exactly what his role would be in intelligence gathering.

"Why are we, as Circassians, involved in intelligence gathering against Germany?" Kadir asked. "Russia is occupying our homeland now." Voroshilov pondered this vital question before answering.

"Circassians have debated for months about what can be done to start the process of regaining Circassia as our homeland on the Black Sea. Before starting the organization, we realized that if we are to re-establish our homeland, our priority is to keep Germany from occupying our territory. At high-level meetings with Russian officials, I received assurances that an independent Circassia is part of postwar planning. In return, I pledged to share our intelligence data with the Russians. The Russians were anxious to find a spying organization. They explained their reason as follows: In the 1860 war with Russia, Circassians proved themselves as skilled intelligence workers, operating in top secrecy. Stalin himself recognized their unique ability and decorated no less than sixty Circassians with the Soviet Medal of Honor for Bravery. Many of the decorated intelligence warriors were women, who led secret raids and operated with the greatest of stealth. The authorities specified that we must deploy as many of our women as possible in our intelligence gathering."

It became clear to Kadir that Voroshilov had given this matter a lot of thought. He knew he could not return home without committing to help the Adyghe Intelligence Organization. "I will be proud to serve Adyghe in Belgium," Kadir declared. "I expect my influence with the king and his entourage will prove to be helpful." Boris felt satisfaction at his success in convincing his visitor to agree to his plan. Kadir had almost forgotten why he had taken this trip to the Black Sea.

"I came to visit you to discuss my daughter, Danya. She is now sixteen, and I would like your advice on how best to raise her as a Circassian. I cannot imagine a more suitable place to have a heart-to-heart talk with a Circassian still living in the homeland, about a family matter that I am trying to resolve. How should I bring up my girl in the alien world of Belgium and still educate her about our customs and traditions? Will she have the strength to develop as a young woman with the courage of a Circassian? Every day, during my morning walks, I ask myself this question." Raising his right hand, Voroshilov interrupted.

"Look, there is no need to torment yourself about your daughter's future. You suffered the loss of your little boy. However, you have Danya. You have passed your Circassian genes to your girl. Do you remember the story of Satanaya, queen mother of all Circassians? She will grow up drawing on her power, as all Circassians. She You have passed your Circassian genes to your girl. is the progenitor of all Circassians, the original daughter of the oldest descendants of the tribe of Eve. She endows us with our personal values and tradition, with the book of wisdom in one hand and the sword in the other. Trust me, on the wings of Satanaya, Danya is destined to heroic deeds," Voroshilov prophesied. Kadir felt better about his daughter's future.

"When I set foot here in our motherland, I started to feel a special bond to our people and their tradition and principles of life. I am thankful to you for reconnecting me with the mystique of our ancestral lands. You have opened up my heart to the soul of this beautiful region," Kadir told him, wanting to share his own experience. "May I tell you something I experienced back home, during my walk in the forest?"

Voroshilov was curious. "Of course, as Circassians, we are accustomed to sharing our deeper feelings." Kadir expressed his feelings about his lost son.

"In the distance of the woods, I heard Danya's name called as I was reminiscing about Sergey; an owl swooped overhead and perched on a high branch in a Linden tree. Through the owl, I have heard my boy Sergey calling Danya. He will live in my daughter; he asked that I bring up Danya as a courageous Circassian woman, Now I learnt here with you how courage runs through our veins through genealogy," Kadir explained as Voroshilov gazed at him in wonderment.

The next morning, the rain had stopped, but a mist remained. The air smelled like fresh-cut grass. Voroshilov and Kadir rode in silence in the car along a ravine with steep rock formations on both sides of the river a thousand meters high that had been carved out over the millennia by the roaring Kuban River. The morning sun pierced through the cracks and crevices, where moss bedecked the rocks, creating the mystique of the Kuban Valley.

Boris looked at Kadir and could not help borrowing from the Sagas. "Danya will grow up as a girl in whose heart lays the valor of a hundred heroes," Voroshilov said, stopping the car to give Kadir a last look at his beloved Circassia before returning home. In the distance, he saw a flock of Demoiselle cranes flying low over the river. "They are the most endangered cranes in the entire world, found only in the Northern Caucasus. The hundred breeding pairs still found here on the Kuban River carry on to preserve through their genealogy their species of the state bird of Circassia," Boris said with a tear in his eye. As they disappeared around the bend in the river, their sad cries faded into the mists, calling on Satanaya to save them from extinction. Their plea symbolized the call of these unique people who, although lost in history, have never forgotten their dream of returning to the homeland one day.

CHAPTER 1

The Mandraskit Family

IN THE SPRING OF 1935, IN THE TOWN OF BRASSCHAAT, a suburb of Antwerp, the dormant trees came to life. Behind the ornate wrought iron gate stretched a lane of stately Linden trees as far as the eye could see. Like the pillars in the nave of a Gothic cathedral, they stood thirty meters tall and straight, reaching into the heavens. The canopy created a tunnel of foliage so thick it blocked the sunlight in full summer.

To the town's people, the Mansion Adyghe had the mystique of a hidden castle, located at the end of a long tree-lined lane. The sign above the gate entrance displayed a strange looking, but artistically ornate wrought iron cutout with the word "Adyghe" in the center. Symbols surrounded this coat of arms from the "Nation of Circassia" as if it were a consulate. Nobody knew where Circassia was. Few had ever set foot on the domain where the inhabitants lived in their secluded world. People in town had little contact with this mysterious family that lived behind closed doors most of the time.

Antwerp was home to the diamond center of the world, where Kadir Mandraskit was a partner in the diamond brokerage firm Zalinsky & Co. He had made a fortune in diamonds.

Kadir's daughter attended a private school in Brasschaat. Danya was reserved and never spoke of her family. She tried to be congenial but kept her distance from her classmates. With that forlorn and sad expression on her face, she could not bring herself to share her feelings of loneliness with anyone at school. As for any sixteen-year-old girl, not belonging to her age group caused an unbearable hardship.

Her parents often reminded her not to talk to anyone in school about her Circassian background, keeping it a secret. There was no need for outsiders to know they were descendants of a faraway people. They would not understand. However, Danya longed for her family to be like those she saw in town, where everyone seemed to get along so well. Without real friends in her young life, she wondered where she could turn for help with finding her way as a teenager.

That evening, when she returned from school, Danya went upstairs to her father's study, as usual. She liked to talk about schoolwork with him.

When Danya went to bed that night, she could not sleep. Perhaps she sensed that tonight would bring change. Things would be different after this night. She would remember this moment in her life forever.

Nowhere was the quiet more noticeable than in Mansion Adyghe. Tossing around like a rag doll, Danya rolled from side to side, with dreams of flashing images she had never seen before racing through her mind. Finally, she fell into a deep sleep.

In the middle of the night, the song of a nightingale in the forest woke her up with its melody from Toselli's Serenade, which she had heard many times before. In the dark of night, she tiptoed to her father's study on the second floor. All was quiet in the old mansion, except for the tick-tock of the grandfather clock downstairs in the foyer.

She had to open the door without making a noise, so as not to awaken her parents. She entered the room in total darkness, except for a beam of moonlight hitting the walnut paneling in the far corner of the study. She could hardly see where she stepped. Opening the drapes just wide enough to let in a streak of bluish moonlight, she groped around the office in the half dark and found her father's overstuffed leather chair. Sinking into the soft cushions, she felt the warmth and coziness envelope her like a cocoon.

The wood-paneled walls, made from the wood of walnut trees from the Northern Caucasus, cast a feeling of mystery upon the young girl. The dark knots and burls were like strange and shadowy images moving in the forest. The wall panels were so rare that Stalin, the dictator of Russia, placed an embargo on the exportation of this commodity from the Caucasus region.

In the corner of the study, a beam of moonlight pierced through an opening in the brocade drapery, illuminating a deep mountain gorge bounded by a sheer rock wall. The mighty Kuban River rushed the waterfalls in the mountains to the Black Sea. She heard the music of the "Song of the Volga." She saw a tiger, poised to jump from behind a boulder and deer peacefully grazing in the valley. Deeper in the forest, angels floated on clouds of mist. Then, out of nowhere, dressed in a flowing white dress, Satanaya appeared through the curtain of Spanish moss to slowly reveal herself in her full majesty as queen of Circassia.

Danya could not take her eyes from the goddess-like figure slowly emerging into her world of youthfulness and uncertainty. She trembled with exhilaration and reached out to the mysterious figure of her ancestors. "It is you, Satanaya ... the one I have read about in the *Book of Sagas*, queen of Circassia," whispered the young girl.

Slowly, the queen approached Danya, clutching the book of wisdom in one hand and raising the sword in defense of the women of Circassia in the other. Danya succumbed to the spell of the goddess, to which her family belonged, awestruck by her presence.

"So often you are in my dreams. Tonight, at last, you are here with me. I am no longer alone," Danya continued. A shiver of excitement bolted through her young body. Euphoria pushed her into the realm of the queen.

In a deep, mellifluous voice, Satanaya spoke. "Danya, you must trust me. I will guide you with wisdom. I will be by your side to give you the strength to be courageous. From here on, you will no longer be alone. You will witness war and famine, maiming and killing. At the bridge, you will toss your tulips in the bloody river. Have no fear I will make sure you have the courage to stay on the path of your destiny. You will drive out the enemy from your homeland. In the end, the liberating forces will hail you for your heroic deeds. Remember, as a child of the Nation of Circassia, courage is always with you."

With the sound of the nightingale barely audible, the image of Satanaya vanished into the mists of Circassia.

Danya sat quietly, enveloped by the scenery of the forest. She worried that Satanaya was no longer there and tears trickled down her beautiful face, as she sat wondering if it had all been just an illusion. How could she be sure that Satanaya had talked to her?

All remained quiet in the mansion as she returned to her bedroom. She pulled the duvet over her head and nestled in for a good night's sleep, dreaming about Satanaya and her birthday party next week.

On the morning of her sixteenth birthday, Danya woke up to bright sunlight streaming through the century-old Linden tree outside her window. She decided to rise earlier than usual and looked outside at the expansive manicured lawn of the mansion. In the distance, she noticed how the trees were in full bloom. For the young girl, springtime was the most beautiful time of the year. She recalled the fun she'd had during the fall season when the Linden trees sent their winged seeds twirling slowly to the ground like parachutes. Children loved to catch them, and their mothers made a fragrant tea from the seeds.

Danya had anticipated her birthday for quite a while, and she made a special wish. "I want this day to be the best. My friends are coming, and I hope they will not tease me about all the Circassian stuff in the mansion." Her dark hair, olive skin, amber eyes tinged with a flicker of gold, and curly hair as black as a raven's wing gave her an exotic look. The lingering glances the boys always gave her did not sit too well with her friends, out of sheer jealousy.

"Good morning, Danya! It's a wonderful day! Happy birthday!" Her mother rushed in with the unique dress she had picked out for this occasion. It was the traditional costume worn by Circassian girls on their sixteenth birthday. Keeping the tradition going was extremely important to her mother. Danya had difficulty following "old Circassian" customs. Fatima was about to learn Danya's true feelings.

"Mother, I am not wearing that outfit tonight. I know how much you want me to wear this dress, but I have another dress in mind, so I don't look so different from the other girls," Danya insisted. Her mother had seen this coming.

"Your grandmother has sewn this outfit for your birthday party. I wish you would wear it," urged her mother. Danya cared little about being a descendant of a faraway people living on the shores of the Black Sea. She could not understand why all the secrecy surrounded her ancestors.

She started to sob. All this controversy was drawing a dark cloud over this critical day. Her mother came over and hugged her.

"Oh, sweetheart, all right then, wear whatever you want; it's your birthday." Relieved, Danya dressed for school. As she left, she saw her mother standing in the hallway with a handkerchief to her face, wiping away tears. Danya changed her mind. The heartache she was causing was not worth it.

"Okay, tonight I will wear the outfit." She smiled at her mother. All was well for now.

Her mother realized more than ever that Danya was growing up in Belgium, in a different culture. Would she still carry on the Circassian tradition as Sergey would have, had he not been involved in that terrible accident? Fatima wondered.

Throughout the day, Danya had difficulty concentrating on her schoolwork, flashing back to the encounter with Satanaya in her father's office the night before.

Returning to her room, she found the outfit for the evening laid out on her bed. Danya's family was wealthy, and her mother had spared nothing to have her birthday ensemble made by Danya's grandmother with the most delicate material, embellished with ribbons and pearls. Danya had seen pictures of the beautiful girls in the *Book of Sagas* in her father's study. She had adored their elegant costumes. The Circassian dresses enhanced the physical beauty of the girl's body; over the years, these ethnic costumes had become trendsetters in the fashion world. Young girls were required to wear a corset in the form of a short, tight-fitting vest made from red Moroccan leather, worn under the chemise. It served to limit the development of the bosom and was to be removed only on their wedding night.

"What is this for?" Danya asked her mother when she saw the corset for the first time. Her mother was too embarrassed to give her any detail. She took the girdle from the bed without explanation, handing her the tiara made from twisted red velvet and multi-colored ribbons and embellished with silver ornaments. She took a quick glimpse in the mirror. She was happy that she had kept her promise to her mother. She was going to make the most of the occasion, and tonight she decided that she was going to be a Circassian beauty. She put on the green velvet skirt, with yellow panels interspersed in the colors familiar to her. She liked the short-sleeved blouse that showed off the exquisite embroidery with beads and sequins in the colors of the rainbow. I am no longer going to hide my pride in being Circassian, Danya silently resolved.

Around her waist, she tightened her belt with an over-sized silver disk adorned with a purple garnet. She smiled, which brought out the dimples in her face.

"Is this the way Circassian girls are supposed to look?" Danya asked. Her mother looked adoringly at her daughter who had grown into a beautiful Circassian girl.

Danya looked forward to the presents on this particular day. When Kadir saw her beautiful outfit, he was happy, yet sad about how fast she had grown up right under his eyes. He had written her a birthday poem about time flying by too soon. He wanted to write a poem she would remember for the rest of her life.

"I just returned from a meeting at the Diamond Exchange, and I rushed home in time for the party tonight. You look stunning in that Circassian dress. Are you ready for my present?" Kadir asked.

"Let me see it, please! I can't wait!" Danya shouted, excitedly opening the carefully gift-wrapped package. Inside, she found the poem her father had composed, titled, "To My Daughter." He had spent many hours handwriting the rhymes in Gothic lettering on original parchment paper. Dainty graphics incorporating the symbols of Circassia embellished the poetry. He had painted little periwinkle flowers and nesting doves fluttering over the parchment paper. Danya remained silent while adoring the figures. In a quiet voice, she read:

"The moment I laid eyes on you and
Crowned you with your name
I knew my life was different and
Could never be the same
Racing past my eyes
Baby crib to boyfriends."

She paused and hugged her father. "Thank you for putting this poem together," she smiled. "I am sure that I will enjoy the rest of the rhymes on my own." The poem ended with these words, but she did not finish the poetry:

"But the end was just beginning
For you have become my friend!"

The significance of the last lines would become more evident with time.

Her friends would be arriving soon for the party; she had to finish getting ready. She heard her mother calling her from upstairs. Danya entered her mother's boudoir and walked into her mom's outstretched arms, receiving a big hug.

She wondered about the present her mother would give her. As if reading her mind, her mother handed her an ornate dark walnut box, decorated with intricately carved ivory figures resembling Egyptian artwork. Danya opened the box to reveal its red satin lining. She drew in a deep breath and picked up the small white flask.

"Happy birthday, Darling!" her mother exclaimed. "The flask is made from alabaster and has been in our family for hundreds of years. It is traditional for mothers to pass it on to their daughters when they turn sixteen. I know you will take special care of this heirloom." She hugged her daughter and kissed her, watching with joy how Danya admired the beautiful figurine of Satanaya in gold leaf inlay. She recalled a poem from the *Book of Sagas* that the ancient people recited during dance rituals in the darkness of night along the shores of the Black Sea:

> "Like a flower's head held high
> Turquoise eyes shining like stars
> Bearer of gladness and delight
> O life's beauty
> You captivate whoever lays sight on you
> All yearn for you
> You are the youth's undying hope
> Our cherished love."

At the end of the ceremony, each member of the tribe would place a single red rose at the foot of the statue of Satanaya.

Danya's mother told her that the flask contained a perfume made from a mixture of fragrant plants from Socotra, in Yemen. In Circassian folklore, the young girls learned early in life about the "Bottle of Enchantment." They believed the fragrance originated with the Nubian queens of Southern Egypt, who used the perfume to seduce Egyptian pharaohs. The mixture was a tightly guarded secret within the sorority of Nubian beauties, until one day, the Circassians overran the capital of Nubia and stole the secret. From that day forward, Circassian women were not only the most beautiful on Earth; they were also some of the most enchanting, thanks to the secret potent aphrodisiac.

"Is this the perfume grandmother spoke of years ago?" Danya asked. Holding up her hand and looking Danya in the eye, her mother answered solemnly.

"I must ask you to keep this gift a secret between us. It belongs to the sorority of Circassian women. To keep the Circassian tradition, promise not to open this bottle until the time has come. But only you will know in your heart when that day has arrived."

When Danya went to bed that night, she could not sleep. Her mother's words of secrecy puzzled her. What is so special about this bottle that I'm not allowed to open it? Holding the bottle, she considered opening it but decided to honor her mother's wishes. Years later, Danya would learn the power of the fragrance. Exhausted, she laid down in bed thinking about this particular birthday, full of mystery.

CHAPTER 2

A Family United by a Common Bond

IT WAS LATE IN THE DAY, AND THE WIND BLEW HARD. The family sat at the dinner table, and, as usual, Manus was late. There was a good reason for his tardiness. The rain came down in sheets, creating deep puddles. He drove into a ditch while looking at a pair of cows lowing their heads off, complaining about the heavy rain. Manus was the compassionate type, and he wondered if the farmer had forgotten about his animals.

The wind howled with an eerie sound through the narrow street in Mill, Holland, where the Habers lived in a small house. Painted in moss green with white trim, the homes in the little cities of Holland resembled a tableau in a classic Dutch painting.

Manus could easily pass for a second-rate hobo. He was not handsome, but was somewhat odd-looking, with shoulder-length hair covering his slumping shoulders and bushy sideburns. His beady blue eyes, pointed chin, and pouting lips, along with his quarrelsome know-it-all nose, gave him away as an individual in search of something extraordinary. He was determined to find it somehow. No wonder his artsy friends called him a know-it-all; he had a firm belief in himself.

Manus arrived exhausted from pushing his bicycle against the gusting wind. With one hand, he steered his bicycle through the deep puddles while maneuvering his umbrella to ensure it did not flip over with the other. Through the driving wind, he could barely make out the roadway. He had to keep his wet beret from sagging over his eyes. His long hair was dripping wet, but he was okay because he knew that mother was cooking bratwurst tonight.

He had attended another lecture at the Academy for Fine Arts. In his class, only three students considered a future in sculpting. The academy did not spend a lot of time or resources on education for sculptors. They had produced several famous Dutch painters, and this was the discipline they favored.

Finally, he reached his home and parked his bicycle in the courtyard, next to his younger brother Arie's. The back door slammed shut with a bang, thanks to the wind. Manus was soaking wet and starving. He quickly dried off. Shoulders slumping, he saw the negative looks his family gave him. One could not help to notice the comical look on his face. To his family's annoyance, he never seemed to worry about the world. He knew where to find good food. He loved red cabbage, boiled potatoes, and bratwurst. Pulling his chair up to the table to start his meal, he noticed his family staring at him in silence. Arie snickered. Manus looked like a tomcat that had crawled out of a well, dripping wet.

"You know what you remind me of?" Arie chuckled mockingly. "You look like a cat who lost her mouse under the sofa." Manus did not care to answer and started to load his plate with food. Everyone started eating again. Manus knew they had been talking about him. He looked at his mother; she was in one of her dark moods. He blamed it on the four days of rain, which depressed her. Despite being tired from cooking all afternoon, she found the energy to address Manus in a stern, shrill voice.

"How old are you now, Manus? Ah yes, twenty-nine. As if I have to remind you, you are still without a job. You are not bringing in a single guilder, yet, every day, you are here for your meal. Oh yes, you want to be an artist. Let me tell you; there is no money in it." His mother was a stoic individual with little tolerance for dilly-dallying. Manus could not get his brain working under his wet, matted hair. Only warm, comforting food could put his mind back in gear to give an intelligent answer. When mother spoke, no one dared to jump in, either to support what she said or to smooth things over for Manus.

His father also remained silent. He preferred to think matters through before speaking. Antonius Habers had been married for thirty-two years and had a lot of patience; he was gentle and caring by nature, as long as he had his pipe. He talked about his pipe smoking as if it were the medium whereby he gained clarity about the future. His wife, Cornelia, wished he would stop smoking, but now that Manus had taken up the pipe, she knew she had lost that battle. Manus had found a common bond with his father.

He decided to jump in. "Manus, did you understand your mother? You need to earn a wage, and until you do, I agree that we have a problem," his father announced, looking seriously at his son. "I looked through your portfolio of drawings and was impressed with your work," his father told him, boosting his self-confidence. "You show real talent. But talent alone does not translate into money. We need to see some income to support this family." He rose from his chair and put his hand on Manus' shoulder. Manus appreciated that his father stood by him and encouraged him to succeed.

The Academy, where he was a guest lecturer held Antonius in high regard. A master painter in his own right, he often lectured about the Old Dutch painters. His favorite subject was how to translate realism into poetry and splendor.

"Our own eyes are the key to making art our guide and solace, our delight and comfort," he told Manus as a wise father and mentor. Manus stayed behind after dinner with his father. He offered him a wad of tobacco for his pipe as they enjoyed a good smoke. Manus wore a hurt look on his face. His father put his arm around him, and Manus felt encouraged that eventually, he would find a way to make money for the family.

His portfolio contained a large bundle of drawings of Mary and Jesus; his father inquired about his choice of subject matter. He was uncomfortable telling his father that his first love was sculpting. "I'd like to come with you to Saint Anna Church, where you are painting the biblical figures," he told his father. That evening, he joined his father and climbed a tall ladder to the church ceiling. They balanced themselves carefully on the scaffolding and started painting. Manus noticed how the pastel colors, accentuated by solids, brought to life the spiritual aspects of the figures on the ceiling. He wished he could find a likewise style in sculpting to call his own. He knew he had talent in drawing figures, but if he wanted to sculpt, moving from two- to a three-dimensional artwork was essential.

Back home, he began to experiment with a new style. Suddenly, as if he had flipped a switch, he started to create multidimensional figures that sprang to life from the paper, telling a story. He began drawing from his heart.

Manus longed to have a place of his own. Laying on his bed, he searched for his pipe to help soothe the frustration. Resting on his elbow, he searched for the tobacco pouch on the nightstand. The pouch was empty; another reminder that he had no money. Late into the night, he fell asleep.

He woke up refreshed, feeling a renewed zest for life. He was making progress with his drawings and would soon take the plunge and start his very first sculpture. Downstairs, his mother had set the table for breakfast, and Manus helped himself to a cup of tea. He grabbed the daily paper. The headline highlighted Holland's economic difficulties, with a 30% unemployment rate.

As Manus turned to world news, his father came in holding his pipe and pointing to the headline: "Freedom of the Arts under Attack in Germany." Antonius started explaining about the Socialists in Holland.

"The Democratic Workers Party in Holland is in a strong alliance with the Nazis. In Germany, the Nazis issued strict guidelines for the practice of the arts. Under the direction of Hitler, who thought of himself as an accomplished painter, the regime banned all modern styles; only classical styles approved by Hitler were allowed if they exalted the virtues of Aryanism." Antonius kept a close eye on political developments in Germany about the arts. He had several friends that were leaders in the art world who were also Jews.

"I am concerned by these developments in Germany. The Democrat Socialists want to import these restrictions to Holland. I will fight these misguided policies in whichever way I can," Antonius remarked adamantly. Manus set his cup down, surprised at his father's uncharacteristic outburst. Was he still angry over yesterday's discussion or was he going to protect freedom of the arts in Holland? Manus knew his father to be a calm and reasonable person.

Arie walked in, eager to relate the news he had heard at the Police Academy. "Guess what?" he began excitedly. "At the Academy, cadets were talking amongst themselves about German agitators forming secret cells in Amsterdam and Rotterdam to create unrest amongst the population by murdering and plundering. We're going to need more officers to deal with this problem." He looked at Manus and waved his hand. "No, no, no! You would never qualify; this is not for you. You have no idea how dangerous police work can be. Chasing German agitators requires agility, fast thinking, and a willingness to pull the trigger. The agitators are well trained in Germany to become terrorists."

"Well, it's a good thing for men like you, Arie!" Manus said, feeling insulted as he left the house in search of work.

Later that night, the rains had stopped, and Manus came in at suppertime with an announcement. "After listening to father, I decided to stand and fight with him in the resistance," he announced, avoiding eye contact with Arie. Arie looked surprised. Had Manus mentioned the resistance? He found it hard to believe that he and his brother agreed about standing up for freedom.

"You mentioned something close to my heart: fighting," said Arie, putting his arm around his brother's shoulder. "We will make you a real man yet!"

Later that evening, their father came home from his meeting at the Academy, his face revealing deep concern. He hesitated to share his news with the family, but given the perils involved, he could not withhold the information. He took another drag from his pipe and placed it in the ashtray. The family knew he had something important to say.

"During my years as editor of the Academy News, I developed close relations with well-known painters and academicians in Germany; mostly Jews," Antonius began. He showed them the headline he had written three days ago: "Never shall we surrender our freedom in the arts to the Nazis."

"I found out today that three of my closest friends were arrested in Berlin while attempting to escape from the clutches of the Gestapo," he told them. "When they searched them, they found a copy of the Academy News, with my name as editor." The Habers sat silently, staring at the teapot on the table. Antonius was a proud man, and he sat up taller in his chair, looking at his sons as he continued in a determined voice. "The Academy director called me in to reprimand me, warning that he would dismiss me from the Academy as a docent and editor of the Newsletter and that he would not tolerate anyone on his staff to be a 'Jew sympathizer.' I advised him that I had every intention to rescue artists and academicians who came to town persecuted by the Nazis. Right there, the director dismissed me." Despite the challenging economic time for the family, Antonius stood firm in his beliefs.

Manus looked at his father, admiring his courage. His resolve sparked him out of his laziness and prepared him to take action. He needed to find a way to join the fight for freedom of the arts.

The dark clouds of war blew in from the east. Antonius informed his sons that his name was on the German Gestapo's list. It was general knowledge that German agitators in Holland were conducting surveillance on any individual who was an enemy of Hitler. He warned his sons that he was a marked man.

"Once Germany invades Holland, the Nazis will hunt me down," his father warned. "I will be sent to a concentration camp in Germany, unless I take decisive action, like going underground. Otherwise, I will not survive the onslaught of Germans," his father said. His words had the desired impact on his sons, who knew they must protect their family in this hour of threat. "There is no doubt in my heart that both of you will have the courage to fight," Antonius said to his sons. "Once the resistance calls on you, I expect you to serve." He spoke these words with the profound conviction of an individual whose ancestors were known for their heroic deeds. But for now, Antonius was not ready to reveal his actual Circassian ancestry.

The two brothers and their father pledged that they would become freedom fighters in the Dutch Underground if Germany invaded their land. Manus reflected on how his father's dismissal had caused his family to unite around a common cause.

CHAPTER 3

A Rookie Policeman & Two Rabbits

ARIE HABERS' DETERMINATION TO BECOME A POLICE officer was paying off. On this morning, the sun was shining brightly on the narrow streets of Mill, where he would take his first steps as a rookie on foot patrol. The chief assigned Arie to the outskirts of town, where farmers lived, scratching out a living for their families. Word went around that you could smell a rookie because of the glossy shoeshine. The boyish expression on his face was another giveaway. He was well aware of this since senior officers had teased him at the graduation ceremony. He looked at his partner to see if he had the same youthful look, when suddenly someone yelled, "There they are! The new graduates of the Police Academy!" They looked in the direction of the loud noise and grinned bashfully. The voice came from a tipsy derelict with an old bowler hat, swaggering down the middle of the street. Arie was not sure how to take this. He felt better when a few citizens went out of their way to say something nice to them, like "Thanks for stopping by," which was a rarity.

They recalled the oath they took when they graduated: "In partnership with the community, I pledge to protect the lives and property of the people in my jurisdiction." These were strong words for a twenty-year-old boy. The value statement in the oath was every bit as sacred as the three Hail Mary's he recited before soccer games.

To Arie's chagrin, his police work in the community did not take off quite as he had expected. During his first months on patrol, he knew he had to make some adjustments.

Walking the streets in his precinct, Arie was amused to see the same little houses that his father loved to put on canvas in pastel colors; the low-slung thatched roofs with stone chimneys, the little doors, and small windows, and a barn with a few bales of hay. He felt his stomach grumble. It was noontime.

"Are you hungry?" he asked his partner, Jos, who had a funny look on his face and answered in his usual quizzical fashion.

"Remember when we were in training and we asked dumb questions? 'Why do they call it the 4-12 shift if it starts at 3?' 'Why do we have to wear clip-on ties?' 'Where do we stop to find a restroom?' The answers were always the same: 'Good luck, buddy.'" Arie nodded, distracted by the smell of nearby food.

"Do you smell that?" Arie asked.

"How can I not?" Jos replied as the two hungry rookies hastened their steps, following their noses straight to Juintje's house. Arie had met Juintje, aka "little onion," and her husband before he was a police officer. The family grew the finest white, sweet, yellow, and red onions in town. Three times a week, Juintje came to town with her horse and cart, yelling, "Best onions in Holland!"

The front door was wide open, as usual. "I smell rabbit stewing," Arie whispered, peering inside the little home where Juintje stirred her pot. With her spoon dripping with delicious gravy, Juintje waved Arie inside.

"Hey, Arie! You made policeman!" She smiled with the warmth of a typical Dutch farmer's wife. "You come from a family of artists—your father a painter and your brother, well, he's an artist of some kind too. What made you decide to become a lawman?"

"Ever since I was a little boy, I've looked up to policemen. I wanted to be like them," Arie explained. "I like working in the open air; I am more of the adventurous type. I would rather be on patrol than sitting in front of a canvas, smelling paint all day," he smiled. "I smell rabbit in the pot," he added, expectantly. Juintje felt a bit uneasy about having police in the house. She hoped they didn't ask how the rabbit ended up in her cooking pot. There was no need for them to know. She served them each a rabbit leg, which they devoured before leaving to continue their patrol, never questioning how the rabbit ended up in Juintje's pot.

"Do you hear that grunting? Listen, it's coming from over there across the street," Jos said excitedly. Arie heard something more than a "grunt," and they rushed over to investigate the noise, now sounding more like a squeal.

"Let's look behind the shed," Arie directed. "It sounds like a pig in trouble." As they turned the corner, they saw a boy riding a pig.

"Get off that animal and let the tail go!" Arie yelled. "You're hurting the animal!" The teenager yanked one more time on the little tail, causing the pig to bolt like a bucking horse and throw the boy to the ground. Arie grabbed the boy, who smelled like the pigsty where he had been working. Mud was smeared all over him. "If I catch you on that pig again, I'll take you to jail for animal cruelty!" Arie admonished in a stern voice, pointing his finger at the boy's face.

The boy ran into the house. His mother was relieved that the officers had come by to teach her boy a lesson. Arie and Jos took another look at the pig, which looked like it was smiling, or so they told each other.

During one of their patrols, Jos brought up an incident that had occurred when they were in training. The Police Academy operated under strict rules. Still, from time to time, something went wrong. The sergeant in charge of instruction had told Arie to start a fire in the stove every morning to warm up the room, so Arie had to arrive early to get the fire started. One morning after a light snow had fallen during the night and the temperature hovered near freezing, Arie found a few sticks in the wooden box, but they were frozen. Returning to the classroom, he noticed a stack of old newspapers. He quickly read a headline: "National Socialist Movement claims to have answers for economic woes in Holland." Arie shrugged his shoulders, thinking. Here they are with their socialist ideas right out of the mouth of Hitler. He had no time to waste. He crumpled up the paper and stuffed it underneath the frozen sticks. His ingenuity jumped into gear as he thought about how to give the fire an extra boost. Grabbing some brown shoe wax from the cupboard, he smeared it all over the paper and threw two lit matches on the wax. The flames immediately started licking at the damp sticks of wood. It would not be long before the classroom was cozy and warm.

Thinking about the headline he had just read, he spoke a few choice words to the flames destroying the paper. "Here you go up in flames ... serves you right, you socialists." He chuckled at the idea that the fire in the stove was destroying the ideals of socialism. He found some anthracite coal and poured a bucket over the fire. As the fire began to roar in the stove, the room quickly warmed to a comfortable temperature. A few minutes into the first class, the instructor noticed flames coming from the pan under the stove. Arie knew immediately the mistake he had made. He had used too much shoe wax, and it had caught fire. After class, the instructor told Arie that his error could have been costly, burning the entire building. Arie mumbled an embarrassed apology and left the building.

"How did it go?" Jos, who had waited for him, asked.

Arie sort of ignored him, before answering boastfully. "Would I do it again? Heck, yes, with a little less shoe wax." Jos snickered when he heard the story.

It was now spring, another beautiful sunny day. They were on bicycles today and began their patrol in the early morning, heading towards the outskirts of town. Arie and his partner became a familiar sight, and when they had a flat tire on their bicycle, people would lend them a hand. To Arie, it was somewhat of a revelation to see the many people who liked them as police officers. In neighborhoods with little crime, the police were part of the scenery, and most people greeted them as if they were one of them. Arie remembered how he used to look up to police officers when he saw them.

"I noticed policemen like I saw mailboxes," he told Jos. "…until I needed to ask for directions or something." Jos said he had the same experience. They both chuckled at the word "mailboxes." Arie realized how much the police were now appreciated, primarily by the elderly, young children, single women and people dressed for work or church. They looked at him with thankfulness, seeing him as a protector against lawbreakers.

During his patrols, Arie had plenty of time to think about his role in the street. When he started out as a policeman, he understood that his primary purpose was to enforce the law. With time, he found a measure of kindness for derelicts and delinquents, inherited from his father.

Things were now different than they were in the beginning when he had reacted in a commanding voice to anyone who complained or challenged him: "It's my job to show up here. Relax; maybe in a week or month, you will have found a reason to love or hate me, but for now, you don't know me."

Arie dutifully reported to his sergeant on duty following each patrol. He quickly excelled in taking accurate statements, making realistic drawings of crime scenes, capturing circumstantial evidence, and more. His sergeant was impressed with his reports. It became clear that Arie was destined for more than just a street patrol officer.

Illegal sale of liquor was high on the crime list. Police were under orders to bring this matter under control. Every night the jail filled up quickly with drunks. Citizens resorted to heavy drinking, seeking relief from the misery of the difficult economic times. In the districts outside town, many of the small homes had a small plot behind the house, where the farmers grew potatoes, carrots, onions, cabbage, and string beans. Those who were a little better off might have a pig or a few chickens in the yard.

Poachers and trappers did their best to evade police. As the result of the economic hardship and poverty, people plied their trade of poaching out of sheer necessity rather than for the thrill of the hunt. Many officers would like to look the other way when faced with poaching, but in the eyes of the authorities, tolerating this activity of killing wildlife without a permit was not an option despite the bounty of wildlife.

Three days had passed without any significant events. Arie and Jos ventured towards the outskirts of town again. On this day they went on bicycle to the outskirts of town, into the woods thick with underbrush. It was late in the afternoon as the sun set in a blaze to the west. In the distance, Arie saw movement in the undergrowth; without speaking, he signaled to his partner to follow him quietly, avoiding sticks and rocks on the dirt road.

"I am sure there is a trapper in the woods," Arie cupped his hand and whispered. Jos was not as anxious to proceed as it got dark, preferring to let it go.

"Come on, why bother some poor soul who is trying to catch dinner for his family? Yes, I know it is against the law, but God knows how many mouths he is trying to feed," Jos answered. Arie was more concerned with impressing his sergeant than becoming emotional.

"I understand your concern. If you are going to make it as a good officer, we may as well start here," he countered. Jos struggled to continue down the dirt road, not wanting to abandon his partner in case there might be trouble.

Knol Brandts was a scruffy-looking forty year old, with a dirty beard and baggy clothing. All his life he had been a trapper, a trade he had learned from his father. He had spotted several rabbit holes and was an expert at finding recent activity. It was there that he set his snares. The two police officers moved slowly through the woods without making a sound until they were a few meters from Knol. He looked up from setting another snare, quickly dropping his wire cutter. His wry smile revealed his mischievous character. For years, he had managed to elude the law. He cursed himself for his stupidity at getting caught by two rookies.

Arie saw the head and front paws of a dead rabbit sticking out of his pocket. In the other pocket, he kept his hand over something still quivering and struggling. "What are you hiding in your left hand?" Arie asked him.

"You two are too green to see what I have in my pocket," Knol told them.

"Show us your hands!" Arie demanded, his voice rising.

The old man showed them another rabbit, barely alive with a mangled leg, ensnared by a trap. The little animal struggled to get free. Arie could not stand the sight of the bleeding creature and commanded Knol to put the animal out of its misery. In one swift motion, Knol drew his butcher knife and slashed the throat of the animal. Then problems started. Brandishing his knife, he turned on the officers.

"Get out of here you rookies!" he shouted angrily. "Do you see this knife? You are not going to take me to jail!" Arie felt a shot of adrenaline coursing through his veins as he tried to manage his anger. As if in unison, they lunged forward at the poacher, who turned quickly and began running. The race to capture him was on. Remembering his high school record for the 100-meter sprint, Arie ran fast, catching the old man without difficulty. The pair walked him to jail in cuffs. A couple of times, between cursing, he spat at the officers.

That evening while Arie worked on his report, he reflected on the case and knew it could have turned out very different if Brandts had been successful with his knife. Catching some crazy trapper with a knife was not in the manual he had read while at the Academy, and Arie was disappointed that he did not feel satisfied with this kind of police work. Had he not learned that he would experience adjustment of expectations during training? That night he thought about his career as a police officer.

"They had to sew his ear back on" was the description Arie heard in the Mill Police Department. A report came in late that Sunday night about a significant disturbance in the district east of town. Arie and Jos were on duty.

The Bierens were a hard-working family. Sadly, they had no luck with their daughter. If the town of Mill were ever to hold a contest for the ugliest girl, the winner in this district would be Belle, the oldest daughter of the Bierens family. With her close-set and beady eyes, nose like a potato, small mouth with crooked teeth and protruding lower jaw, she was no beauty. She was flat-chested and had scraggly red hair. No boy in town would lay his eyes on her, and they all joked about her appearance. Until one day, she met Frans Dries, a twenty-two-year-old weaver.

Belle's parents had told their daughter to stay away from Frans. He had run up a conviction for stealing chickens, for which he had served six months in prison. They had hoped their daughter would end the relationship at once. Nevertheless, Belle saw in Frans her last chance to find a partner, and she would not hear of abandoning her Frans.

"I will not break up with Frans," she made clear to her father. "Where am I going to find another boy?" Her father looked her up and down, shaking his head.

"I agree with you," he told her. "With that kind of body, you are better off not being married. However, no matter how desperate you are, do not stoop this low, going out with a chicken thief."

That Sunday evening, Frans showed up at the Bierens' farmhouse after Belle's parents had gone to sleep. He knocked on Belle's bedroom window; after a few minutes, she came outside.

"I am afraid to tell you, my father no longer wants us to be together," Belle tried to explain in a hushed voice. Frans flew into a rage, flailing his arms and jumping up and down.

"What? You listen to me!" he shouted. "You're fortunate to have me as your boyfriend ... who else would go out with you? Tell your father that we stay together. I do not care if he is angry with me." Tears rolled down her cheeks, as she looked away from Frans.

Her father appeared, grabbing her by the arms and swinging her around towards him. "As for you, young lady, you go inside!" her father commanded loudly, pointing towards the back door before suddenly lunging at Frans and pushing him into the street.

Shortly after, Frans returned with a knife, attacking Belle's father as he sat in the dimly lit kitchen. Her father was surprised to see Frans wielding a large knife in front of his face. It was over in a split second. Frans managed to cut the tip off his fat potato nose, picking up the missing body part and running outside in jubilation.

Arie arrived at the crime scene first and helped Bierens with his bleeding nose. Once in a state to talk, Bierens told him to go after Frans.

"Now, go and catch him; he is drunk and has a sharp knife on him." Arie caught up with Frans, took the bloody stump of the nose from him, and returned it to the owner. Doctor Smit, who lived on the same street, stitched the missing part back on. Bierens thought long about the incident as he looked every day at his sadly aggrieved daughter.

At the wedding of Belle and Frans, six months later, father Bierens thanked Arie for his quick action in returning the tip of his nose.

During his first year as a police officer, Arie found some appeal to police work: the spontaneity and variety, picking up a criminal, the pursuit on foot, and intervening in disputes. He had learned to lend an ear to people's hardships: robberies, beatings, heart attacks. When he had to deal with someone who had died in the house, he had a hard time getting used to the stillness of the body; it transfixed him. In the living organism, he saw at least a rhythm, shaking or trembling.

Being present in life and death situations was all part of his job to become a good lawman. But something was missing. At night, when he went to sleep, he had recurring dreams of doing more, like fighting for freedom. His father's words lingered: "There is no doubt in my mind that my sons will have the courage to fight to the death for the ideals of freedom. Once the war starts and the resistance calls on you, I expect you to serve. The blood that courses through our veins is Circassian. In due time, you will find out about your ancestors, a special people. At that time, you will better understand why you have courage in your genetic make-up." Arie became restless, wondering when that time would arrive to understand his family heritage more fully.

CHAPTER 4

Himmler's Professor

THE TWO CHILDREN BROKE OUT IN SONG, MOCKING the fascists of Mussolini, "The Macaronis of Italy," that they'd heard on the BBC. Anxiously, their young mother looked around to assure herself that nobody was listening to their singing. Anyone who listened to the lyrics on the radio by the British Broadcasting Corporation in London knew what the words meant. However, they had to be careful with any display of anti-fascism in Holland. German infiltrators were becoming bolder in harassing people in the open. Despite the risk, the Dutch could be heard whistling the tune while walking down the street or riding the tram.

The German government had no qualms in making it clear that they financed the National Socialist Bond (NSB) in Holland. The organization received thousands of guilders to support their clandestine operation, with the aim of subverting Holland's legal government. As the NSB grew more aggressive, increasing incidents occurred. Beyond mere verbal altercations, beatings and murders were now becoming a daily occurrence. Their purpose was to create unrest in the country so the general population would then perceive the government as weak and incompetent against anarchism. They would eventually demand law and order—the same strategy that had worked for Hitler.

Pope Pius XII had not yet publicly condemned fascism, and the Catholic Church in Holland tacitly tolerated a fascist regime.

As she anxiously looked around to see if her children's song had offended any pro-Germans, she was relieved to see only reassuring passengers. The tram riders covered their faces to suppress snickers at the innocent display of mockery by these children. They gave the mother a friendly wink and went on with their journey.

Willem van Lansfoort, sitting opposite from her in the tram, also smiled and quickly nodded, signaling he had recognized the song and that all was well. Yet, he was deeply concerned about the future of these children. The danger of a German invasion loomed larger every day. He feared that the threat was not somewhere in the future. Willem had strong feelings about the impending war but kept his thoughts to himself.

The invasion of Holland is now more likely than ever before … it may come sooner than these people realize, and we have no defense against their Panzer divisions, built during the last decade, despite the prohibition under the Treaty of Versailles. He had become a member of the intelligence division of the Dutch Armed Forces, thanks to his relationship with Prince Bernhard of the Netherlands, with whom he had been friends since his golfing days.

Willem was born with the proverbial silver spoon. His father, R.J., had served as mayor of Amsterdam and was now running a major financial institution. Queen Wilhelmina had appointed him as governor of the Royal Court. The family lived in a castle on the outskirts of Amsterdam. At a young age, Willem had shown great interest in playing golf, a sport reserved for the upper class. He earned the title of Junior Golf Champion of the Netherlands at the young age of 15.

The van Lansfoort family belonged to an elite organization of Circassians, which they kept secret from friends and associates. Their pledge demanded that the family patriarch maintain secrecy about their offspring. Their ancestors came from the Black Sea and the Caucasus Mountains. Being Circassian meant that Queen Satanaya was their primordial progenitor, the most ancient ancestor.

Willem, in his early twenties, came to the realization that banking was not in his future. He set out to explore a career in something more exciting than living in an office. His parents were concerned that their son started life out as a carefree youngster, interested only in golf.

R.J. showed on Voroshilov's list when he recruited him in the previous year to join the Adyghe Intelligence Organization. His assignment had to remain top secret, even from his family. Voroshilov confided that there was also an Adyghe Intelligence network in Germany which had spearheaded the most recent plot to murder Hitler. One of the key members was a mysterious professor who served as a principal advisor on Himmler's staff. Voroshilov had shared his name with R.J. Written communications within Adyghe network were prohibited. Only telephone contact could be made over a secure line. The code name for telephone contacts was "Ma'anata" (Eagle in Circassian). The language used over the telephone was "Adyghe." R.J. had only a marginal knowledge of this complicated language. For the mysterious professor, Adyghe was one of the exotic languages he had mastered during his time in service to Nicholas II, Czar of Russia. Voroshilov had recommended him to R.J. as a teacher of the Adyghe language, but he had not gotten around to contacting him.

R.J. decided it would be a good idea to send his son Willem to Nüremberg to see Hitler deliver a speech to the people. It was not going to be easy to get Willem a pass to the convention. However, he decided to give the professor a call. Remembering the codename Ma'anata, he introduced himself as Gustav von Habers, Professor at Gottingen University, a hotbed of occultism, favored by Hitler. Here, R.J. learned that he had been appointed to Himmler's Supreme Council on Purity of the Aryan Race, the organization responsible for the execution of orders to annihilate Jews, Gypsies, and Eastern Europeans, part of Hitler's Final Solution. However, the professor was a traitor who belonged to the high-ranked German officers who formed the plotting committee to kill Hitler. Obviously, Voroshilov in Sochi had pulled some strings in this complex network. As they approached the end of their phone conversation, he suggested to R.J. that they meet some day in Eschelbach, a short distance over the border between Holland and Germany so he could introduce him to Gertle von Habers, whom he described as an exciting character. Not much else was shared about Gertle.

"I shall be delighted to receive your son, Willem, in Nüremberg," the professor agreed. "We will go to the Convention Hall to hear Hitler give his speech. If luck is on my side, I may introduce Willem to Himmler." R.J. could not have been more astounded by the conversation. He delivered the news to his son with a dose of excitement beyond his wildest dreams.

At the train station in Amsterdam, Willem bought his ticket for Nuremberg. The train made an intermediate stop in Frankfurt where he got his first glance at the real Nazi Germany. Two members of the Gestapo seated themselves opposite him in the first-class compartment. They were exactly as he had pictured the Aryans: blond hair, blue eyes, and swastika armbands on their leather jackets. What really caught his attention was their brand new heavy black boots, ready to crush anything that got in their way. Were the SS already following him, after he barely crossed the border into Germany?

When he glanced at the headlines in the *Frankfurter Zeitung* newspaper the SS man was reading, a cold chill rolled up his spine. On the front page, in bold letters, it read: "Fuhrer to address Nazi Party in Nuremberg." Unsure whether the SS had noticed the surprise on his face, he recovered as much as he could. They looked him over in some form of nonverbal interrogation and ignored him for the remainder of the trip.

He must keep his composure. Then curiosity about Hitler took over as he thought about going to see and hear this lunatic rave and rant about the Jews and Nazi supremacy policies. He had heard Hitler so often on the radio. Now he would see and listen to him in person.

He anticipated seeing him on stage pounding his little fist on the lectern. The caricatures of Hitler he'd seen in the Dutch newspapers came into his mind: Hitler practicing his speech in the mirror, admiring the subtle quiver of his mustache. Another newspaper picture showed him standing on stage wearing nothing but shorts and suspenders embroidered with tiny swastikas. They spoke of his squeaky voice making his point about wiping the flotsam of human undesirables from the face of the Earth.

Riding through Germany, Willem was aghast at the lines of swastika flags waving from buildings and homes. How could it be that so many Germans had fallen for this dictator and elected him chancellor? A long line of Mercedes-Benz taxis waited for passengers. Willem took the first one and directed the chauffeur in perfect German to drive to the Kaiser Wilhelm Hotel. Large flags adorned the front of the hotel. It took no time to locate the monocled Professor Gustav von Habers in the lobby. With his massive mustache and unruly hair, he had to be the professor. He held a glass of Schnapps in his hand as he kept an eye on the front door. As soon as he recognized Willem, he walked straight to him.

"Welcome, welcome, Willem!" he shouted. "How was your journey from Amsterdam?" While Willem wanted to recount the scene in the tram in Amsterdam, he decided against it.

"Fine, very uneventful, although the weather was dreary and overcast, not offering a good view of the German landscape," Willem answered, holding back his comments he really wanted to make about the abundance of flags waving at him from every structure.

"How is your father?" von Habers asked eagerly. "How is the banking business? I heard that Holland is coming out of the recession in good shape."

"Father is doing quite well, and he continues to devote a lot of time to his work."

"Is it true that you hold the title of Dutch Junior Champion in golfing?"

"Let's say that I was lucky on the golf links." As Willem talked a little about the game of golf, it quickly became evident that the professor had never held a golf club. It would be wiser not to continue this line of conversation. Willem knew that von Habers was a real expert in foreign languages, mainly Adyghe.

The next day Hitler arrived in Nuremberg, and Willem and von Habers decided to take a stroll to the Conference Hall where the Party Congress would take place. During their walk, the professor offered him a cigar. Willem declined. With a broad gesture, the professor announced that he wanted to share something of great importance.

"Willem, you may know that your father and I have a common ancestry, which goes back hundreds of years. We are Circassians. Because of our origin, we are uniquely qualified for clandestine intelligence work. For this reason, we have chosen to stay in the shadow of world history." Willem listened quietly, impressed by his company.

"Recently, I have thought a lot about my future," Willem told him. The professor had been waiting for this opportunity.

"You made a success in playing golf. What is the one thing you would like to do in life after golf?" the professor asked him.

"I would like to be in a job that is exciting, such as traveling. I am not sure that I can find work in that line. I respect my father's advice; he would like me to enroll in the military. My friends are less enthusiastic about the idea. Maybe once I can show them what my plan is, they will see it my way," Willem shared.

"Now you are making progress," von Habers continued. "To fill you in on something important like joining the military, I suggest you consider intelligence work. Here lies some interesting work for you with travel opportunities. I would like to recruit you in our Adyghe Intelligence Organization. To make it more exciting, consider serving in a dual role, intelligence work for the Dutch Armed Forces and working for the Circassians at the same time. You could call it being a double agent. You will find that we have parallel goals. You will not be alone ... we will stand by you as a brother-in-arms, in the way of the Circassian brotherhood. Give it some serious thought." He looked Willem in the eye and noticed a smile on his face.

"I will rush home to tell my wife!" Willem answered excitedly.

"From now on, remember that your involvement in intelligence comes with secrecy—no sharing of information with relatives, even your wife," von Habers said sternly.

The next day Willem arrived back in Holland on the 10 a.m. express train from Nuremberg. The train arrived ten minutes late in Amsterdam Central Station. The shrieking noise of the train's brakes pierced the foul-smelling air, stopping the train just in time to avoid a collision with the hydraulic arrest bumper.

When it rains in Holland, it always feels wetter than it does anywhere else on the continent. Outside the train station, he waited for quite a while in the drenching rain for streetcar number 7. The tram took him to his home situated along one of the picturesque Amsterdam canals. His heart beat faster in anticipation of returning to his beautiful wife, Annette. The memories of Hitler's fiery speeches peppered with vitriolic overtones of Aryanism and hatred toward the Jews the previous day were still drumming in his head. With their right arms outstretched towards the Fuhrer, as though in a gesture of adoration to the Teutonic deity of Adolph Hitler, the crowd had shouted in endless cadence: "Heil Hitler! Sieg Heil!" Willem had stood out in the group for not raising his arm. How had this lowly corporal from Austria managed to become this Aryan deity?

Riding home in the tram, images of the frightened mother and her two children came back to him. War was not too far off. The stage was being set for an invasion of Holland. Holland was still a free and neutral country, and maybe it was not too late to take action.

In the fading sunlight, the sky displayed a spectacular scene of many colors of red and purple in the evening horizon, as if serenading the fall season. The colors in the leaves along the canals were preparing for that beautiful tapestry of yellow, red, and brown.

This is my country, free and colorful, just like in the paintings of our famed painters. No Hitler is going to take that away. It will come to our commitment and willpower to stay free, Willem thought. As he exited the tram, he was unable to shake the image of the young mother and her children.

We must protect our children's future, he thought, cementing his resolve to keep his country safe. A week later, he joined the Dutch military, but he was not sure how to share his decision with his wife.

Annette was happy to see her husband return from Germany. She rushed to the door, anxious to embrace Willem as he arrived home. Immediately, she noticed he had something on his mind. He was not his usual jovial and relaxed self. She saw in his eyes a man with a mission. Their little dog Skippy came over for a quick hello. Willem bent down to pet the little Schipperke. He wanted to tell her all about his adventure in Germany, Hitler speaking in Nuremberg, and his meeting with von Habers.

As darkness settled over the city, the gas stoker came by to light the street lamps, one by one. Willem struggled to find a way to tell Annette that he had decided to join the military. "After I listened to Hitler's speech, I made the decision that I must do something to help preserve our national freedom," he began. "The invasion of Holland by the Germans is closer than we think." He told her about the children singing on the tram. "Seeing the children singing taught me an important lesson. I cannot wait to enlist in the Dutch Military. I must join the fight so these children will live in a free country." Annette hugged him. She noticed his determined look. She was in awe.

Together they walked to the far wall in the drawing room, where a line of fading sunlight hit an antique framed document bearing the coat of arms of the van Lansfoort family. It was dated 1589. It had been in the family for hundreds of years. They had never paid much attention to it before. Now, Willem stepped close to the picture, and he fixated on the ribbon on the bottom of the document, bearing the family motto: "Courage is Victory over Fear."

"Now I know that I made the right decision," he said.

Annette wiped a tear from her cheek, looked at Willem, and put her head on his shoulder as he held her in an embrace of endearment. She knew him well enough to understand that he wanted to live by the family code. Now she was the wife of an officer in the Dutch Armed Forces and became fully aware that he would find himself in harm's way. Underneath the ribbon in the coat of arms was the symbol of the Circassian Nation with "Adyghe" printed in the original language.

CHAPTER 5

Death of the Queen

A CLOUD OF MIST RUSHED INTO THE HALLWAY AS HE opened the front door of the mansion. Kadir Mandraskit picked up the newspaper, soaked from the morning rain. It was a dreary-looking day. He spread the paper out on the kitchen table to let it dry. When he looked at the front page, a large border in black ink struck him like a bolt of lightning. He did not need to find his reading glasses. The headline in bold letters read: "Queen Astrid of Belgium Dies in a Motor Vehicle Accident in Switzerland." Kadir's world came to a sudden halt. In shock, his eyes would not let go of the front page. He looked at the picture of the queen, wearing her diamond and sapphire necklace, with matching earrings. Had the accident occurred while she was wearing this jewelry that he had personally designed for her?

"This cannot be true," he whispered. He desperately wished that it were different. The news hit him like a rock. "No, this cannot be true." He looked around for Fatima, who was still upstairs getting ready for the day.

Queen Astrid was adored by young and old for her beauty, charm, and simple lifestyle, qualities rarely found in European royalty. She lived with King Leopold III in a small villa on the palace grounds in Brussels, where she prepared the meals for the king and their three young children. National newspapers often featured photos of the queen taking a stroll with her children along Avenue Louise in Brussels. The press followed her daily life and, as the Belgians read the captions like "Princess of the People of Belgium," they were instilled with immense pride in their small nation. Finally, as was the case in so many European countries, the Belgians had their own royalty with whom they could identify.

Belgium experienced the difficulties of the worldwide economic depression as so many countries throughout the world, and the queen wanted to do something about it. She genuinely cared about the plight of women, children, and the disadvantaged, writing about it in an open letter to the people titled "The Queen's Appeal."

Especially the young people in Belgium had found their idol in Queen Astrid. For Danya, she was extra special. Queen Astrid was more than just a queen. She had come to Belgium as a foreign princess that had married a Belgian prince ten years earlier. The queen was born a Swedish princess and Danya often wondered why the people of Belgium liked her as one of their own. Danya herself felt like a foreigner and was treated as an outcast in school. Jealousy often crept into the ridicule behind her back. Her loneliness caused her many restless nights. For sure, she was pretty with her curly dark hair and beautiful eyes. So, the queen was unique to her; how had she managed to become so adored by a foreign people? And so, she became Danya's only friend. Someday she hoped that things would change in school and that she would be included in the circle of favorite girls.

She remembered the day her father received an urgent call from Dierk de Jong, adjutant to King Leopold. "I am contacting you as a global diamond trader. I wonder if you could be of help to the royal family. The king wants to surprise the queen with a beautiful diamond necklace for their anniversary." Kadir was the right man to contact for such an order. He had the exclusive distributorship in Belgium with the world-famous diamond firm De Beers in South Africa.

Kadir immediately arranged for a dinner meeting at Restaurant Rubens in Brasschaat. He had invited the king's adjutant and requested that he bring along a rendering of the necklace, embodying the wishes of the king. When Kadir mentioned how much Danya adored the queen, the adjutant insisted that she come along. In the back of the restaurant was a room reserved for private meetings.

Once they settled in, Kadir was eager to show the selection of diamonds from the vault at his firm. He retrieved an ornate leather pouch from his inner pocket and let the diamonds roll slowly from the pouch on the black velvet cloth, spread out under the bright light over the table. Large and small diamonds sparkled as they reflected the brilliance in each facet. Mixed in was a deep blue sapphire. For Kadir, this was like a ritual he had carried out so many times before, with the aplomb of an international diamond trader. de Jong was impressed with the display of glitter and glimmer. For young Danya, seeing her father at work as a global diamond broker was a first. Her eyes reflected the sparkle of the jewels displayed on the table.

"Can I take a closer look at the sapphire?" she asked, tilting her head and smiling. "May I pick it up and look at it more closely?" Her father nodded and placed the precious stone in her palm. She felt like a grown-up, no longer the child of yesterday. This particular moment in the relationship between father and daughter did not pass without notice by the adjutant. The jewel she held was destined to become the centerpiece of the queen's necklace. de Jong gave his stamp of approval on the plan for the necklace design.

"The king will be pleased with the jewelry you are creating for the queen. Just imagine how the sparkle in the sapphire will match the beauty of the azure color in the eyes of the Swedish-born princess." Danya could not take her eyes from the brilliance of the sapphire she had held in her hand minutes earlier. She must hold on to this experience forever; none of her schoolmates had such a memorable moment to relish for the rest of their lives. In this way, she could claim her own connection with the queen.

In August 1935, the king and queen left incognito on holiday for a trip to Switzerland. At the end of the day, they went for a ride in the mountains before returning for the night. While the king drove their Packard One-Twenty convertible, the queen looked at the map of Lucerne, where they were staying. She told the king to take a left turn in the road, destination Kussnacht am Rigi. The car swung around an unexpected large boulder that had fallen on the roadway. The king lost control as the vehicle careened off the road and down a steep embankment, where it slammed into a tree. During the fall, the queen opened the door to try to escape, but the impact ejected her with force. Her body collided with the trunk of a huge pine tree. The car rolled down the steep hill to plunge into the lake below. Despite his injury, the king managed to rush down to the queen, but it was too late. She had died instantly on impact. He knelt next to her, holding the lifeless body in his arms. The queen, pregnant with her fourth child, died from her injuries in Kussnacht.

Kadir saw his little girl happily hopping down the staircase, as she did every morning. Suddenly, she stopped in her tracks and looked at her father, seeing a tear trickling down his cheek. She had never seen him like this before. He was always the influential figure in her life, not quickly giving in to emotion.

"What's wrong?" she asked with widened eyes. Arms outstretched he approached her. He wanted to hug her, but she gently pushed back. She looked into his eyes and asked in a worried tone of voice: "What happened, Father? Tell me." Thoughts of bad happenings started to uncontrollably spiral through her young mind. Without speaking, he took her hand and gently guided her to the kitchen table with the newspaper spread out. When she read the headline, embossed with the heavy black border, she understood immediately why her father was so distraught. He lifted the paper from the table, where it fell limp, damp from the rain. He tried to stretch out the newspaper, but it tore in half. The headline jumped off the page like a thunderbolt. There was no doubt about the graveness of the tragedy. Danya only saw the headline. She turned away from the kitchen table, covering her face with both hands.

"Why is she gone? Where did it happen?" she stammered, sobbing. It felt like a boulder had crushed her. In a flash, she turned around, heading for the stairs; she wanted to flee the scene of the accident. "I will never see her smiling face again!" she screamed angrily at the top of her lungs. She rushed upstairs to the solitude of her room. Lying in bed, looking through the window, Danya stayed awake with the memories of Astrid's sapphire spiraling through her mind. She wished desperately that it could be different. All she wanted was to be alone in her room with her grief and anger. It was raining outside. If the sun had been shining, she would have been mad. She jumped up from her bed, and angrily stomped to her dresser where she kept a picture of the queen. With both hands, she firmly grabbed the frame with the photo of the queen. She raised it to smash it on the floor. Before doing so, she took a final look, to bid her goodbye. With her eyes glazed over, she spoke to her queen for the last time with a simple word, "Goodbye." Why keep this picture? I will never see her smiling face again.

At that moment, her mother entered the room. Danya

felt ashamed about what she was planning to do. Her mother hurried over and took the picture from her. When her mother looked at Danya, she saw anger she had never seen before. Danya had hoped that her parents would never see her like this. Her mother placed the picture frame back on the dresser.

"Just tell me it is not true. I do not want to hear anything else," Danya pleaded. Her mother seated herself on her bed. Deeply concerned with Danya's reaction to the sad news, she tried to embrace her, stroking her hair as if she were still a little girl.

"Everything is going to be okay," her mother soothed. However, Danya did not hear her words; nothing eased her sorrow. At last, she dried her tears and found a few words to explain her grief.

"It is so difficult to tell you how I feel. The queen was my world, my idol." Looking away from her mother, Danya started to talk about her schoolmates. "I am looked at as different," she said in a low voice. "When I am alone I cry a lot." She explained the connection she had felt with the queen.

"I loved the queen because she was my only hope that things might change at school," Danya shared. Fatima felt the bitter hurt her daughter had been enduring since the queen had died; she wondered if they should not have hidden their Circassian heritage.

Fatima mentioned the funeral service in Brussels. However, Danya was too absorbed in the tragedy of the accident to listen to her mother. Royalty and dignitaries from Europe and around the world attended the funeral service at Sainte Gudule Cathedral in Brussels. Kadir, Fatima, and Danya sat in reserved seats behind the rows of dignitaries. The choir performed the famous "Missa Rosa" composed of four voices. At the end of the mass, eight men carried the flag-covered coffin to the hearse as the choir sang "In Paradiso." It was a fitting tribute to a queen adored by all. The hearse, drawn by six Brabant horses, carried the coffin through the streets. The Flemish and Walloon people, often at odds over politics, stood shoulder to shoulder in unison. In silence, heartbroken, six deep, they tried to catch a glimpse of the funeral procession as they wiped away their sorrow.

The Mandraskit family left Brussels in their Minerva automobile, returning to their home near Antwerp. Danya sat in the backseat, and her mother glanced back at her from time to time to see how she was doing. Nobody spoke. Danya watched the raindrops trickling down the window.

Back home and exhausted, Danya could not fall asleep. She searched for something to take her mind off the sadness of the day. Her eye fell on the wooden box holding the bottle of fragrance from her mother. She heard the voice of Satanaya whispering not to open the box and smell the distinctive fragrance. Would she open the bottle of enchantment tonight, in defiance of her mother? Danya held the bottle, careful not to drop it. She put it back in the box and placed it on the dresser in the corner of her room. She was proud that she had found the courage to resist the temptation.

She desperately needed somebody to share her worries in a trusted way, like a brother. Sadly, the only family she had were her parents, who wanted her to be a real Circassian girl. Yet, she felt she must break away from the traditions and customs of Circassian life. Walking over to the poem hanging in a frame on the wall, she read the words her father had written for her sixteenth birthday. She heard her father's voice speaking to her as if he were there:

"I did not realize
How fast that time would fly by
I turned around to touch you
And heard you say goodbye
Our days of parent and child had come to an end ..."

Had the time fallen upon her already when she must face the reality of moving away from her family? She fell into a restless sleep, trying to come to grips with being separated from her parents.

Later that day, she tried to organize her thoughts on how to make the best of her lost world. She was still a Circassian girl, but she realized she must be strong and show she was more than just a little girl. She would be a real daughter of the Mandraskit family. That she carried in her DNA the gene for the courage she now needs, she could not know. She thought about it for a while and returned her mind to the image of the Circassian queen. It was like a flashback to her meeting with Satanaya in her father's studio. Had she not promised to stand by her in difficult times? She needed a source of courage and found it in her.

She reached for her book with drawings and looked for the sketch of Queen Astrid she had drawn months ago. Walking to the window and opening the curtain slightly, she saw the full moon shining into her room like a crack in the window to her future, bringing a ray of hope that she would find the courage to overcome the hurt she had endured for so long.

An absurd idea flashed through her young fertile mind. She should create a statuette of Queen Astrid to keep with her forever.

Fatima and Kadir were unsure how to bring Danya out of her state of dejection. Fatima had seen Danya's drawings in her bedroom but had not told Kadir.

"Last night, when I was with her, she surprised me. She showed me her drawing of Queen Astrid. I was astounded at the fine artwork she created. You should have seen the incredible resemblance to the picture in the newspaper. She even included the beautiful necklace and sapphire. You know how she talks about it all the time. Do you know what she told me? I am going to make a statuette of the queen."

"I am confident she will grow up as a Circassian girl," Kadir said, as his eyes misted over. Fatima told him that she had already contacted her sister, Althea, an instructor at the Academy of Fine Arts in Mill, Holland. She'd spoken to her about Danya's interest in sculpting. Her parents agreed that Danya should move in with her aunt in Mill and enroll in the Academy. Her mother broke the news that evening.

"I talked to Aunt Althea, and if you like the idea, you can stay with her to get your degree at the Academy in Mill." Danya was shocked and thought of the poem foretelling her separation from her parents. Now she understood the meaning of the last verses of the poem.

Rumors about the loss of the beautiful necklace circulated widely, particularly among the young girls. Weeks later, on the second page of the newspaper, Kadir saw a picture of the pendant dangling from a branch in a pine tree near the lake where the accident had happened. When he recognized the necklace, it impaled him like a dagger of sorrow, further tearing open the wounds caused by the tragedy. When Danya saw the picture, she felt a ray of hope. The necklace had not been lost in the lake as was first believed. When she returned to her room that morning, sunlight lit up Queen Astrid's picture on her dresser. For the first time in a long time, Danya felt happy; her pouty little mouth stretched into a charming smile.

At the royal palace, starting his work as a spy for the Adyghe Intelligence Organization, he needed to find a way to work with de Jong. He was not exactly comfortable with this game changer, creating credibility as an intelligence officer, but he had a plan. He was going to present himself as part of a secret European Intelligence Organization in defense of the German threats of war. This way, he gave himself a chance to gain the confidence of the Belgian military. He was confident that by mentioning the Intelligence Service in Holland he would garner the trust of de Jong.

Kadir lifted the phone and wasted no time initiating a discussion about his role as an intelligence agent. "I have become the Charge d'Affairs for the European Intelligence Organization in Belgium. We are starting a Western European Defense Program against Germany's aggression. In Holland, the military has already installed its intelligence network. Yesterday, I spoke with my counterpart in Holland, van Lansfoort, who works closely with Prince Bernhard of the Netherlands. He briefed me on the news that Goering, Germany's Minister of the Air Force, is concentrating aircraft, especially heavy bombers, near the border of Belgium." Until then, de Jong had remained silent, but when Kadir mentioned the aircraft concentrations near the Belgian border, he became agitated.

"The King raised his concern about this danger to Colonel de Greef, Head of the Belgian Intelligence," he said. "I will set up a meeting with de Greef as soon as possible. King Leopold is in close contact with Queen Wilhelmina of the Netherlands, and he would not object to a collaborative effort between the countries."

Kadir was proud of his progress, establishing his role as an intelligence officer. However, he had to make sure his work with Adygha Intelligence remained top secret. Following his telephone contact with the Belgian authority, he contacted Voroshilov in Sochi to deliver his first report of success and receive further orders.

CHAPTER 6

The Death Mask

TODAY WAS NO DIFFERENT THAN ANY OTHER DAY. Manus walked around with a frown on his face. He could not wrap his mind around a career in sculpting. Then, suddenly, an unexpected opportunity arose, despite the fact that creating "death masks" was the last thing on his mind.

With just three days before Mrs. Moller's funeral service, Manus had to find a handbook showing how to make death masks. The only place in town to see such a guide would be in the library. The problem was that a couple weeks prior, he had returned two long overdue books for which he had no money to pay the fine. He decided to secretly leave the books without paying the fine. She had yelled at him as he fled on his bicycle. The incident had left a sour aftertaste with the old woman. She was a disciplinarian. Someday she would get him for it, and that day came soon enough.

Manus had no choice; he returned to the library. Upon entering, he walked up to the reference desk, where the same old woman with a wrinkled face and owl-like eyes peered through her thick glasses. At first, she stared at Manus, then shook her finger at him.

"I believe we have met before. You still owe money from the last time you were here." Manus pretended he did not hear her and asked where to find information about making death masks. Still angry, she leaned forward and gave him a stern look. She thought that Manus was playing some ghoulish joke. "What is going on?" she asked with a frown. "You are the third person today inquiring about this subject."

Manus had no clue why anyone else would be asking about death masks. He noticed the gruff librarian's glasses had slid down to the tip of her nose as they fogged up. Perhaps reading his feelings, she squinted over her glasses. Manus had walked away before she could give him a response.

"Go to the letter 'D' on the shelves and look under death masks!" she shouted at his back. She mumbled: "Move on, you oddball, with your long hair and bushy sideburns. I hope this is the last time you show up here. You give me the creeps." She had an inkling that the other youngsters from the Academy of Fine Arts, who had visited before Manus, were playing a game with her.

Manus found a booklet with a detailed description of the subject, titled, *The Art of Making Face Masks*. On the cover, he noticed the face mask of Henry III, reportedly the oldest mask displayed in the state museum in Amsterdam. He began reading: "A death mask is a plaster cast of a mold taken directly from the face of a dead individual." He cringed at the idea and hesitated to continue. Somehow, the more he read, the more captivated he became with the subject. He learned that the mask serves as a memento of the living and commands high reverence; the face is symbolic and perpetuates the final impression of the human spirit. Manus found himself captivated by the mystery of the mask, standing between two phases of man's very existence: life and death. He found it a noble undertaking that he wanted to explore.

Ensuring he was out of the librarian's sight, he hid the booklet in his briefcase and left the library without checking it out. As he departed, he felt compelled to take a parting shot at the old librarian, but he thought it wiser to keep his thoughts to himself. He mumbled: "She should be my next customer; she has a face I would like to immortalize in a death mask."

Manus' father started his day with a pipe brimming with tobacco and a cup of black coffee. However, today was far from ordinary. He could not forget last night's dream. On her deathbed, she had told him about their Circassian ancestry for the first time. The family had migrated three hundred years ago from the Northern Caucasus Mountains to Holland, where they were persecuted by tribal hordes who invaded their lands from the East. It was the start of the first genocide in Europe. The Circassian people had no choice but to leave their homeland. During their northward migration, they had lost many members of the Habers family troupe; she told Antonius they had fought back with valor to maintain life and freedom. During his mother's last hour, she expressed the hope that Circassians would someday return to their ancestral lands on the shores of the Black Sea. Since her death, Antonius had kept this information to himself as a secret.

Yesterday, in an old shoebox, Antonius had found his mother's prayer card that was read at her funeral. It showed a picture of her when she was a young and beautiful woman. Black curly hair and a radiant smile gave her a seductive look. The name on the card said "Anna Maria Petrovsky," a Circassian surname and, according to family lore, she was hot-tempered, never hesitating to vehemently speak her mind. After her funeral, Antonius became fascinated with the Circassians. But he did not share his feelings with anyone. At the local library, disappointment awaited him with the scarce resources on the subject of Circassians. He had found a copy of the *Nart Sagas*, ninety-eight stories about the traditions and family customs of these people. He read that the Circassians were considered the oldest ethnic population in Europe. Over the millennia, they developed a strong tradition of raising their children in the "Circassian" way. They were a unique people, best known for their deep-seated pride in their ethnic identity, combined with a love of freedom and a strong fighting spirit; they would defend their beliefs to the death.

Antonius wondered why he had not delved deeper into the history of his ancestors. He knew that he had inherited the courage and perseverance to achieve success in his artistic endeavors from his mother, and he was an accomplished artist. Still, as the family patriarch, had he failed his family? Should he not have raised his sons more openly under the Circassian family principles? He felt his responsibility more than ever to take action as the family patriarch.

Manus struggled to find the ideal image of the Virgin Mary in his drawings.

While a student at the Academy, Manus had shown talent drawing religious figures, such as Mary and Jesus. But he failed to come up with his own style. Day after day, he diddled and dawdled with pencil and paper to refine the facial expressions in his sketches. Finally, his father took some time to review his son's work. He detected in his drawing a common element in the facial expressions: the downcast eyes, reflecting the uncertainty of life and the longing to find a light somewhere in the distance. Their mouths showed a determination to succeed, but the corners curled up into a question mark as if pulling back with hesitation. These were faces showing doubt and defeatism. Manus was shocked when his father first pointed out the similarities in the faces he had drawn. It was as if Manus had looked in the mirror and painted his own face on paper. His father's observations helped Manus realize that he had incorporated his own inner life combining the restlessness of a man searching and questioning life's trials and tribulations. He must find a way to allow his own style to take hold, to supplant his reaction to despair.

Sometimes a stroke of luck brings fundamental change to a troubled individual. For Manus, good fortune presented itself as the opportunity to make death masks. He thought about how it had all come about quite unexpectedly.

Manus had ridden his bicycle in the rain to the Academy office to pick up paperwork for his father. The rector of the Academy, Dr. Moller, was having second thoughts about dismissing his father over the editorial issue. Had he been too harsh? He saw Manus across the street and waved him over.

"I need to discuss something important with you!" Dr. Moller called. Walking his bicycle across the street and parking it against the building façade, Manus removed his raincoat and followed the rector inside. He pointed to a chair opposite him and looked Manus in the eye. "Did your father mention that my mother passed away yesterday after a long illness?" Dr. Moller asked him.

"No, my father has not mentioned it," Manus responded, shaking his head. "My condolences, Rector."

"Thank you for your expression of sympathy. I want to discuss a matter of importance," explained Dr. Moller. "As has become tradition, my family decided to have a death mask made of our mother. They want to have it ready for the funeral in three days. Your father told me you are an aspiring sculptor, and even though making a face mask is not exactly what you may be looking to do, I wanted to ask if you would take on this task as a learning experience for becoming a sculptor." Manus felt like he was sinking into a well of disbelief. He had no experience in this field, and when Moller told him that he'd already asked two other students at the Academy, Manus shrunk to think he was the third choice.

"Why did you choose me?" he asked in disbelief.

"Let me get right to the point, Manus. We are fully aware of your financial struggle to become a sculptor. About a month ago, your father and I had a long conversation about your future. I want to help. Descriptions of death masks are found in archaeology books, going back to ancient Egypt. In the thirteenth century, European sculptors made death masks before creating busts and statues of royalty. In museums, you will find masks of Henry III, Edward III, Isaac Newton, and Napoleon Bonaparte as evidence. This practice helped sculptors shape the form of the head. Manus felt a surge of interest; now he was getting interested. He had discovered a new method of creating a better way for the facial expressions in his drawings, and eventually his sculptures. He wanted to know more.

"Where are death masks kept?" he asked.

"As in many cultures, family members like to keep the memory of their deceased for as long as possible ... they usually display the mask on the wall in the drawing room. A death mask stands as the gateway between life and death," explained Moller. "It bears a supernatural character, very different from our experiences of sunrise, nightfall, and another day. While being molded, something of the mystery of death passes through the hands of the maker into the mask itself." Manus looked at his hands, realizing they could become part of the mystical transformation of the living face into the plaster form. He felt bewildered, yet anxious to get started. "None of my students have shown an interest in helping us. You are my only candidate. Are you interested?" Moller inquired. "You will receive a substantial financial reward if you undertake this project. Due to the economic recession, not many people have the money for a death mask. They have barely enough to cover funeral costs. But I see a resurgence of this art form. Most importantly, it will help you to develop your own style." Manus recalled his father's comments about his style in the facial expressions, but he was still not convinced he should take this job.

"Are you not looking for work?" Moller prodded. "Here is a start that could launch your career." Manus went into a panic about drifting into an area in which he had no experience. Never in his life had he considered making death masks and he had no idea where to start. He would have to overcome his fear of touching the cold face of a deceased individual. "You are the logical candidate, and I know that your father will be able to guide you through the process." Manus was surprised at this conciliatory remark about his father. To ensure that Manus was up to the task, he asked, "Do you have any practical knowledge of working with plaster models?" Manus knew he had to bluff if he wanted the job.

"I have worked with clay models and plaster forms. I have the necessary tools in my workshop," he answered truthfully, realizing he was now committing himself to the task.

Riding home on his old bicycle with the rickety chain that needed grease, he could not wait to announce the good news to his parents. "Guess what? I got my first assignment!" he blurted out. "Rector Moller asked me to make a death mask of his mother, who just passed away." His family, already seated at the dinner table, dropped their eating utensils in unison, looking at each other without a word and rolling their eyes.

"How does this sit with you?" asked his father, surprised at Moller's offer. "Will you take it on?" Habers had good reason to ask since Moller had dismissed him as editor of the newsletter. What made him so kind to his son? Or was there something else behind this offer, he wondered.

Manus knew that he had no experience in making masks, but, with his face in his food, he nodded as he ate dinner. A cloud of silence, like chunky pea soup, drifted over the dinner table as the family let the news slowly sink in, one pea at the time. They looked at each other in disbelief. The idea of making face masks is ridiculous, his mother thought. She could not bring herself to believe that something positive could come from it. Still, Manus would earn ten guilders, a hefty sum for the time, which would help with the family finances.

"Well, Son," his father began, breaking the uneasy silence. "It is a start, and this will help prepare you to become a student sculptor after all." He wondered if this was the time to bring up their Circassian courage to take risks and undertake challenging tasks. To help Manus make a decision, he father suggested, "Go to the cemetery, where you will see several grave sites with tombstones carved with religious reliefs and statues of Jesus and Mary." By the end of his meal, Habers stuffed a wad of tobacco in his mouth and started chewing. Without saying a word, his mother left the table in a dark mood, wondering what was to come of Manus. Alone, Manus sat at the dinner table finishing his meal. What would his brother say about him making death masks? He should be home soon.

For several days, Manus did not feel well but was too embarrassed to tell his family about the physical problem with which he suffered. Here it was again—a boil on his bun! What an embarrassing problem! Sitting became a real pain. The problem grew larger every day. The last thing he wanted was to be melodramatic about it. He decided to try a quick cure he had heard about involving Epsom salt.

Late at night, while his parents slept, he filled the washtub with warm water to give himself a soak. Lighting a candle, he placed it on the floor next to the tub. Naked, except for his French beret and pipe, he lowered himself in the tub, spilling half of the water on the floor. He would clean it up later. With the newspaper in hand, he started to read.

Just then, the back door swung open, and Arie arrived, heading for the kitchen. Not quite making it to the kitchen door, he backed up a few steps toward the tub in the darkened room, suddenly stopping, turning, and looking down at the crumpled figure covered by the newspaper in the washtub. What a bizarre scene, he thought. Was his brother sitting in the water, barely fitting in the tub, his kneecaps touching his nostrils? Arie laughed uncontrollably.

"What in the world is this?" he asked, snorting incredulously. "Why are you reading the paper in the tub? I have never noticed how scrawny you are!" Arie continued. "What happened today?"

Manus was embarrassed to tell his brother about the death mask. "I got my first commission to make a death mask of Rector Moller's mother, who just passed away," he finally brought himself to mumble. "I'm in the tub because I have a painful boil on my rear end," he confided, looking away from Arie. The expected ridicule came in full force. Arie burst into wild laughter, tears streaming down his cheeks.

"I wish I could marry these two ideas, face masks and bun boils!" he guffawed. "This makes my day! Show me the boil." Manus answered by splashing water on Arie's face.

"Get out of here!" he yelled, pointing at Arie with his pipe.

The next day, he arrived late to begin his assignment at the home of the deceased. Moller led Manus to the drawing room, where he adjusted the heavy curtains to let in a beam of daylight. The corpse, dressed in a white linen gown, lay on a Victorian-style bed. Six lit candles were spaced throughout the room, which was permeated by an eerie silence. Manus stood in reverence at the foot of the bed with Moller. This was Manus' first experience being near a cadaver. As he walked around to take a closer look at her face, he noticed right away the deep sunken eyes and protruding cheekbones, indicating she had lost weight before her death. Much work awaited him, including correcting the noted features to make her face look younger.

Moller turned towards the dresser and pointed to a photo of his mother, taken twenty years earlier. Manus hoped he had brought enough cotton balls to fill up the sallow cheeks. He soaked the strips of plaster gauze and gently applied each to cover her facial features. He was pleased with the effect the cotton balls had on filling in her oral cavity. Worried that he might have missed some essential element, he stepped back to survey his work and let the mask dry. Moller invited him for a cup of coffee in the kitchen.

"It looks to me like you have the technique well under control. Are you sure this is your first mask?" Moller asked. His words of encouragement lifted Manus' spirits.

Taking his leave, Manus carefully placed the plaster negative in his satchel, making sure not to break the form as he headed home. At home, he hung the negative plaster form from the kitchen ceiling to dry.

"Is this for real?" Arie mocked, unable to resist teasing his brother. "It looks like you still have a lot of work ahead of you before it becomes a death mask. Here is an idea: How about a face mask of Hitler? It'll sell like hotcakes in Holland!"

"One day when I'm a famous sculptor, you'll be surprised at my creations!" Manus retorted, trying hard to keep his temper. "You'd better leave before I make a death mask of you!" Arie stomped off in a huff.

Three months later, Manus would make a death mask of his own mother—his most exceptional work of art to date.

CHAPTER 7

The Rembrandt Tulip

IN MAY, PAINTERS IN HOLLAND SWARMED THE FIELDS, capturing the beauty of the multi-colored tulips. This year, they were after the notorious Rembrandt Tulip. For several years, a select group of growers had worked in secrecy to enhance the color and markings of the Rembrandt's petals. During this same time, agricultural researchers were working on a new method of engineering unique colors with colorful striping in the petals. Scientists at the University of Leyden achieved this feat by injecting a transmittal virus into each bulb. They were confident they would succeed beyond their wildest imaginations, naming their masterpiece the "Rembrandt Tulip."

Within the next weeks, the Rembrandt would be at its peak, revealing its full blossom. The scientists successfully created a stunningly beautiful tulip. Its intense and stunning coloration earned it the prestigious and rare Queen Wilhelmina Tulip Award. Once a year, the judges considered all entries based on splendor, color, and uniqueness in the markings on the petals.

Despite its beauty and accolades, the Rembrandt tulip's fame was short-lived. As the growers celebrated, this tulip variety had captured the attention of the Dutch Department of Agriculture. The government subsequently issued a ban on farming Rembrandts, sure to doom its destiny. Notices went out to all growers requiring them to immediately cease cultivation of the Rembrandt and ordering them to destroy and burn all related plant materials, including bulbs. The government said the virus injected into the plant to cause its transmutation could spill over into the human gene pool, with dire consequences for Holland's people.

The news about the impending destruction of the new tulip variety growers had counted on to revive the sluggish industry dashed any expectation of improvement. As the tulip industry suffered severe losses in sales due to the economic recession, the death of the Rembrandt caused the tulip growers to sink into despair.

The people of Mill were angry with the government and demanded answers. The City Council scheduled an emergency meeting at City Hall in response to the public's outcry over the government regulation. On the day of the meeting, the hall filled quickly with agitated growers and ordinary townspeople. They stomped on the floor in unison with their wooden shoes, "a-one and a-two," while clapping their hands as if executing a war dance. They wanted action. In the end, the City Council came up with a solution to honor this unique flower in a painting. The council wanted to immortalize the Rembrandt on canvas, in all its glory and splendor. Antonius Habers was the unanimous choice for the assignment.

When he received word that the City Council wanted him to paint the famous Rembrandt, he was overjoyed and immediately set out to create several sketches on paper. He wanted to make sure that he captured not only the glorious beauty of the Rembrandt but also the sentiment of "a memorial" of the vanishing tulip. However, before he could put his first brush strokes on the canvas, he needed a vase for the tulips.

Time was of the essence, with the government order to destroy all Rembrandts immediately. He needed a dozen tulips from the most reputable grower in town, Dierckx Growers. They delivered the first grown tulips every year to the Royal Dutch family, earning them the reputation of purveyor to the Royal Court.

Antonius dispatched his son to gather twelve of the famous tulips. Swept up in the excitement of his father's commission, Manus enthusiastically headed to the tulip fields outside the city. He took off on his bicycle with a newspaper rolled up under his arm. He decided he needed to tell his friend the good news first and hurried to the local tavern, his usual hangout, for a cup of tea. His best friend, Jope, was already there. Manus greeted him before ordering a cup of Douwe Egbert's tea and a speculaas cookie made from almond paste. He unfolded the paper and showed Jope the article about the endangered Rembrandt. Manus read the headline, written in bold letters on the front page, aloud: "Death Sentence for the Rembrandt Tulip." When Manus explained that his father was going to play a significant role in the final chapter of this flower's existence, Jope understood why Manus had the paper with him. He wanted his friends to know his father was going to paint the last Rembrandt, as the article mentioned. The news made Manus proud.

"Do you know where the Northern Caucasus Mountains are?" Manus asked Jope unexpectedly.

"I know they border the Black Sea," Jope answered, looking at Manus with a puzzled expression and wondering why he had asked the question. "Why are you asking?"

"The article says tulips come from Circassia," Manus explained. "In the second half of the fifteenth century, as the result of a major exodus caused by the marauding bands from the East, the surviving caravans of Circassians found their way to Holland and Belgium. Here they found the same soil conditions as their native Black Sea home. The dark clay soil was exactly right for cultivating their prized tulips," Manus read. Jope listened attentively.

"The Circassians carried large supplies, including clothing, food, and bags of tulip bulbs, which they highly valued and used as a food source when needed. The tulip was their sacred flower. Despite numerous attempts by the Greeks to trade tulips for their goods, they constantly refused to give up this prized commodity," Manus continued reading.

"The Circassians decorated their wagons with colorful flags, streamers, and banners, and the women's clothing showed a color-rich pattern of yellow, blue, red, black, and green."

"Wait!" Jope exclaimed, holding up his hand to stop Manus. "The colors you just mentioned are the same ones found in the famous Rembrandt tulip!" Jope pointed out. "I wonder if the geneticists at the University were Circassian, trying to reproduce the colors in their new tulip?" he asked, as both friends stared at each other in awe, considering this possibility.

Manus suddenly interrupted their reverie and motioned Jope to follow him to the fields. He had to find a dozen of the most beautiful Rembrandts before dark. They raced to Toon Dierckx's field.

The sun was setting, and the air was cooling down, offering ideal weather for cutting tulips. When they arrived at the tulip farm, Manus knew he was at the right place.

They parked their bicycles and walked to Dierckx's office. Toon Dierckx immediately recognized Manus as Antonius Habers' son. For years, he had spotted Habers in his fields, amidst the painters, with his easel, canvas, and paintbrush, creating some of the most spectacular portrayals of the flowering meadows. Habers was one of the painters with the ability to capture the intimacy of color of these flowering bulbs on canvas. It was no wonder he was a docent at the Academy.

"We are fortunate that your father lives amongst us to paint the Rembrandt," Toon told Manus. "We need to act now. Tomorrow, horses will be plowing the Rembrandt bulbs under for good. I have no choice in the matter," he said sadly. "I feel like the executioner of this gorgeous flower. You will find the best Rembrandts in a single row by the end of the road; look for a little sign in the row that says: 'Cultivated exclusively for the Royal Dutch family.' I will permit to pick a dozen tulips from this row only."

Manus and Jope hastened their steps, passing row after row arranged in broad swatches, by color and variety. It was an incredible joy for the eye to take in the magnificence of the scenery. They suddenly stopped, having reached their destination. They eyed the Rembrandts, standing in awe and admiring the exquisite tulip seen by so few. They knelt to admire the flowers close-up as if it was a sacred moment. The foot-tall stems in dark green were bearing shining blue flower petals, colored white inside with black veins and a yellow and orange glow like a sunburst. The edges of the petals showed the curly-crinkled fringes that made these flowers so unique.

"No wonder they gave this variety the Queen Wilhelmina Award," commented Manus. "It's sad that nobody will see them again after tomorrow. I am so happy my father has the opportunity to paint these tulips, so that generations from now, people can still admire them in his painting." Manus wiped a tear he hoped Jope had not noticed.

"Why did you pull those tulips with their bulbs attached?" Jope asked. Manus looked down at the ground, remaining silent. He had plans for the bulbs. Placing the tulips in his basket, he went to the office to thank Toon.

"My father will be happy with our choices, and I am sure that he will do justice to these tulips on canvas. Thank you!" Manus said.

"Please thank your father for us," Toon told him. "How grateful we are in Mill to have someone with an artistic background paint these spectacular flowers. The city manager has already agreed to hang the painting in the entrance to City Hall so that everyone entering will notice it."

Riding home, glowing with the excellent news and pleased with his tulip selection, Manus put the tulips in a unique vase before presenting them to his father. That evening he laid the first brush strokes of paint on the canvas destined to become the most spectacular painting in Mill. He knew the freshly cut Rembrandts in the vase would only last a few days before wilting.

Retreating to his room, Manus had cut the bulbs from the tulips he had harvested to keep for himself. He placed them in a paper bag to dry and hid them amongst the socks in his dresser drawer. He was not sure if he would ever plant them, but he would figure out something to do with them.

Days later, late in the evening, Manus heard the violin in the living room. It could only be his father, who was celebrating the completion of his painting. Manus walked up to the easel where the picture rested. He could not believe what he saw. He was quite familiar with his father's paintings and admired his masterpiece. It represented the culmination of many years of experience. He stood there in awe and then looked at his father in tears.

"The people of Mill will honor you for it," he said, hugging him.

Before returning to the violin, his father adjusted the strings with his pitchfork. As he played, the notes rolled off the violin with a vitality and joy Manus had never heard before. He had no trouble recognizing the song, "Juliska vom Budapest," about a young girl in her native costume twirling jubilantly. On this particular evening, his father played with a joy and passion drawing Manus into the music. He joined in the celebration of the moment by smoking his favorite tobacco in his pipe and blowing little smoke clouds. As the music floated through the highs and lows, he had a vision of a stunningly attractive and exotic girl in a faraway country spinning in a colorful dress, with streamers floating from her headdress like a parasol. They were the same colors as the Rembrandt. The music waxed to a crescendo once more before hauntingly trailing off into the silence of the last bar.

Manus stayed in the room long after his father had gone to bed. The vision of the dancing girl held him in a mesmerizing spell. She was gorgeous, dainty, and full of life. As he took the last puff of tobacco from his pipe, Manus let the girl slip away from his dream, but only for now. He knew he had seen the girl who would become the model for his sculptures. Returning to his room, Manus found a crayon in an old shoebox. He opened his sketchbook and pressed it flat against the little table in the window alcove. He brushed his long hair out of his face and with his tobacco-smelling fingers started to glide the crayon across the sheet to form the figure he had admired in the cloud of smoke. She had curly jet-black hair, a youthful face, and beautiful dark eyes, with a glint of gold. She was joyful and demure looking. Her features on paper grew even livelier than in real life. He squinted for a moment, smiling. As he slept, Manus wondered about the tulip bulbs drying in his room. Why was he defying the government's edict to destroy all Rembrandts? Now was not the time to align himself with the government, as an accomplice in the extinction of the famous flower. In the end, maybe he was the one who would save the Rembrandt from destruction.

Once Habers finished his painting, he received a visit from Toon Dierckx who stopped by to check on his progress.

"You painted a treasure to commemorate not only the Rembrandt but also the people's devotion to this tulip," Dierckx told Antonius with a wink.

A month later, the mayor unveiled the painting at a ceremony in City Hall. The hall filled up with national and local dignitaries. When the city manager removed the sheet from the frame, the crowd broke out in lively applause. Everyone wanted to get a closer look and congratulate Habers for the beautiful artwork he had rendered, capturing every detail in the colors of the Rembrandt. Through the magic of his artistic ingenuity, he had succeeded in depicting the sadness that came with the loss of this national treasure.

CHAPTER 8

Madonna Danya

THE MORNING WAS COLD AND DARK. MANUS WOKE up late. He had fallen behind on his assignments at the Academy and was unsure where to start. Yesterday, a friend had given him a book on Peter Paul Rubens, the famous painter in Antwerp. He could not wait to discuss the masterpieces with his father. However, to study Rubens close up, he wanted to be in the city where Rubens had lived.

His father had advised him to explore ecclesiastic art, and he was anxious to show his work. He had made multiple sketches of Mary and Jesus. Upon reviewing his portfolio of drawings, he became unsure whether he was capable of depicting Mary in a way he called "exalted."

With the book on Rubens in one hand and his sketchbook in the other, he stumbled around the kitchen to find his usual chair at the table. His father read the paper, enjoying a cup of coffee. He looked up at his son, noticing that his face had changed from his familiar quizzical expression to a somewhat squeamish one. For a while, Manus sat quietly staring at his half-empty cup of coffee. His clenched fist rested on his portfolio as if he were on the losing end in his struggle to continue his sculpting future. Indolently, Manus fumbled for his pipe in his pocket. It made no difference; he had no tobacco. Without saying a word, his father noticed his predicament and opened his pouch, offering Manus a wad of his preferred brand. He saw Manus' clenched fist and looked him in the eye.

"Why are you are hiding your sketchbook?" his father asked. Manus shook his head, puffing his pipe and slowly handed over his portfolio. He had been living on a thin rope of hope in which he featured himself in the stone carving art world. He feared his father's criticism. It would not take much to unravel the thin thread of hope.

"Might as well get it over with," Manus said. "Since the last time we talked about it, I have tried to improve my drawings, which I hope you will like." Manus had not expected to encounter a genuine admirer of his work at this point, especially in his father, a lecturer at the Academy. Habers leafed through the portfolio and smiled languidly.

"Compared to a couple of months ago, you've made considerable progress in your work. Bravo!" Had his father not admonished him to study the images in his sketchbook and compare them to the sadness in his face, his eyes aimlessly searching for perfection? He remembered that day when he had looked in the mirror and seen the face of a lost and terrified artist. He had recognized the forlorn look in the eyes. At the time, he had concluded that his father was right.

Had his father come around? Had he become a genuine admirer of his work?

"I am finding deeper expressions of passion; however, I still have a long way to go. Now that I have made several death masks, it makes a difference. It has become clear that death masks can be a communication channel with the deceased," Manus explained. He looked at his hands and continued. "It feels like the spirit of the dead travels through my hands, using them as a vehicle to communicate with my inner self. It opened up a window into my soul, where I now feel passionate about my artwork."

"Son, you just told me something that very few of us in the art world realize. Let us put this knowledge to good use. You will remember from Art History class how the Renaissance painters became masters of deeper feelings. They found a way to convey their passion into the paintbrush. In your case, you will find the power to create with your hammer and chisel. You will find Rubens' art a great help in your development as an artist," his father told him.

"You gave insight into my drafting, as I never had before. I am very excited!" Manus showed him the copy of the Rubens book he had brought to the table. Judging from the little slips of paper peeking from its pages, Habers noticed he had spent a lot of time studying Rubens. Small pieces of paper marked the picture of a masterpiece.

"There are two Rubens paintings that specifically to me. First, there is the painting called 'Bathsheba Receives Message from David.' I have studied this painting in depth. Do you see how he creates a vivacious effect by playing the colors in the skin of Bathsheba, the black messenger, against the bright sunlight of the architectural structures contrasting with the transparently blue heaven?

"Bathsheba is one of the most important biblical figures. She was the wife of Uriah and later, the spouse of David, King of Israel. She had a child with David, who became King Solomon. By her motherhood of Solomon, Bathsheba became the 'Queen Mother of Israel.' According to the Bible, she is a Hittite, a descendant of the Nubian queens of Ancient Egypt. Their smooth skin, olive color, and graceful posture make Nubian women the most elegant and beautiful ever. Queen Bathsheba and King David are the ancestors of Mary and Jesus. Ecclesiastic scholars have argued for centuries that God would have wanted the mother of Jesus to be a descendant of these beautiful females." Habers agreed that this would not be an unreasonable conclusion.

The next painting Manus was particularly fond of was "The Little Fur," depicting Helena Fourment, Rubens' sixteen-year-old second wife, scantily wrapped in a black fur. Helena was a frequent model for Rubens. The white of her skin contrasted with the dark softness of the mink fur she was wearing. In his sketchbook, he had several drawings of Helena Fourment.

"Someday I will find my own 'Fourment Girl' as my model," a little voice inside him whispered. With encouragement from his father, Manus packed his bags and took the train to the city of Rubens, Antwerp, Belgium for the first time in his life. He exited the train from Holland at Central Station and started immediately on the task of finding a place to stay. With the few Belgian francs his father could spare in his pocket, he wandered from the main boulevard toward the River Scheldt, in the seedy district of the city, where he located an attic room in the Lange Nieuwstraat, upstairs from a bordello in the Red Light District. Bordellos were popular with sailors from around the world on leave from their long voyages. Manus was not a man of the world. He did not realize until later where he was bedding down. The property owner was Madame Giselle, who kept her parlor downstairs, where she entertained her clients. During the "off hours," usually during the daytime, she presented herself in the window, which she had adorned with a single strand of red neon light. Dressed to the nines and overloaded with cosmetics to look much younger than she was, she sat in her luxurious armchair. With her pussycat in her lap, she held a book, pretending to read. No one believed she was a sophisticated bookworm, but that is how she wanted her upscale clients to see her.

On his first day of class at the Royal Academy of Fine Arts in Antwerp, Manus wanted to make sure he was on time. He wandered for a while in the old district of the city, noticing the old homes, showing the toll of several years of economic downturn in the inner city.

Full of anticipation, Manus looked forward to his first day at the Academy. It was more than the fact of having arrived in the city of Rubens, but also that he was at a turn in his sculpting career. Walking through the front portal of the Academy, he was shocked to see the lobby nearly blocked by smashed pedestals, broken plaster arms and legs, and decapitated torsos. In the corners of the darkened rooms, he could make out cobwebs dangling from the ceiling. It struck him as ironic that he found himself in a graveyard of an iconoclastic tornado that had swept through the halls of this massive institute. In the courtyard, he saw a uniformed guard seated on an old cement bench with a cup of coffee, aimlessly staring at the demolished pieces, as if there was some art left in them. Was this not to be the place for art education, where he had hoped to learn to become a sculptor? Stepping gingerly through this broken world, Manus felt dispirited when he reached his classroom. The first lesson of the day dealt with the history of Renaissance art. He tried to overcome his negative sentiments and did his best to understand the professor's broken Flemish. Manus guessed he must be from Brussels, a francophone.

The Royal Academy of Fine Arts in Antwerp was founded in 1663 by David Teniers, official painter to Archduke Leopold of Austria. Since then, the Academy had earned a reputation as an internationally acclaimed fine arts institute. Rubens had played an essential role in the establishment of the Academy, as had Vincent van Gogh, one of its most notable students.

When it was time to pay his rent, Manus was shy and kept his distance. Giselle climbed the rickety stairs to Manus' attic room to collect the rent.

"Hey, there. Here is something for you to eat," Giselle said compassionately, setting a bowl of soup on the table in front of him. "I am a woman who has decided to live my life the way it suits me. Every day, I remind myself to live this life, never having to repent not having lived it this way." She smiled at him and gave him a slip of paper that said, "It is no good trying to bridge your loneliness on your own. At times, I can take care of filling the gap. But you have to wait for that special moment." Manus recognized it as a quote from *Lady Chatterley's Lover*.

"I must tell you something, young man," she continued in her raspy voice. "You walk through the Red Light District of the city and think of us in only one way. The Chief of the Fire Department is a friend of ours. If a fire broke out in the Cathedral of Our Lady, we would be the only ones awake at night and ready to help put out the fire. As an art student, you know about the cathedral paintings by Rubens, Teniers, and Jordaens. They are our national heritage, and we are just as proud of them as any other citizen is. If a fire broke out during the night, we would be the only ones awake to save the paintings. We agreed to risk our lives to preserve the heritage of this city." By the time she had finished speaking, Manus wanted to believe her story.

After classes, Manus made it a practice to walk to the River Scheldt, which flows a mile wide to the North Sea. Antwerp is a major international port city, and Manus often walked the banks of the river, leaning on the railing to gaze at the slow-moving ocean freighters. Intrigued by the strange names on their bows, he took out his notepad, jotting down the ships' names: "Luceria," Cadiz, Spain; "Hurricane Wharf," South Carolina, USA; "Julio Miranda," Rio de Janeiro, Brazil; "Brunwulf," Kiel, Germany. Someday he planned to visit these faraway places.

The sun was setting in the west, but there was just enough daylight to sketch the rippled waves stirring in the river by a mild breeze. Overhead the sky was purple with strands of pale yellow, signaling the last rays of the sinking sun. A low-hanging mist formed over the river and started to obscure the contours of the left bank. It was almost dark, and he heard a girl singing a lullaby. The lovely voice came through an open window in one of the stately homes lining the river walk on the east bank. He turned the page and set out to draw a young mother seated in a rocking chair; her head turned toward her infant in a tender embrace. "Hush, baby, hush" the music trailed off and became muffled by the sound of the rippling river. The baby had fallen asleep. This sketch became one of his favorites ever, and he placed it in his portfolio: Sketches of Mary and Jesus.

It was Saturday afternoon, and there were no classes at the Academy today. The sun grew steadily stronger by the hour, heating up the city until it was stiflingly hot. Manus had made a few friends at the Academy, and on this sweltering hot day, they needed a beer. They stopped at Café Sinjoorke. Someone had left the daily paper on one of the tables. Its headline left no doubt about the sad feelings of the people: "Despite Economic Recovery, Flemish People Remain Oppressed by Brussels."

Always fascinated by politics, Manus listened to the students' debate. During the past several months, unlawful conduct during street demonstrations had landed numerous students in jail. The Flemish people stood by their students, and Manus found himself in the crosshair of the political opinions of the students: those who favored the NSB (National Socialist Bond) with its Nazi ties against those who sympathized with the plight of the Jews in Germany.

Yesterday, Manus had met a new friend, Jacob Schwarz. Jacob's parents had recently come from Germany, escaping the roundup of Jews in Koln. They had fled from the Gestapo during Krystal Nacht, the "Night of the Broken Glass." A week earlier Gestapo agents in Germany had ransacked hundreds of synagogues. Gestapo troopers had sacked thousands of Jewish shops and rounded up tens of thousands of Jews whom they deported to the concentration camps. Schwarz's parents had managed to escape just in time, thanks to friends in Antwerp's diamond district. Manus listened to his story of the harrowing escape from Koln.

After spending several months at the Academy, Manus moved from entertaining a fantasy in which he featured himself as a sculptor, to finding the reality of being a sculptor with his peculiar art style. At the Academy, his hands were at home working with plaster forms, similar to the work he had performed shaping death masks. His ultimate goal was to create a statue of the Virgin Mary from a block of granite, the most challenging stone to carve. He familiarized himself with the tools of the trade, such as chisels and scrapers, and learned how difficult it was to carve granite.

It was late afternoon when Madame Giselle came upstairs to deliver a letter from Manus' father. The message was clear: "You have been designated by the architect of the chapel on the Moerdijk Bridge to carve a life-size monument of Mary and Jesus from stone. The Catholic Church plans to inaugurate this statue in the roadside chapel within six months. Your return home is urgent so that you can meet the deadline for the inauguration of the chapel." Manus immediately made plans to leave Antwerp and return to his hometown of Mill.

Upon arriving, he learned what was behind this project. The Catholic Church in the Southern Provinces of Holland wanted to make a statement aimed at the Protestants in the Northern Provinces: "As you cross the Rhine River, we welcome you to Catholic Holland." It did not take long for Manus to grasp the enormity of the task ahead.

He wasted no time laying the groundwork for the monument by drawing a rendition on paper. However, he continued to worry about his lack of a live model for the Virgin Mary. He had to quickly find someone who could indeed represent the beauty of the Virgin Mary. He thought perhaps Rector Moller at the Academy could help him find a model. Moller asked Manus for a clear description of the model he required for his sketches.

"She needs to be a young girl who brings together the art style I adore the most as we see in the paintings of Rafael and Parmigianino. May I show you my portfolio of the sketch I made of the Madonna figure I have in mind?" Manus asked him. Moller knew what he was after and was willing to lend him a hand. A newly registered student at the Academy might fit Manus' requirements. He told Manus he would let him know whether the candidate he had in mind would agree to an interview.

The sun warmed Manus as he headed to his usual gathering place at the local tavern. In the corner, he noticed three young girls having tea and cookies. He joined his friends, who were discussing Hitler's politics. Suddenly, one of his friends broke off the conversation, nodding discreetly in the direction of the girls.

"Look at that attractive and adorable girl with the dark olive-colored complexion ... those exotic eyes," he said. "I wonder who she is? Has she been here before?" Manus knew who she was, but he was too embarrassed to tell his friends she was the girl he had seen in his mind when his father had played "Juliska vom Budapest" on the violin. He looked towards her and as if by a miracle, he knew it was her. He had drawn her image so many times and now, here she was in the flesh. Had Moller come through for him and set up a meeting with her at the tavern? He could no longer contain his excitement.

"It is her, the one I have sketched so many times," he whispered to his friends. "She is the perfect model for my Madonna statue. Just look at her elegant figure, the long neck, like the figures in Parmigianino's paintings."

Danya noticed the attention and looked at her friends as they started to giggle like teenage girls. Manus had to act now; gathering his courage, he got up from the table and approached Danya.

"Are you a student at the Academy?" he asked gingerly, a little unsure of himself. Danya looked up at him shyly.

"Yes, I am a student," she responded. She boldly asked: "Are you the sculptor who is looking for a model?"

"Yes, I am looking for a model for my Madonna statue, for the chapel on the Moerdijk Bridge," Manus told her, feeling reassured. "Time is short. The statue needs to be ready in six months." Danya remembered reading about this important project in the newspaper. She reminded herself that she was a mere sixteen-year-old girl attending the Academy to become a sculptor. How could this man think of her as a model for such important work? She summoned her courage by reminding herself that she was Circassian. She was unsure how her family would react if she took this assignment. She let her mind wander to an earlier time in her father's studio with Queen Satanaya. Was this one of those moments that she had promised to stand by her side? She heard a voice from deep inside her: "Time is here to experience life through the Circassian spirit ... the courage is already in you to take this role as a model for the Madonna, the Virgin Mary."

As her friends left the tavern, Danya hesitated to stay by herself with Manus. She was frightened, being young and inexperienced. However, here was an opportunity to learn the trade of becoming a sculptor from the inside by being a model. She had to rely on Satanaya to help her through this phase. Manus noticed the aristocratic look on her face, and it made him uncomfortable. He saw the tension in her face and wanted to put her at ease.

"What is your name?" Manus started out correctly asking with a smile.

"Danya Mandraskit." Her last name fascinated him. First, he needed to explain what he had hoped to see in his model.

"I am looking for someone who looks like the Virgin Mary, as she was depicted in the paintings by the Italian masters. I have studied the different styles, and you fit the image of the ideal Mary figure."

"I feel honored, but I'm not convinced I should be the model for the mother of Jesus," Danya began. Wanting to put her at ease, Manus asked about her life and short-term goals.

"Did you move from Antwerp to Mill last year?"

"Yes, I am staying with my aunt."

"Tell me about your parents …"

"Well, my parents live outside of Antwerp in the suburb of Brasschaat. I was going to private school there until I decided I wanted to learn the art of sculpting. The academy in Mill is the only school in Europe where they accept female students in their sculpting program. I am planning to return home after my studies."

"I'd like to ask you a question about your last name … Do you know where your family originally came from?"

"Hundreds of years ago, our family came from the Northern Caucasus Mountains; they were called Circassians … my parents told me our ancestors go back to the Hittites of Egypt."

"This explains your unusual last name," Manus commented before he went further with the connection with Mary's ancestry. "In the Gospel of Matthew, I read that Mary, Mother of Jesus, was also a Hittite. What an incredible coincidence!" Danya stayed quiet as she tried to absorb what he had said. "With you as my model, the monument in the chapel on the Moerdijk Bridge will be the most beautiful figure of Mary ever to be carved in stone. The Protestants will know that they entered Catholic territory."

CHAPTER 9

Intel Arie

A NEW POSITION IN THE ARMED FORCES POSTED ON the bulletin board at police headquarters stirred a lot of interest amongst the younger officers. When Arie noticed the letters "IB" in the posting, he learned from his colleagues that it stood for "Intelligence Bureau." The wording "intelligence" caught his attention and he decided to find out more about the opportunity.

To compete for the position, Arie resolved to learn all he could about the craft of intelligence. He found a book about the origins of intelligence gathering in the library and was astounded at how long the knowledge of intelligence gathering has been part of warfare. He read about the Romans and their secret spies.

Several months ago, the chief of police had promoted Arie to Investigative Police Officer, seeing that Arie was capable of doing more than patrolling the streets as an ordinary officer. Shortly after Arie's promotion, the chief gave him his first chance to prove himself with the murder investigation of Mrs. Van Sluister. In record time, Arie concluded the investigation quite adroitly, leading to the indictment of Mr. Van Sluister for murdering his wife and filing a fraudulent insurance claim.

During the investigation, Arie had worked closely with Willem van Lansfoort to solve the case. The managing director of the company V.L. Insurance and Surety in Amsterdam, Van Lansfoort had been appointed to a critical position in the Dutch Intelligence organization by Prince Bernhard of the Netherlands.

As a police officer, Arie had impressed van Lansfoort to such an extent that he received a call about a position in intelligence. Van Lansfoort arranged for Arie to meet with Colonel Harry Ternouw at the Intelligence Bureau in Amsterdam. For an opportunity like this, Arie wanted to prepare diligently by studying military intelligence and its history. As Arie leafed through the *Origins of Intelligence Gathering* in the library, he came upon an interesting footnote about the Roman legions and their intelligence unit. Arie learned about the encryption system used by Julius Caesar. He wondered how it was possible that Caesar created a system to send coded messages to his generals on the battlefield more than two thousand years ago. The book explained how to encrypt text using a simple algorithm known as "Caesar Cipher." The code substitutes a letter with another letter of the alphabet by using a constant. For example, when the constant is 3, shifting three positions down in the alphabet, the letter "A" becomes the letter "C." Arie was excited about this game and caught on quickly. In anticipation of his meeting, he experimented with the code by creating a brief message in Caesar Cipher. He added the cipher experience to his resume, which added to his accomplishments in the best light.

The next day, Arie left the house wearing his police uniform. He wanted to make a "military" impression on the interviewers. Riding his bicycle, he loved to whistle, and this morning was no exception. He could not put out of his mind the tune his father had played on his violin the night before: "Song of the Volga," based on the story of a soldier sitting on the banks of the Volga River, dreaming of his girl back home.

Will I become that soldier? He mused. He looked at the cloudy sky and wondered when it would start to rain. To stem his darkening mood, he continued whistling. Overhead, grey clouds rolled in from Germany. Arie saw these clouds as an omen for what was to come for his family in Holland. He had good reason to feel this way. Two months ago, without warning, German storm troopers had invaded Czechoslovakia and Austria. Emboldened by their success, Germany continued its military buildup of armaments and troops in direct violation of the Treaty of Versailles.

Earlier, at the police post, rumors floated around about a Dutch spy who stole documents from the office of the Abwehr (the military intelligence service of the German Army) in Berlin. The captured documents revealed Hitler's intention to attack Holland within the next eighteen months. In a footnote, initialed by Hitler, he declared that Holland would be quickly overrun, given the Germanic ethnicity of the Dutch people and the ties of the Dutch royal family to Germany's imperial family. Because of these historical perspectives, Hitler predicted that the Dutch people would welcome the invading troops with open arms.

Arie arrived at the Intelligence Bureau with his curriculum vitae and the encoded message he had written the night before hidden in an old World War I gas mask. He wanted to impress the interviewer with his ingenuity of hiding documents.

Arie entered the unfamiliar building and peered around the corner in the hallway, seeing Colonel Ternouw's nameplate. He cautiously turned the doorknob and found himself in a dim room. It took a while for his eyes to adjust to the darkness.

Ternouw entered the room after him, and Arie handed over his curriculum vitae. Ternouw glanced at it briefly before speaking. "Willem van Lansfoort, whom you know from your police work, briefed me on your background," he said curtly. "He provided your background information and spoke highly of your accomplishments as a police officer. Willem is a founder of the Dutch Intelligence Bureau. He works directly with Prince Bernhard, head of the bureau." Ternouw went on to explain the importance of intelligence for the Dutch Armed Forces.

"Remember that Holland is a small country. When war breaks out with Germany, intelligence gathering will make the difference between victory and defeat. It will fall upon our efforts in the bureau to collect vital information on troop movements and equipment before the invasion."

Just then, van Lansfoort entered the room, walking straight to Arie and greeting him warmly as an old acquaintance. Van Lansfoort also knew Arie's father, whose paintings his company had insured. He regretted not being present when Arie arrived to introduce him properly.

"Yesterday, I attended an urgent meeting of the Intelligence Bureau, presided over by Prince Bernhard," van Lansfoort began. "The German Armed Forces are amassing in huge numbers on the border with Holland. We must immediately send a spy to the border region in Germany to give us an accurate assessment of the military situation. We require an individual who can leave on short notice to spy on the Krupp Werke (Factories) in the Ruhr Region. Krupp is the manufacturer of heavy military equipment for the German Army. We are deeply concerned with the manufacturing of the Panzer Tanks, which are superior in speed and accuracy to any tank on the European Continent."

On the table, Ternouw studied the coded message Arie had written in Caesar Cipher. "You know Arie well enough from the police force that I recommend Arie as a candidate for the position of an intelligence officer," he said, pointing at the message. "Take a look at Arie's message, encrypted in Caesar Cipher. Pay attention to the content he chose."

> "The life that I have is all that I have
> The love that I have for God, Queen, and Country
> Is yours eternally."

"This speaks volumes to his pledge of courage and commitment," the colonel stated.

Van Lansfoort nodded. "I agree with you," he whispered. "He is our man. We must immediately start his training to go into Germany."

"In one week, you will be on your way," Ternouw informed Arie. "Tomorrow you will start formal training on the essentials of intelligence-gathering operations. Never give away your cover. Intelligence gathering requires a high level of secrecy and resourcefulness to maintain your cover. We want the outside world to speak of you as a 'man hard to place.' You are no longer of use to us once your cover is blown." Arie felt excited and worried at the same time. He knew he had placed himself at serious risk. Taking comfort from his coded message, he saluted as he departed.

"I am ready to serve," Arie assured, having just joined the Dutch Military Intelligence Bureau.

When he returned home from his meeting in Ternouw's office, he found his father in a state of excitement. He had already received a phone call from van Lansfoort to discuss Arie's assignment. They needed a particular location in the Ruhr Valley for Arie to undertake his espionage work. Eschelbach, situated in the Ruhr Region, was the city of choice for Arie's spy work.

Before Arie had a chance to talk to his father, van Lansfoort had already briefed him via telephone about his first spy mission in Germany. When Antonius asked why he was going to Eschelbach, the professor only mentioned that his sister lived in the Ruhr Region. When van Lansfoort explained that she could be trusted entirely, he left out the fact that she provided the locale for clandestine meetings of the German officers plotting to kill Hitler.

The fact that she had been in a thriving practice as a leading prostitute in town, serving high-level German officers, he also left out of the conversation. Once a very attractive woman, age and a sagging figure had caused her business to fall dramatically, forcing her to switch from prostitution to a new profession. She became a foot care specialist, hanging a new shingle: PEDICURIST. Her former clientele stayed loyal and returned for foot treatments. Gertle was not shy in admitting, "If one has to start again, it may as well be at the bottom, the feet." With the German officers in her pedicure salon, she remained on a first-name basis, amiable and pleasant as ever.

On his way to Eschelbach, Arie reminded himself that he traveled under the alias of an insurance agent for van Lansfoort's company. His instructions were clear: collect as much information as possible about troop concentrations and equipment on the border of Holland.

Arie arrived in the late afternoon at Gertle's in Eschelbach and was amused by the new Pedicure shingle, quickly realizing this was the perfect ruse to keep the Gestapo at bay. He pulled the chain to the doorbell, and a lively, middle-aged woman opened the door with a smile. She spread her arms to embrace Arie, as she had been expecting his arrival.

Without uttering a word, she quickly led Arie through the hallway into the kitchen. As they walked through, Arie noticed the pedicure salon on the right, separated from the kitchen by a curtain. She offered him coffee and strudel, motioning for him to take his luggage upstairs. She whispered in his ear that she was finishing a pedicure on her last customer of the day. Arie sensed that she had a German officer in the salon. After depositing his travel bag upstairs, he decided to stay close to the pedicure salon to overhear their conversation.

Gertle's clients usually enjoyed a glass or two of Schnapps during their visits. It helped them relax and open up about more sensitive matters. They often shared their deepest secrets, military or personal, with Gertle. Today's client was Colonel Hank Strössel, a highly-positioned officer at Krupp Werke. In a loud voice, he talked about the pressure put on him by the German Army to increase production of tanks, artillery pieces, and marine parts.

"The SS is unreasonable," he told her. "There is no way that I can meet the demands being made by Hitler. Unfortunately, this may put my promotion in jeopardy if I do not meet the quota." He paused and then continued. "I may have a solution. Have you noticed how frequently the trains roll by at night?" he asked her.

"Yes, the increased rail traffic keeps me awake," Gertle replied. "At night, I see train after train, with lots of cattle cars …"

"You must keep this between us. I have come up with a solution. I ordered an increase in the cattle cars transporting Jews from the concentration camps to the Krupp Werke. The German authorities put Jews to work assembling Panzer tanks. Jews should be grateful that we give them the opportunity to work towards their freedom. After all, the sign above the gates of the concentration camps makes that clear 'Arbeit Macht Frei' (Work Will Set You Free). If they can read, they will understand the true meaning of the slogan: it is an elegant and mystical declaration of self-sacrifice in the form of labor, which brings a kind of spiritual freedom. This idea leaves an incredibly powerful impact on each prisoner," he explained passionately.

Unsure whether to go along with Strössel's interpretation, Gertle did not dare challenge him. In Germany, very few people were true Nazis, but many enjoyed the return of German pride. They were too busy with their lives, leaving no time to care about the plight of the Jews. As a German, Gertle had no choice but to go along with the idea that Jews must pay the price in rebuilding Germany after WWI. Strössel looked at his feet, where Gertle was filing his big toenails.

He abruptly changed the subject. "Shortly, I will be up for promotion. I will need to prove to my superiors that I deserve it. Only something spectacular will convince them that I deserve it." He paused as he admired her masterful work on his gnarly toes.

"I have been working on the development of the Biber mini-submarine manufactured at Krupp Werke under my direction," he told her, getting more specific. "Germany has no port on the North Sea adequate to field test this new vessel. The engineers in the program have set their sights on a port on the North Sea, in Holland." Gertle thought immediately of Arie. Gertle decided to tell Arie. Here was something Arie could bargain with. She offered Strössel another Schnapps. As she completed filing his toes and proceeded to polish them, she allowed him to down his drink.

"Would you be interested in talking to someone about this?" Gertle asked him, not knowing whether Arie had any connections with the government in Holland. He put his glass on the little table next to his chair, raising his eyebrows with a skeptical look on his face.

"Do you know someone?" he asked.

"Let me fetch him from his room." She pushed through the curtain to find Arie, telling him what he wanted and advising him to deliver on the deal. Arie was unsure what Strössel was expecting of him.

"May I introduce Arie Habers?" Gertle asked, back in the salon. "He is in town on business."

Strössel felt the excitement building in him … this could be a stroke of luck. He repeated what he had told Gertle about the Biber submarines, carefully watching Arie's face for a reaction. Arie remained stone calm, as he mulled over his response in his head. Gertle was no stranger on how to move conversations along smoothly. She poured another round of Schnapps, this time including Arie. If Arie played his cards right, he could benefit the Dutch Military. Arie took a deep breath and mustered the courage to bluff himself through this deal making.

"Scheveningen in Holland is situated on the North Sea. The Dutch Government recently built new docking facilities, which may be of interest to you. The lighthouse covers an area of ten kilometers, with a light beam flashing at intervals of two and seven seconds, the only port on the North Sea with this unique feature. It may come in handy for your test maneuvers." This information impressed the colonel.

"This is exciting news!" he said. "What are the drawbacks of your facilities?" Arie moved closer to the colonel, looking at the footbath where the colonel's feet were still soaking. The shallowness of the water in the tub gave Arie a quick idea about how to answer this tricky question.

"The port of Scheveningen lies on shallow water, not suited for deep-sea marine traffic," Arie said with a smile.

"This should be no problem since we are testing mini-submarines in shallow water," the colonel assured. Arie took a deep breath, problem overcome. They both looked at the shallow water in the foot tub and chuckled. It broke the tension between the two men. Strössel was not convinced of Arie's authority to make such a deal.

"Are you sure the Dutch will approve?"

"There is no doubt in my mind that they will okay this deal," Arie told him. Arie smelled success in his first endeavor as a spy. "I wonder if you could assist my company with our business expansion in Germany."

"And what might that be?"

Looking the colonel straight in the eye, Arie explained, "I work for V.L. Insurance and Surety Company, Marine Casualty, as an insurance agent. In Europe, we are the only insurance carrier in the marine industry. My mission is to establish our company here in Germany." Strössel became cautious, ever mindful of the prospect of his promotion. He let Arie continue.

"My company has an interest in Krupp Werke. We only provide insurance to a small portion of the industry. The inventory sheet needs to be completed, to prepare a quote on the premium for an updated policy." Strössel saw no difficulty with his request.

"The head of engineering at Krupp is a close friend. I will set up a meeting for tomorrow," he told Arie, who could not believe his good fortune.

He and Strössel arrived the next morning at Krupp headquarters to meet with the manager of the Engineering Division. Both had a Schnapps headache. It all went okay until Arie pulled out the insurance questionnaire. The engineer insisted on obtaining approval from his superior. Strössel became impatient and demanded the engineer take action immediately, explaining the urgency of finding a testing site for the Biber submarine. He insisted that finding a seaport on the North Sea for the Biber experiments took precedence over his small demand for pre-approval. Strössel assumed the approval for this deal.

"Admiral Raeder is insisting that we start testing immediately. We must make sure that the minis are up to our operational standards under seafaring conditions. We cannot wait any longer. Let's complete the questionnaire and get on with the testing," Strössel urged. When the engineer heard mention of Admiral Raeder, head of the German Navy, he dropped his demand and completed the form. Arie watched the engineer write the numbers on his form. He could hardly believe his eyes when the engineer provided exact data about armaments production at Krupp.

When he returned to Gertle's that afternoon, he took a few minutes to read the engineer's report. He was amazed at the details he saw in the report. The daily production for Panzer tanks was two hundred and twenty-five; the numbers for production of heavy artillery, navy guns, and munitions were also astoundingly high. Here he saw with his own eyes the buildup of power of the German war machinery.

Gertle was proud of her role in this intelligence caper, which had started in her pedicure salon. More so, she told Arie how proud she was of him for succeeding beyond the expectations of what only experienced intelligence agents could hope to achieve after months of surveillance. It was apparent to Arie that she had been involved in this type of operation before. She had something to celebrate his success: a meal of smoked eel, rye bread, and dark beer … a rarity for Arie. She unrolled the newspaper in which she had stored the eel, bought that morning from the fish cart. As Arie readied himself to gorge on this delicacy, Gertle put a damper on his enthusiasm.

"Look how exhilarated you are with your exploit," she exclaimed. "Do not let that go to your head … you will find yourself in deep trouble if you throw caution to the wind. Let me show you what I mean." Taking Arie's fish and placing it on a wooden block, with a hammer, she nailed a horseshoe nail through its eyeballs. With a knife, she circumcised the collar, grabbing the eel's casing and tearing the skin free from the body with one rip, like taking off a wet glove.

"I am showing what will happen to you if you become too adventuresome and brash," she told him, pointing at the naked eel body. Arie looked at the eel and lost his appetite, leaving the table with nothing more than the image of a skinned spy. Upon his return home, Arie did not waste any time before visiting Colonel Ternouw. When they reviewed his intelligence data, they congratulated him on his accomplishment. Arie was the first Dutch intelligence agent to capture a detailed picture of the buildup of Germany's war machine. If he succeeded in convincing his superiors to base the testing facility for the German mini-submarine in Scheveningen, he would have a double success story to his credit. His caper would allow them to research the Biber Submarine in the North Sea.

Something else gnawed at him; he must tell his superiors about the use of Jews as forced laborers in the Krupp factories. In 1938, the use of forced labor was only a rumor. No confirmation existed until Arie detailed it in his intelligence report. Ternouw immediately informed Prince Bernhard. The next day, newspapers in Amsterdam, London, and New York carried the story about forced labor in Germany.

In his final intelligence report, Arie failed to mention the "eel affair," despite the memory loitering in his nightmares.

CHAPTER 10

Castle Lindendale

MANUS HAD RECEIVED THE MOST SIGNIFICANT COM-
mission of his career with the Stations of the Cross in the open-
air park behind his parish church. The space at his parents'
home was too small to store fourteen enormous granite blocks
from which to carve the stations.

This morning, he woke up late and went straight to his
shop. He'd had a bad night's sleep riddled with nightmares
about where to find a larger space.

Holding a cup of tea, he kicked open the door and surveyed the chaos. He could hardly believe the disarray he had
created over the years. Broken clay models lay helter-skelter
throughout the workshop, dust-covered and connected with
spider webs. Spiders crawled aimlessly in search of food scraps.
Manus was not particular about left behind food crumbs.

Yesterday, he had managed to finish the death mask for
the deceased Mrs. van Aalst, bronzing it with a high gloss. It
was his best one so far. In the distance, he heard the church
bells toll, summoning parishioners to her funeral. Just before
10 o'clock, he delivered the mask to the undertaker, who placed
it on the lid of the coffin.

He decided not to attend the funeral mass. Instead, he stuffed his pipe and set off for a long walk in search of an expanded room for his atelier. He hoped to take a long walk in the woods at the outskirts of town. The solitude cleared his cluttered mind, allowing him time and space to ruminate about life. His beret askance on his head, he turned onto Castle Lane, where weeds had overtaken the dirt path. The old tracks used years ago were barely visible. The trees on both sides gave the road an aura of aristocratic dignity. The only life in the woods was a raven, taking an angry swipe at his beret, hoping to distract him from finding a solution to his space problem.

Suddenly, through the shadows of the trees, he saw the outline of an old castle. The three-stepped structure with capstones in the windows revealed its seventeenth-century architecture. The old brick walls reflected in the water of the moat surrounding the castle. He stopped at the ramshackle drawbridge, pondering whether to cross the broken boards. Unsure whether they were safe to walk on, he moved gingerly forward, sidestepping the broken pieces of wood.

He hesitated. How could he afford an atelier in a castle? Above the entrance of the portico, a weathered sign announced the name: Castle Lindendale – 1677.

He rang the clapper and heard the sound resonating throughout the castle proper. After a few minutes, he heard the shuffling sound of someone approaching. A senior woman opened the heavy wooden door with squeaky hinges. She was dressed in black and wore a white apron. With her plump appearance and smile, she came across as a friendly character.

"Hello, young man," she said. "Are you lost? I am Clara Habers. What is the purpose of your visit?" Manus was surprised that she went by the same name as his family. He was so nervous that he forgot to introduce himself. Not daring to look at her, he stumbled over his words.

"I am a sculptor, and I was thinking ... " When she heard the word "sculptor," she raised her hand and stopped him mid-sentence. She showed him into the courtyard paved with cobblestones. In the stable, Manus saw a horse munching on hay. In the back of the stable, he spotted an old carriage from the nineteenth century. The gold leaf patina had peeled off long ago. They stopped at the main entrance to the castle hall.

With a sweeping gesture, she opened the massive oak doors and announced in an exaggerated manner, "You are entering the Hall of Knights." Manus had read about old castles often having formal halls like this one. He looked up at the tall ceiling, convinced the rafters were sturdy enough to hold the tackle required to lift the granite blocks from which he was going to carve the Stations of the Cross. Large paintings in dust-covered frames hung from the walls, displaying portraits of the previous owners. Manus stopped at the canvas with the nameplate Gustav Habers I – 1779-1830. Clara pointed to a distinct looking medal on the nameplate with a green national flag of a country unknown to Manus: Circassia. Manus could not take his eyes from the peculiar looking features of the face in the portrait. Judging by his attire, he surmised that he was of nobility. Clara looked Manus in the eye, turning away as she shook her head in disbelief, not uttering a word. He looked like her brother. Manus had eyes similar to the ones in the portrait.

"I apologize, I never introduced myself. I am Manus Habers," he said awkwardly. "I shall be going now ... " She looked at him intensely and stopped him.

"You are the son of Antonius Habers, the famous painter of the Rembrandt Tulips, right?" she proclaimed in a firm voice, wagging her index finger at him.

Manus nodded, wondering what this had to do with the portrait. Was it because her name was also Habers? After all, no one else in town had that name.

"I wonder if I should be the one to talk about your family history," she went on after a pause. "I have just come to realize that we are relatives. The reason you have not found out about your family provenance is simple. We live with a vow of silence never to talk about our family secret. I wonder if the time has come to speak the truth about Anna Petrovsky, my mother." Clara kept talking.

"As my mother grew old, she became more anxious to show her family pictures from the days she lived in Maasbree, Limburg. Raised in an aristocratic family, she was a beautiful and quite lively girl, especially with the boys in town. Her family were descendants of an old Circassian aristocratic family that had migrated from the Black Sea in the early half of the nineteenth century. The boys in town sought after my mother, being the Circassian beauty that she was. Her free spirit caused a lot of shame to the family. To spare further embarrassment, her parents sent her to Marianna Habers at Castle Lindendale. One morning, they simply sent her off in a horse-drawn carriage with a large sum of money and a letter of introduction to her aunt in Mill. That was the reason why she came to live here," Clara concluded.

Reality dawned on her that here stood the son of her estranged brother. How far was she prepared to go to tell Manus the whole truth about the goings on at Lindendale Castle? She could not resist asking, "Are you going to tell your father that you visited Lindendale Castle? It is up to him to fill you in on the family history."

"I must tell my father about the beautiful portrait in the Grand Hall; he will be fascinated," Manus answered.

"Before leaving, I'd like to give you some exciting information about Gustav Habers I. He was the Duke of Saxony. In the second half of the nineteenth century, the Russians expelled most of the Circassian aristocrats from their homeland. With his family, he migrated to Germany, where they became part of the German aristocracy. Thanks to their connections with the elite Federation of Circassians living in the diaspora and paying large sums of money, the German Emperor Wilhelm I bestowed him with the title of Duke.

Clara paused, studying Manus' face and wondering whether to keep revealing long-held family secrets. As she stood up to get more tea, her cheeks turned to a rosy blush. Back in her chair, she re-arranged her bonnet and pondered how to proceed. Manus became restless.

"I should go now," Manus told her.

"You haven't explained why you came here in the first place," Clara said.

"I received my first major commission for the Stations of the Cross for the parish church. The planning commission requires life-size stations for the park behind the church in the Via Dolorosa. I need to carve fourteen stations out of large granite blocks, about 3 meters long, 2 deep and 2 high," he demonstrated with his arms. "Unfortunately, I have run out of space for my atelier at my parents' home. Fourteen large granite blocks are on order, and I have no room to have them delivered. I am depending on this delivery to start my commission." Clara turned to pour another cup of tea. She pictured fourteen Stations of the Cross under construction in her Hall of Knights. It would fill her with pride to have the sculptor of these monuments on the premises. She adjusted her apron.

"As you can see, I am the only one living here, and I have a lot of open space," she told Manus, gesturing with pride at the kitchen and bakery oven. Manus had never given much thought to cooking or washing dishes. He found it beneath his dignity to exchange his sculptor's tools for a dish rag. "It would be an honor to have you on the premises." Manus had his doubts about sharing the kitchen with her. "Perhaps we can work out an arrangement that will make it possible for you to transfer the atelier from your parents' home. Will the Hall of Knights suffice for the delivery of the granite blocks?"

Quickly estimating in his head, he declared, "Yes, there is adequate room for the delivery." He could hardly believe his luck, but there was still a problem, as he explained to Clara. "This is my first commission, and I've already spent the advance on purchasing the granite for the project." Clara squinted, looking away from Manus before returning to face him.

"You have no money for rent?" she inquired, forcing Manus to admit to the raw truth about his financial situation.

Downcast, he murmured, "I shall be leaving now." Clara was not ready to let an opportunity slip through her fingers without trying.

"Let me suggest something that may appeal to you," she offered. "You are a sculptor, and if you agree to my terms, you may stay here free of rent. I have been planning my funeral arrangements. I need someone to make a tombstone and death mask. Besides, I would like a statue of Mary and Jesus on my grave." Manus was inclined to accept this arrangement. However, he was not so sure it was wise for him to work for Clara. He had to talk with his father first.

"Before I can accept your gracious offer, I must go home to tell my father the good news." Foremost, Manus wanted to discuss matters with his father about the family history. He had not worked through the story he had just heard from Clara. Holding her hand out to Manus, Clara shook his hand.

"I understand," she said with a nod. Taking leave, Manus hurried home to tell his father about his find in the woods.

As he filled his pipe, his father steadied himself by holding onto the back of his chair, as if preparing to deliver a sermon from the pulpit. "For all these years, I have remained silent about the family secret. Castle Lindendale is our family's ancestral home. There is ample reason for my silence. By turning into the woods outside town, you found my sister, Clara

Habers. We have not spoken to each other since mother passed away. What happened within the castle walls has been a secret for sixty-eight years. By revealing the secret, I remind you that our family honor is at stake.

"In 1870, Duke Gustav Habers and Anna Maria Petrovsky met for the first time at Castle Lindendale. She had just arrived from Maasbree with a letter of recommendation addressed to her aunt, Marianna Habers, who resided at the castle. The letter addressed to Professor Gustav Habers pleaded with him to rehabilitate Anna Maria in the Circassian traditions. He was the Professor of Ethnic Populations of Southeastern Europe with an emphasis on Peoples of Circassia. He was an expert on ethnic populations in the Black Sea and Northern Caucasus regions and a guest lecturer at the University of Leyden in Holland. He needed a stopover during the long trip by horse and carriage from the University of Göttingen in Germany."

Antonius took another puff on his pipe, hesitating for a moment and pondering whether the time had come to reveal what had happened at Castle Lindendale so many years ago.

"It was early February on a cold and foggy day. The professor had been on the road since early morning. He arrived at the castle late at night. Anna Maria was cleaning up after dinner. When she heard the clapper, she hurried to open the gate. After he announced himself, she let the professor's horse and carriage through the gatehouse. In the kitchen over tea and sandwiches, they became quickly acquainted. He was a distinguished looking individual, debonair and charming. They exchanged views on the cold weather. He told her he lectured in languages unique to the Black Sea Region of the Northern Caucasus.

"That fascinates me because my family comes from that region," she told him, hearing his story. "Few people are aware of Circassia." The professor wondered if she was familiar with Adygha, the native tongue of the Circassians.

"Have you heard of the Circassian people?" he asked in Adyghan, exploring this possibility.

"I was raised in a Circassian family and learned to speak the language when I was a child," she replied in Adyghan. Habers had always dreamt of finding someone with whom he could converse in this uniquely distinct language. However, there was more to his feelings than the love of linguistics. He looked into her beautiful eyes.

"You are an exceptional woman. I've often dreamt of meeting a Circassian beauty like you. You are like a dream coming true for me," he told her. Anna Maria knew that the magic of love had revealed itself.

"I suspect you have lived under the shadow of the Circassian tradition. Time has arrived to unveil yourself," he continued in his professorial fashion, as he touched her cheek and spoke of her raven black tresses brushing her angelic face. He gently stroked her cheek and called out her name in Adyghan. When he looked into her eyes, he saw her longing to explode in passion. Anna Maria scarcely believed her rapture, and it empowered her as never before to perform to the fullness of his pleasure. With their act of love, they wittingly sealed their Circassian bond.

A couple of months later, she knew she was pregnant.

When Habers returned to Castle Lindendale, Anna Maria invited him for a walk in the forest. "Much has happened since you were here last," she told him, no longer able to wait to tell him the news. She looked him in the eyes. "I am carrying your child." He stopped walking, taking her into his arms and kissing her. He acted like a man in love with his new bride.

"A mortal did not conceive you. The spirit of Queen Satanaya is your progenitor, as she is the progenitor of all Circassians, as foretold in the *Book of the Nart Sagas*," he told her with joy in his face. Everything was going to be all right. They walked in silence, holding hands. "Of course, I must follow the code of the aristocracy," he commented, which sounded alarming to Anna Maria. "It is the protocol that I protect the honor and title of my family name. The child cannot be born here at the castle. Do not worry, my dear. I will make the necessary contacts to arrange for a place where you will deliver, without causing any dishonor to my family." His honor as a duke and distinguished professor was at stake. He could not let his title tarnish his reputation of Duke of Saxony. Anna Maria could not hold back tears. He tried to reassure her. "Everything will be well with you and the child. Soon, you will know where to deliver your baby." With his handkerchief, he wiped away her tears. Had he said "your" baby? Was it not "ours"? Anna Maria mused.

In the middle of the night, her coachman helped her enter the black carriage with gold trim. She was all alone in the darkness of the richly appointed coach, curtains drawn. The noise of the four horses trundling over the drawbridge in the stillness of the night startled her. She tried to sleep.

As the first rays of the sun rose over the horizon, she peeked through a crack in the curtain. They passed farmers, with their horse-drawn carts loaded with produce on their way to the market. It took several more hours before they arrived in 's-Hertogenbosch, where they turned on Duke's Lane, lined with elegant bourgeois homes. The coach came to a halt at a massive iron gate. The coachman dismounted and pulled the chime of a convent house. A friendly face in a nun's habit appeared and hurried over to help her down when the coachman announced her arrival. The convent of the Sisters of the Holy Cross was the only delivery hospital in Holland where nobility could drop off their pregnant charges in total anonymity.

Ten days later, she delivered her child, a boy. Sister Amanda provided the nursing care during the delivery. She brought up the birth certificate, filed with the city. Anna Maria had named Duke Gustav Habers I as the father. Sister Amanda needed clarification.

"Are you and Duke Habers married?" Anna Maria turned her head away from Sister Amanda.

"No," she murmured in shame. Under these circumstances, the city registrar always made the customary entry: "Said child is born out of wedlock." Anna Maria could not hold back tears. Was she now entirely on her own and abandoned by the professor?

Three days later, Habers visited. He kissed her, then gently cradled the baby in his arms. A glow of happiness came over him, as he admired his son. Anna Maria wiped away a tear. She picked up the birth certificate from the nightstand and handed it to him with a shaky hand. He read the registrar's notation: "Said child is born out of wedlock."

He brushed away a tear from her face and kissed her. She looked adorable, yet forlorn. Torn between the urge to protect his family name and his duty as a Circassian, he chose the latter. He went to the registrar's office that same day and signed his name on the birth certificate as the father of the newborn baby. He had decided to abandon his aristocratic name, giving up all privileges that came with it. He adopted Gustav Habers without a title as his new name.

Three months later, Anna Maria Petrovsky and Gustav Habers were married.

"I can no longer keep the family provenance to myself," he said. "Anna Maria Petrovsky is my mother." There it was. Manus now knew who his grandmother was. Left to question the need for all the hush and secrecy, he wanted to hear the rest of the story.

"The day before mother died, she called me to her bedside. She was ailing with pneumonia. In a broken voice, barely audible, she talked of her ancestors. They were members of a well-respected aristocratic family, expelled from Circassia during the war with Russia. They migrated from the Caucasus Mountains to Germany and Holland. As she lay dying, she spoke of the burning desire of Circassian people to one day regain their lost motherland. She looked up at me and said in a strained voice, 'I will not live to see my beloved Circassia on the Black Sea again.' Tears welled up in her eyes. In her last words, she directed me to find an important document 'Go to the attic and look for a wooden box. There you will find your birth certificate. What you read in the margin of the document, you must keep to yourself. In a final gesture, she brought her hands together and started to pray in her native Adyghan."

"The next day I looked at my birth certificate. I could barely make out the notation in handwriting: 'Antonius Petrovsky - Born out of wedlock on September 12, 1870, in Hertogenbosch, Holland.' The certificate showed Gustav von Habers, the father of the child born to Anna Maria Petrovsky." Manus hugged his father as they silently thought through this brand new revelation about their ancestral lineage.

Later that morning, a Jewish family arrived at the Habers' home. Judging by the Star of David sewn on their coats, they were German refugees. The husband, wife, and their three children looked hungry and desolate, having slept in the fields for several cold nights. The man explained how they had crossed the German border on foot, penniless and with only one small satchel of clothing. Before granting their exit visa, the Germans had demanded they sign over all their belongings, including money, jewelry, and artwork to a "trusted attorney" in anticipation of their eventual return. These "attorneys" were traitors who worked as collaborators with the Gestapo. Gertle in Eschenbach, who had helped Arie with his spy work a year earlier, was asking for a return favor. She had given the family the Habers' address in the hopes they might find shelter in Mill. The Habers took them in, giving them food and a place to sleep. The next day, Manus moved from his parents' home to Castle Lindendale to make room for the Jewish family.

CHAPTER 11

Invasion

ALL WAS QUIET IN THE CASTLE. IT WAS 10 A.M. WHEN he stretched in bed. He pulled the cover up and rolled over on his side to continue snoozing. After a few minutes, he opened his eyes and noticed the old Linden tree in the window shade, branches waving in the wind, as if coaxing him to get up. The image on the window shade reminded him of the stained-glass window by Tiffany "The Magnolias." He decided to make a quick sketch of this unique scene.

He was so pleased with his work that he decided to find room in his drawing of the Garden of Gethsemane, in the first sculpture of the Stations of the Cross.

The sputtering of Arie's motorcycle broke the serenity of the spring season in the forest as he steered his vehicle between the broken boards of the castle drawbridge. He let the clapper down with a loud bang. When Manus did not appear immediately, he banged the clapper a second time with more conviction. Manus hurried to the gate and opened it, as Arie rode his motorcycle inside the courtyard. Manus left the gate open as he often did in his careless way. Arie had come to warn his brother. Although he knew how naïve Manus was about world politics, he still cared for him enough not to wallop him into reality. His visit was short and to the point.

"Manus, you must listen carefully. I have a message of great importance. It has to do with your friends Jope and Joris. You must stop meeting with them right away. You have no choice in the matter."

"Why are you ordering me around?" Manus asked, with a surprised frown.

Arie was not accustomed to sharing his sources of intelligence with anyone, but he made an exception for his brother. "Yesterday, at the Intelligence Office I found their names on the list of the NSB as sympathetic to Hitler's policies. You have probably never heard of the organization. It operates in secrecy, collaborating with the Nazis in Germany. Once Holland is invaded and occupied by the Germans, they will spring into the open and become the core cadre in Holland of the German Regime, which, I promise, will be installed soon after the invasion."

Manus was shocked. That they were German sympathizers was unthinkable. He vaguely recalled a few passing remarks by them about the Jews. "I am not entirely surprised," Manus said, after a brief pause. "Their casual remarks about the Jews did not register well with me. There were times when they hinted at their hatred for Jews and how they would like to see them expelled from Holland." Arie intercepted him.

"Let me clarify … they were not 'hinting about the Jews' … they spoke their beliefs. You need to see them for who they are. They will try to recruit you, and before you know it, you will fall into their clutches," Arie warned. The second reason for Arie's visit was to tell Manus the invasion was imminent. "To show you how imminent the war is, let me tell you about an incident that happened last week. British and German military officers gathered in secrecy in the town of Venlo. They are part of a plot to overthrow Hitler. General Schellenberg of the German Army insisted on including an agent from the German Intelligence Office at the next meeting. I had been suspecting that Schellenberg was a double agent, working directly for Hitler. Before the meeting could take place, Germans ambushed the car in which the British agents were traveling and promptly hauled them off to a concentration camp in Germany." Manus sat quietly through Arie's account of the incident. He looked at his brother with a degree of respect for his position as a spy with the Dutch Army.

"You were fortunate that the Germans did not execute you as well," Manus told him.

"Hitler will use the 'Venlo Incident' as a pretext to invade Holland," Arie continued. "My contact in the Dutch Embassy in Berlin told me that Hitler had set the deadline for the invasion of Western Europe one week from today." Manus began to panic.

"Large tank divisions are poised at the border to roll at a moment's notice," Arie went on. "The Dutch Armored Divisions consist of old tanks, left over from World War I. I am worried that we have only one modern experimental tank ready to go into battle."

To soothe his feelings of anxiety, Manus needed a break from the news about the war. He walked to the window to find solace in the spring blossoms in the forest. His brother joined him.

Suddenly Arie turned his attention towards the courtyard where Danya was walking. He had never seen her before. He turned to his brother slowly.

"Is that Danya in the courtyard?" he asked, captivated by her at first sight. He noticed how she walked in beauty, her black hair flowing with every step. As she entered the room, Danya looked elegant and demure, eyes downcast. Manus introduced her to his brother.

"Danya, meet my brother, Arie. He serves in the Army and has come for a visit. Danya has been helping me with my drawings for the sculptures of the Stations of the Cross," Manus told Arie.

Arie looked into Danya's eyes and admired the curls in her long black hair, her raven tresses slightly brushing her face. He struggled to focus on his duty as an officer. However, he could not take his eyes from Manus' drawings of Danya. He decided to derail his feelings towards her by complimenting her as a model.

"My brother could not have found a more perfect model for his work," Arie told her. In the silence that followed, she felt something strange in his words, something that caused a breathless flutter in her chest. Not much more, she told herself.

She turned her eyes to the medals on Arie's uniform. Danya wanted to reach out to this man of courage and strong character. For a brief moment, their eyes locked into each other's soul. Should war come to Holland, she would want someone like him to protect her from harm. It created a kernel of agony that Satanaya was not the one to help her out in difficult times of war.

"I shall go now," Arie announced, taking another look at Danya. Clutching his helmet, he walked through the grand hall where the granite blocks were stacked ceiling high. "Earlier, you showed me Danya's drawings. She is even more gorgeous than you drew her in your sketches," Arie told Manus. With that thought, he wondered about his brother's feelings towards her.

As they walked through the hall, they passed a row of death masks, dangling to dry at the end of piano strings, slowly twirling in the gentle breeze. Hitler's facemask caught Arie's attention. The hair lock across the forehead, the tidy mustache, sweating gypsum, fresh from the clay mold, gave away the perfect likeness of the German dictator.

"Did you make this?" he asked with a wink, poking Manus in the ribs as he pointed at the mask.

"My friends dared me to," Manus replied. "Hitler's time will come soon enough … I will be glad to deliver the mask in person when I get word that the plotters have succeeded in eliminating him."

"I will be the first one to let you know," Arie said, shaking his head, as he smiled and left their father's home.

Ars Brabantia was the publication to which every artist subscribed in Southern Holland. When Arie got home, he saw the paper on the kitchen table. Antonius Habers had written an editorial about the repression of free expression in the arts in Germany. It was a scathing rebuttal to the Nazi policies. Not everyone at the Academy was happy about his editorial. Rector Muller summoned him for a reprimand for his critical commentary. It did not take long for Habers to realize that Muller was a member of the NSB, a staunch Nazi sympathizer.

Arie had no interest in politics, but upon seeing the article, he became infuriated with the Nazi policies. When his father walked in, Arie stood up and pointed at the paper.

"I am proud of you, that you have written this editorial. You may as well get your true sentiments out about German politics before it is too late. It portends to show what will happen in our country when the Germans invade Holland," Arie told him. As if to add fuel to the anger floating in the kitchen, he added, "The invasion will start next week." His father looked at Arie in disbelief. He noticed the resoluteness in his face.

"As I see it, the Germans will call an end to our freedom, for which the Dutch are well known. We must dispel that there is no hope of getting rid of the Nazi vermin. I still remember my mother's words to fight with courage to the death," his father formally declared.

Habers paused as if to ponder the wisdom of bolstering what he just said. With the invasion at hand, the time had come to tell his sons how they must stand together under the leadership of the resistance, which was to form during the war.

"Our family are descendants of the Circassian people." Manus had heard of these exceptional people through Danya. To Arie, they were unknown. Driven by his inquiring mind, he became curious about his family's provenance.

"Who exactly are these Circassians?"

"The Circassian spirit runs through our blood," Habers answered. "They are a people driven from their homeland by the Russians, some one hundred and fifty years ago. To this day, they are fighting to return to their homeland in the Northern Caucasus Mountains. In history books, they are the forgotten people, called Circassians ... the original Caucasian Europeans known for their courage to fight for freedom to the death. Not many people can make that claim. We are proud to belong to these people."

Danya spent a long day modeling and had to hold a kneeling position looking up at Jesus dying on the cross for a long time. Manus asked her to keep her arms outstretched to portray the agony of the moment better.

After such a long time on her knees, Danya became exhausted from holding that position. Finally satisfied with his work, Manus showed the drawing to Danya. A cold chill rolled over her, as she had never felt before. Overwhelmed by the drama of the scene, she broke down in tears. Manus should have chosen someone else as his model. Confused, she sat in the corner of the room and silently wept.

Manus put his arm around her shoulder to console her. Words failed to come to his mind.

The time had come for Danya to call on the one who had promised to stand by her to overcome this painful moment. She knew Satanaya would not abandon her.

That evening, she returned home, where she found her aunt with the newspaper. She had a worried look on her face as she read about the impending war. She put the paper down and offered Danya a cup of tea. She started to tell her about World War I when she was a young girl. She shared the horrors she had experienced during that conflict, twenty-five years earlier. The government had incarcerated her parents as enemies of the state. They had both died in prison before the war ended. Danya felt devastated as she thought about her parents. The news added to Danya's fears of the future.

On May 10, Danya arrived at the castle earlier than usual. Manus invited her for a walk in the forest. Tall sycamore trees lined the road, their branches reaching up to the sky, forming an archway to shield them from the spring sun. Danya noticed the blackbirds flying around, feverishly hunting for grasses and sticks to build their nests. She wondered what happens to these little creatures when war comes. Nobody would be there to protect them from harm.

War was on everybody's mind. After hearing her aunt's story, she asked Manus, "Do you think the war will start soon?" Manus had no choice but to tell her what he had learned from his brother.

"Yesterday, through his secret channels, my brother found out that Hitler has set a date for the invasion." Danya's eyes widened with fear.

"Did he say when?"

"It will be next week. Although the threat of war hangs over the entire continent of Europe, his troops are poised to invade Holland as the first country in Western Europe."

"What can we do? Where will we go?" Danya wondered.

On their walk back, they heard the clop-clop-clop of a horse and cart moving towards them. Manus recognized his neighbor.

"Did you hear anything about the war?" he asked. Before he could answer, they turned their gaze towards a droning sound in the sky. A single airplane with the German Airforce

Cross on the sides buzzed high overhead. As it came closer, it grew louder. It sounded like glass clanging in a steel cup. Then, it changed to a whistle, like a kettle about to blow up. Out of the tailpipe of the plane, a white contrail drew its pathway against the blue sky.

Somewhere in the forest behind them, a massive explosion rocked the air, sending shockwaves through the trees. Seconds later, they gazed at a flotilla in the sky, looking like birds flying in formation ... airplanes. The Germans were in Holland!

Danya halted, crying out in panic. "What is that piercing sound? It terrifies me!"

"The air raid sirens are going off! They are giving us warning that bombers are on their way. We must hurry back to the castle!" He took her by the hand as they ran home.

The massive granite blocks in the great hall offered the best site to seek shelter. Hidden between the stones, Manus lit a candle. The air stank of dust, chalk, and mildew. When another bomb fell in the woods near the castle, dust fell from the rafters and two rats scampered by, trying to find safety. Manus wished he could offer shelter for his friends the rats before they disappeared in a crack in the wall. The continual droning of airplanes kept them hunkered down.

As evening fell, the "All Clear" air raid siren sounded a reprieve from the onslaught of dropping bombs. Danya left her hiding place to take a quick look through the window. In the far-away sky, she saw British Spitfires chasing German Stukas. There was no way of knowing who was winning the air battle.

The air raid sirens went off again around 10 o'clock at night. The bombardment continued endlessly through the night. With shrieking noise, shells fell around the castle, setting fires in the woods on the East and South sides. The granite stones where Manus and Danya were hiding vibrated with every explosion. They huddled through the deafening noise, which kept them awake through the night.

In the dark of night, they listened to the news bulletins on the BBC. The news from London was dreadful. German Panzer tanks had overrun the Dutch Defense Forces on the border. The Dutch fought with bravery to protect the bridges over rivers and canals. Despite the enemy's difficulty taking the bridges, they rapidly advanced to Den Haag, the seat of the Dutch royal palace. The Germans planned to capture the queen and her government officials as quickly as possible.

At last, it was dawn when an eerie quiet fell over the city of Mill. It felt worse than the continuous noise of bombs raining down from the sky. Danya worried about the town where her aunt lived. "I hope my aunt is alright. I wonder how many homes are still standing in the city?" she asked.

She went to the window to survey the damage. "Manus, look! The drawbridge is still standing!" she joyfully announced. "At least we can get across the moat."

"That is good news. Do not stand by the window," Manus cautioned. "It is too dangerous. Airplanes may return any time …"

Together, they left on bicycles, listening for the blare of the sirens. They worked their way to the center of town, circumnavigating the craters in the roads. A few houses were still smoking. People were desperate to save what they could.

Closer to town, they noticed more chaos, heavy dust, and wheezing crowds. The streets were a living, breathing dragon of humanity inching away from the center of town, moving westward, fleeing the invaders. The roads resonated with a cacophony of noises, honking horns, people yelling for help, babies crying, elderly moaning, and the smell of sweat heavy in the air.

At the station, the trains of the "Nederlandsche Spoorwegen" stood aimlessly in rows, as if they were discussing where to roll today. Smoke from the engines puffed up towards the arching ceiling. Somewhere, a whistle went off. Immense iron wheels began to churn towards an uncertain destination. On platform number 4, young men carried suitcases, women kissed them goodbye, and children reached out to daddies, begging them to stay home. Slowly, the train took off, and the platform trembled beneath the heavy weight of the machinery.

Danya wondered at the vast crowds of military men at the train station. She craned to see what was going on. In the distance, she recognized Arie in his military uniform giving directions to the young men, who were off to the front. He looked self-assured and confident in his role of commanding officer.

Back on the road, files of shuffling refugees swelled in the streets. Automobiles, bicycles, carts, and children's wagons loaded with boxes, suitcases, and bags were everywhere. Already the young and old were falling behind and losing hope.

Manus and Danya worked their way in the opposite direction towards the center, where they met with the ravages of the first day of the war. Suddenly, Danya dismounted her bicycle and dropped it to the ground. They had arrived at her aunt's street, but there was nothing left of her residence. A bomb had made a direct hit and completely razed it into a pile of rubble. Half a dozen neighbors with Red Cross armbands worked feverishly, tossing stones, rocks, pieces of cement, and broken beams in a frantic search for survivors.

Danya held Manus' arm and stood frozen, gazing in disbelief as she observed people moving in silence hoping to catch the sound of a human, listening for a cry for help from the rubble. Danya walked up to the broken front gate, hanging loose on one hinge. Here, the team leader of the rescue crew met her.

"Are you Danya? Is this your address?" Danya almost missed the entire question. She immediately knew what was coming.

"My aunt and I were the only ones living here," she answered in a low voice.

"We did everything we could. Emergency personnel transported your aunt's remains to the morgue. Is there a possibility that others were living with your aunt?" Sobbing, she shook her head.

A neighbor showed up with a wooden chest she had retrieved from the debris. Danya slowly opened it. She spotted the Circassian traditional dress that she had worn at her birthday party in the bottom of the chest. Inside was the walnut box with the fragrance bottle her mother had given her on her birthday. She quietly closed the chest. Today, it had such little meaning. Manus walked over to dry her tears.

In silence, they returned to the castle, which was now Danya's new home. War had closed her world of dreams for good.

With massive troop movements along the entire border, the German Army charged into Holland with overwhelming force. They failed to capture the queen and her government though, who evacuated to England on May 12.

The Dutch people felt abandoned, left to face the enemy on their own. After the fall of Rotterdam, the German invaders forced the Dutch Armed Forces to capitulate.

Life for the Dutch people under German domination had started in earnest. During the four-year occupation, the Dutch people showed how dear they held their spirit of freedom. They mounted a fierce resistance movement, in which Danya and the Habers brothers would shine as heroic warriors.

CHAPTER 12

Married by Force Majeure

THREE WEEKS AFTER THE GERMAN INVASION, THE local commandant of the SS summoned Arie. Dutch military personnel was ordered to enlist in the Political Police, under the command of the SS. Their responsibility was helping to enforce the Nazi regime's policies, such as rounding up the Jews. Arie thought this repulsive and unthinkable.

He immediately consulted in secrecy with van Lansfoort, head of the Dutch Intelligence Office in Holland, which had gone underground. Arie had been in close contact with him since the invasion. He had given a lot of thought to joining the underground movement. All he needed was someone to provide him with that final push to enlist.

At the meeting with van Lansfoort, Arie learned they were looking for a few intelligence officers with previous experience in the Dutch Army. Van Lansfoort explained they needed to identify a candidate as a double agent, enlisting in the SS Political Police while at the same time serving as an informant for her Majesty's Intelligence Bureau in London. With a handful of other Dutch Army officers, they would be the eyes and ears of the people, spying on German military activities on a full-time basis.

"I want you to be one of our double agents," van Lansfoort told Arie bluntly. "We already saw you at work in Eschelbaum. Once enlisted in the SS Political Police, you will be called on to join the Gestapo in roundups of Jews destined for German concentration camps. Your goal is to perform to such an extent that you rise to the highest levels in the German Command structure. Once you sit in on high-level planning sessions, you will be able to capture valuable intelligence and transmit it to London. You will excel for these reasons: You speak German without an accent, and your physique, flaxen blond hair and blue eyes make you a certain Aryan type. What is even more significant is the fact that you are Circassian. Working under stealth conditions is part of your genetics. With both hands on Arie's shoulders, he recited the pledge of loyalty to the Dutch Royal Crown: "For God, Country, and Queen." Arie remembered his father's words about fighting with courage to the death. The moment had arrived to allow himself to be a full-blooded Circassian. Gratified to find his niche as an officer finally, he was not going to disappoint.

Arie's tall, athletic physique, blond hair and blue eyes— hallmarks of a pure Aryan—made him a shoe-in for a critical position with the Gestapo. The Gestapo Commander appointed him to the chief, in charge of the Census Bureau for the city of Mill. Arie could not believe his good fortune to join the enemy's top-secret bureaucracy. Now he had direct access to essential population lists, with sensitive details about the ethnic origin of each civilian. The Gestapo based their round-ups on local census records to determine whom to send to the concentration camps.

With this source of information, Arie grew enthusiastic about the fact that he held a position allowing him to interfere with the deportation orders issued by the Gestapo. In his job as an agent with the Gestapo, he had no problem manipulating the census files to help the people of Mill, who were scheduled for deportation. Special notations in the census files with the letter "J" (Jew) denoted that they were destined for concentration camps. Arie took on his job with vigor, knowing he must act carefully, in secrecy. Would he dare to remove and destroy census records of Dutch citizens under the nose of his Gestapo superiors? A few hours into his research, he noticed the name Danya Mandraskit. The notation next to her name, "C" (Circassian), immediately sent him into an alert mode. Danya was in imminent danger of being arrested. He had to see his brother at the castle.

Two white swans were nibbling each other's necks, leisurely floating in the moat around the castle. It was spring and love was in the air for this pair of stately birds. War was not to interrupt their joy.

Arie's loud motorcycle disrupted their courtship; their massive flapping wings startled Arie as he dismounted his new Messerschmitt machine adorned with the Gestapo insignia on the handlebars.

Manus met him in the courtyard, shocked to see his brother for the first time in a Gestapo uniform. "You are a disgrace to our family for joining the Gestapo!" he said scornfully. "How could you lower yourself to take this step?" An angry tear rolled down his cheek. "Were you not there at the meeting with father, where we pledged to stand together against the invader? I feel like ripping that uniform from your body!" Arie could no longer keep it a secret that he was a double agent.

"Brother, calm down," Arie said calmly. "I'm here on a mission to save Danya's life. Let me explain why I became a double agent. Van Lansfoort, who persuaded me to serve in the resistance, contacted me. Simultaneously, I joined the Gestapo Political Police. I expect you will keep this secret. You must trust me." Without further delay, he came to the point. "I am worried about Danya's safety. The records in my office list her name under deportation." Manus looked shocked. He was not going to share the safeguarding duty of Danya with his brother. She would be safe with him, hiding in the castle. Arie noticed the torment in his eyes.

"Let me try to help. In my position as head of the Census Bureau, I may be able to keep her out of prison. There is a provision in the Gestapo Directive, which states that Jews and other undesirables in a 'mixed marriage' can obtain an exclusion from deportation." Manus looked at his brother in disbelief. He did not appreciate his brother getting involved in Danya's personal life.

On the other hand, he had never given any thought to the idea of Danya becoming part of his life. He offered so little regarding a future as a struggling artist. However, come what may, he was not going to abandon the girl who had served him faithfully as his model.

Manus decided to tell Arie that Danya would be well protected in her hideaway in the Great Hall. In case of an inspection by the Gestapo, they would not think of searching inside the hall where the Stations of the Cross were.

For weeks, he had diligently worked with hammer and chisel to refine Maria's face in Station IV "Jesus Meets his Mother on the Way to Calvary." At last, he'd found the perfect facial expression of grief and agony. When he stepped back from his work, he realized that he had unwittingly created the facial expressions of Danya, the image of a young girl in torment. Was this a signal to build her hideaway underneath Station IV? He spent hours shuffling dirt to create an underground opening to serve as a hiding place in case the Gestapo came looking for Danya. Arie was alarmed at his brother's naivety when he heard about the hiding place. Manus was underestimating the ingenuity with which the Gestapo carried out their relentless searches. Their agents were experts when it came to rounding up people from hidden locations.

"It lies in your power to save Danya from being imprisoned. Marry her! Once she is married to you, I will sign the certificate of mixed marriage to keep her safe from deportation," Arie urged. Manus did not know how to respond.

"Well, will you consider my proposition, or do you know of another gentile who would be available for marriage?" After a brief pause, Arie pressed on with his brother to get an answer. Manus did not answer, and with a hint of jealousy, Arie added, "Consider yourself lucky getting married to a beautiful girl." Manus was not amused. "Time is running out. You need to decide. Remember, my neck is in the noose as well. If the Gestapo learn of what I just did, they will execute me along with Danya! By the way, where is Danya?" he asked, looking around.

"She is in hiding in the Great Hall." Suddenly, she emerged, surprised to see Arie dressed in a Gestapo uniform. She stared at him, looking down at his black boots. Despite her disheveled hair and simple clothing, she looked exotic. Her amber eyes, angelic face, and enigmatic look made her special to Arie. Without a word, she turned to the fireplace and sat on a low stool. For a while, she buried her face in her hands, remaining silent. The silence in the room became unbearable. Finally, she looked at Arie.

"I am not sure that you belong here," she said in a calm voice, looking him in the eyes. "I should have stayed in hiding …." Arie tried to put her at ease.

"May I explain my uniform?" he began. "Prince Bernhard recruited me as a double agent, working for the Dutch Resistance. I am here to keep you from being deported. Gestapo agents may already be on the way to arrest you." He repeated what he had told Manus about "mixed marriages."

While shocked at Arie's proposition, Danya realized his idea could save her life.

Arie looked at Danya as if he had come to the rescue as her knight and savior. Danya felt bewildered and alone. She needed more time not to be so overwhelmed by the news.

She spent most of her time inside the castle. On a rare occasion, they risked taking an evening walk in the forest around the castle. They had to be careful. Unsavory elements often roamed around in the woods at night trapping rabbits. On this balmy evening, they needed fresh air. They snuck out and walked down a narrow path. Manus wanted to talk with Danya in the stillness of the woods, between bombing raids.

Through the trees, Danya saw the last rays of the fading sun. "Ever since my aunt died, I have felt alone. I have no contact with my family," she said somberly. "I miss my parents. I wonder about my father, who is close friends with the royal family. Will they be able to count on the support of the royal family? What will become of them under the German occupation?"

The only friend in Danya's world today was Manus. On their walk, she took his hand as they strolled through the woods. As they walked amidst the trees, the evening sky turned red and purple. With her dark curls tenderly bouncing off her shoulders, Danya looked like a fawn abandoned by its mother.

The song of the nightingale resonated through the woods, like the music of "Toselli's Serenade." Unsure of how to start the conversation about marriage, Manus gathered a ray of self-confidence. "My brother explained how a 'mixed marriage' would protect you from deportation. Can we talk more about it?" She let go of his hand and walked away in silence. Torn between her safety and marriage to a man she did not love, a voice inside whispered, *what does love have to do with this?* She was a Circassian girl, destined to follow her life's dream of finding that unique individual her mother had spoken about when she had given her the bottle of enchantment. Manus was someone she compared to a great pretender, living in a fantasy world, in his dilapidated castle, without food and with plenty of rats. She realized that her dream of becoming a sculptress was vanishing in the chaos of war.

Manus had never openly shown affection toward Danya. Until now, she had been a precious young girl, standing in for Maria, mother of Jesus. He was not going to violate that special bond he had with her as her teacher and changing her role from a model to a lover was unthinkable. Alternatively, he wondered if he should give it some thought.

In silence, they walked side by side, until the nightingale sang no more. Deep shadows fell behind the trees. Thoughts of imprisonment and deportation flooded Danya's mind.

When morning came, Manus made ersatz coffee from burned carrots. They shared a small portion of porridge, left over from the day before. Manus was the only one who received food ration coupons. Danya was not on the official register to receive her share. He gladly shared his food allotment with Danya.

In the room adjacent to the kitchen, he saw to it that the rats had something to eat too—leftovers, a crust of bread or rind of the old cheese. Manus explained to Danya that killing rats would do no good. If you feed the critters in a fixed location, they stay in that area; he told Danya. He had read this in a handbook on how to raise rats.

It was mid-morning when Arie returned to the castle with bad news. "The roundups of Jews are in full swing. Long lines of lorries are taking them to Westerbork, a Dutch transit prison, where the Germans held detainees for processing to concentration camps in Germany and Poland." Danya shuddered at hearing Westerbork. She had heard the name on the radio a couple of weeks back. Arie paused to take a long, hard look at Manus and Danya, trying to determine where they stood on the idea of marriage. "I have arranged for both of you to present yourself tomorrow in the basement at City Hall," he said, breaking the silence. "The registrar will be present at 10 o'clock sharp. You must do everything to keep the wedding a secret from the Gestapo." Manus looked stunned and turned to Danya. Looking at the floor where her shelter was, she shook her head. After removing the cover, she returned to her hideout to be alone.

"Danya cannot be seen in public while she travels," Arie continued. "Manus, find a way to smuggle her into town. Make sure she is not spotted." Arie suddenly turned and disappeared without further words.

Manus kept a tricycle for delivering statues and death masks in the old stable. All he had to do was manufacture a false bottom in the tricycle, just roomy enough for Danya to hide.

The next morning, Manus was on the road on his tricycle, with Danya in the secret compartment. In the lobby of City Hall, Manus caught a glimpse of the "Last Tulips" painting, so beautifully painted by his father a couple of years ago. In the lower office of City Hall, Manus and Danya were married, correctly signing the marriage register. The local magistrate had summoned two men to stand in as witnesses. They stumbled in from across the street, where the city café was. They were drunk. In case the Gestapo became suspicious, the magistrate wanted the witnesses in a drunken state to help them forget the marriage ceremony. After the wedding, he demanded ten guilders for each witness to cover the cost of the liquor they consumed.

Once outside, Manus pulled her toward him and kissed her. Danya turned away; to her, the marriage license was nothing more than a scrap of paper, a formality to save her life. After all, the occupation would not last forever, she thought. Once liberated, she would be free to find her real prince for life.

Manus and Danya were married only for the law. Afterward, in Catholic Brabant, couples traditionally also married in the church. That did not happen with Manus and Danya. The couple would have to remain abstinent.

German troops crawled through the town, consolidating their grip on Holland.

Day after day, Danya stayed inside, taking on kitchen chores for Manus. This morning, she peeked through the back window, looking out at the forest. A black piece of canvas flapped in the wind, tangled with ropes in one of the trees. She could barely make out the form of a man, slumped towards one side. He struggled to stand. Calling Manus, they looked at what was going on in the woods. Manus had an idea.

"I know who that is," Manus said. "A parachutist landed in our woods! Look at him in the branches. See his parachute tangled? I heard his plane last night. It must have been shot down. We must help him. Let's go!" They hurried through the woods and were upon the downed aviator in minutes. Manus noticed he was English by his uniform. They approached cautiously. He was badly injured.

"Hi, do you need help?" Manus asked him. At first, he failed to respond, but slowly he opened his eyes.

"I am a Royal Air Force pilot … my plane was shot down one kilometer from here. I was able to parachute out. As I climbed down from the high branches, I lost my footing and landed hard on a tree stump, breaking my leg. I am hurting badly." They heard search dogs barking in the distance.

Between the two of them, they helped him hobble on one leg to the safety of the castle. Danya sprang into action and boiled water to treat the open wound. Manus gathered food and a drink, which the aviator gladly accepted.

"We will hide you from the search party," Manus reassured him. "I know whom I should contact. He is with the

Dutch Underground." Within days, the flyer recuperated and became anxious to return to England.

Manus received word from Arie to drop the aviator off at a specific location outside of town. He reminded Manus that the tricycle he used for Danya was the perfect transport vehicle.

It was a rainy day, and Danya decided to handle the transport by herself. She needed to dress in disguise. Once the aviator laid down in the secret space of the tricycle, Manus loaded debris from his carvings on top of it to hide the false compartment.

Danya was not too happy with the heavy load Manus had piled in the tricycle. After pedaling in the pouring rain for a couple of hours, exhaustion set in, making it impossible for her to reach her destination. Just then, she heard German troops ordering her to stop at a checkpoint.

"Papiere!" they yelled. Danya produced her false passport. She told them the stones were for construction on a small dam in a tributary. Due to the heavy rain, the Germans believed her story, waving her through. The fear of being arrested made her tremble inside, but outwardly, she remained calm.

She followed directions to the letter, avoiding more checkpoints until she arrived at a farmhouse where she was to use a specific door knock and have her password ready: "Schort raapje." The Dutch Underground was partial to pass-words from the vegetable world, with words challenging to pronounce for the Germans.

Finally, she spotted the little farmhouse with its thatched roof nestled between rows of poplar trees. She rode her tricycle around the back to the rear door. First, three short taps on the door, then two long pause taps. She waited anxiously for some-one to come to the door. The curtain in the little rear window moved slightly, and she saw the face of a smiling older woman. She had arrived.

The rear door opened and she stated her password. The elderly woman indicated her reply code in a firm voice: "The frogs are still dancing." Danya rolled her tricycle inside the farmhouse.

Her elderly husband came out to see what the commotion was. His wife warmly embraced Danya and proceeded to help free the flyer from the false bottom of the tricycle. He had lost consciousness. After a few minutes, he came to, and she offered him a cigarette, followed by food and water. Soon, he was feeling better.

Danya was amazed to find these seniors with the courage to take in an RAF aviator. If the Germans were to find out, they would kill them both. It was not the first time they had helped parachutists who landed in their fields. In their eighties, they found the will to fight for the Dutch Resistance Movement. To Danya, they were the real heroes of the Dutch Resistance. During her trip home, she reflected on her life with Manus and compared it to the sharp will and dedication of the elderly couple to fight the enemy together. She felt exasperated that Manus failed to be a Circassian with a mission. She wondered if the time had arrived to join the resistance on her own.

That evening, back in her hiding place, Danya fell asleep, resolute in her decision to join the resistance the next day. She must get in touch with Arie.

CHAPTER 13

The Resistance

ON THIS FALL DAY, THE SUN SET IN A FESTIVAL OF reds and purples. Danya took time to dress warmly in her old woman disguise. The wooden shoes made her disguise all too authentic, but not so easy to ride her bicycle. She was getting good at eluding the guards at the checkpoints. They had no problem recognizing her as "the old lady from Castle Lindendale." After helping the aviator in the woods, Danya assisted others who were friendly to the resistance movement. She had yet to join the resistance movement officially. She wanted to prove she could take the risk of joining the ranks of underground workers.

Her first job involved delivering stolen food stamps from the Census Bureau to the family De Ruys. Arie had a hand in the theft of the two hundred food coupons. Danya picked up the bundle and bicycled it to the designated address. All went well until she attempted to repeat the drop three days later.

The resistance warned her that the Gestapo had set a trap to catch underground workers at this address. Two agents hid in the De Ruys' house, ready to entrap anyone arriving with false food stamps. She decided to take a significant risk.

Wearing her usual disguise, she hid a bottle of red ink to mark the house as a Gestapo-occupied domicile to be avoided at all cost by the underground.

It was raining on the evening of the mission. As Danya turned onto the street, she noticed an elderly couple with an umbrella walking home near her destination. She made a quick decision to circle the block and return, hopefully with a more successful result. This time the street was wet but empty. Without hesitation, she grabbed the bottle and smashed it forcefully against the wall of the façade. She was surprised at how big a mark the red ink had left. At the same time, she was worried about the noise of the breaking glass. She pedaled home contentedly, proud of her action, despite the falling rain. Success.

The resistance movement in Holland had started soon after the invasion. Dutch people showed enormous courage to resist the occupation in a variety of ways. There was something else they took pride in—teaching Hitler a lesson. During the planning stages before the war, the German General staff believed that Holland would be a country easily overrun. They thought the Dutch would welcome the invading forces with open arms. While it is true that the Dutch are of Germanic ethnic origin, this did not stand in the way of their intense national pride. Hitler had miscalculated the joy the invasion would bring to the Dutch, who instead greeted their invaders with scorn and hatred. The Dutch were too much in love with their freedom. They stood ready to fight to the death for their beliefs.

Soon after the invasion, many Dutch military personnel escaped from German prison camps and started the Underground Movement. Known for their skills in the military as experienced organizers, they wasted no time setting up a distribution program for food. In large numbers, people opened their homes, offering hiding places for members of the resistance. They became big supporters of their clandestine operations of spying and sabotage. With the increase of British airplanes over Holland, the Germans improved their anti-aircraft artillery, resulting in more significant numbers of airmen coming down over the Dutch landscape. The lucky downed aviators landed in the Dutch farming fields. As soon as they were spotted, civilians rushed to their rescue, beating the Germans in their search.

Early on, Arie in his role as double agent took a leadership position in the organization of the rescue efforts of aviators. However, his Gestapo uniform did not always earn him the respect of the citizens who had known him as their police officer. Few people knew he was a double agent, and Arie wanted to keep it that way. On occasion, he attended the clandestine resistance meetings, where he evoked mistrust amongst his peers. Some of them privately expressed their feelings that something unusual was going on with Arie.

At one resistance meeting in the basement of the church, Arie showed up with bogus food coupons and stamps made by Manus. Everyone at the meeting was astounded at this trove. Arie wanted to impress them and show he was on their side. A week earlier, he'd made a surprise visit to his brother. For Manus, Arie was an unwelcome sight in his uniform. Manus let him enter with a grudge: "What brings you here?"

"The resistance needs your expertise as a sculptor. In your hands lies something we need urgently. With your chisels and fine artwork, you are the best person in the entire region to carve out stamps for false passports and other documents, like food coupons." Manus was not keen on cooperating with the resistance in such a dangerous activity. It would mean the death penalty if caught. He thought about the meeting with his father where he had discussed their commitment to fight for freedom, no matter the consequence. Had that time arrived?

The next day, Manus had set to work diligently carving many different stamps, as precise replicas of the official seals. He found plenty of pieces of granite in the Great Hall.

When Arie came by to collect the first batch of stamps, he was surprised at the quality of his work and the speed at which his brother had completed it.

"Brother, I want you to know how much this means to the downed aviators and Jews in the underground escape program," Arie said gratefully. "The presses completed the blank ID cards and passports ... all we needed were these stamps to affix to the documents. Tomorrow, we deliver passports to two hundred Jewish children waiting in a secret location in Amsterdam. Through the underground escape program, they will travel through Belgium and France and cross the Pyrenees to Spain on their way to Lisbon, Portugal. There they will board a ship heading to the United States of America. Know you played a key role in rescuing these children." Manus let the weight of his help sink in and felt a sense of pride to be a part of the mission.

"You should also know that we need more stamps to arrange for falsified documents for the resistance couriers, who make regular deliveries of newsletters and pamphlets at the risk of being arrested and executed," Arie told him, delving deeper into the importance of Manus' work.

Manus was unaware that Danya had attended a few meetings with the local resistance group. Arie was not sure how much Danya had told him about her toil as a designated resistance courier. True to his role as double agent, even with his brother, Arie remained silent about Danya's involvement.

Danya felt lost amongst the large crowd in attendance at her first meeting of the resistance in the basement of a church, until she saw Arie. At the head of the giant table, she spotted the team leader, who announced the presence of the recruits for the week. Danya's name was on the list. Arie, dressed in civilian clothes, addressed the group.

"We are glad that Danya has joined our team. She has already suffered the death of a family member in the war. She has demonstrated her courage to transport downed British aviators." By stating this, it resulted in the group immediately understanding why Danya had joined the resistance: getting even with the Germans. The resistance considered this a prime motivator for joining their group.

The team leader took over and reviewed the organization's protocol, to which everyone had to adhere if they were to survive. He started by focusing on how the enemy "agents-provocateurs" held false conversations in public places and followed with the Rules of Conduct for all resistance members.

"Stay quiet about what you hear or learn in our meetings … no conversations, even with husband or wife. Make no new relations—even a friend of a friend can be a Nazi. The shortest route into custody is to give your address or telephone number." Danya was a fast learner and had no problem comprehending the importance of the rules.

When she came home, she found herself in an uneasy situation, unable to share with Manus what she had learned at the meeting. She must stick to the rule of talking to no one about the goings on at the meeting, and that included Manus. During the day, she carried out her daily routine with an air of self-determination. She had found direction in her young life. At the same time, she became withdrawn from Manus and their relationship became strained.

As time passed, Danya rose in the ranks as a trusted resistance worker. She proudly accepted the lead role in the downed aviator assistance mission. She could be counted on to deliver British airmen to their designated locations. When she wore her disguise, looking like an elderly Dutch woman in wooden shoes, she enjoyed deceiving the Germans. At checkpoints, she knew how to look flirtatious without giving in to the advances of the German guards. She knew exactly how to play on höflichkeit (the German way of gentlemanliness). However, she fully understood the danger of being killed if the Germans captured her with an aviator in transport. However, in no way would it deter her from fulfilling her obligations.

Her assignment had shifted to delivering essential packages. Today, she was in charge of transporting three hundred falsified food coupons one hundred kilometers from Mill by train. When she stepped on the train, she carried the German language newspaper *Deutsche Zeitung*. The train was packed. Boldly, she opened the door to the first-class compartment, where she took a seat opposite a German Army Officer. She smiled, and he took the bait.

"I invite you to sit with me in first class, reserved for German officers," he gallantly invited. Danya thought he wanted to impress her with his hoflichkeit (courtesy). She unfolded her newspaper and read page after page without showing any interest in the subject matter. The officer left her to herself until they arrived at her destination.

"Auf wiedersehen," he said, smiling. He stayed on the train. As soon as she arrived at her destination, her local contact picked her up, and she delivered the coupons without incident.

Not all of her disguises were pleasant. On one occasion, she used the olfactory disguise technique, packing four hundred coupons in the pockets and seams of her clothing. Then she added a sun-ripened sea bass in her handbag. The idea was to keep the Germans at arm's length because of the fish stink. What she had not counted on was the stench of rotting fish becoming overwhelming, even for her. The Gestapo agents wrinkled their noses and gave her a dirty look. In the end, she made a successful delivery.

The Dutch girls who walked around the city with German soldiers on their arms enraged Danya. They were known as

"Moffen Maidens." She had a difficult time accepting how they could lower themselves to drag the honor of the Dutch women through the mud. It left an indelible impression on Danya, while she sacrificed her safety every day as a resistance worker. She must not forget these "Moffen Maidens"—they must pay the price when the war is over—she would personally see to it.

It was a cold, blustery night when the sky lit up with an enormous explosion. Two of their best explosives experts in the resistance had flawlessly executed their plan. There was much celebration about the mission's success among the resistance workers. Their joy was short-lived when they realized they had to go deep underground if they were to avoid arrest immediately.

The explosion had severely damaged the town's electrical grid, interrupting electricity at the prison, where resistance workers were locked up for execution. A number of them belonged to the "Orange Militia," a top-echelon leader group captured during the "Beinema Affair." Beinema was the founder of the underground movement and had played a vital role in organizing a network of secret shelters in farmhouses. His capture was a severe blow to the morale of the resistance. A call went out to the local "Knock Team" to liberate Beinema from jail. These teams specialized in kidnapping and killing the enemy in revenge for the Gestapo's roundups. They were fierce fighters with total disregard for their own well-being.

As soon as the electricity went out, the entire prison fell in total darkness, putting the German guards on high alert. They grabbed their rifles and spread throughout the facility as best they could, groping through dark cellblocks as if moving in a blackened maze.

Knock Team A-1 immediately put their plan into action. The team consisted of twenty-three members. With the lights out, they launched their attack. The group split in two: half executed the rescue and exit strategy, and the other half waited in a nearby school for Phase 2. Around 8 o'clock, the "School Team" slipped into the library and moved to the second floor, where they ate doughnut balls and smoked cigarettes. The boys checked their weapons and loaded their pistols. Notwithstanding the mounting tension in anticipation of the raid, the atmosphere was ebullient.

Around midnight, Arie, dressed in Gestapo uniform, made another round walking the darkened streets outside the prison. He was in constant contact with the two knock teams and gave the okay to proceed. By 2 a.m., the door opened every two minutes to secrete the boys of Knock Team A one by one. They slid through the night as ghosts, stopping at every street corner, skulking for danger. Moving close to the houses, they shuffled onward, ever alert for any noises, taking cover in alleyways. At every street crossing, they listened with sharpness, piercing the dark, with every nerve in high tension.

Killing the prison guards was the most dangerous work the underground had undertaken so far. They walked close to the houses, avoiding German detection, hiding a sten gun under their jackets, hand grenades in the pockets, pistol in hand. The boys knew all too well the danger they were facing. They did not hesitate for a moment. What made them so determined? At the meeting a few hours earlier, they had made it clear: the rescue of their leader Beinema. Arie provided the cell numbers where each inmate was housed, adding a personal touch to the rescue mission. Each of the boys had a particular reason to participate: revenge for the horrors of torture endured by their friends.

It began snowing by the time the attack started. The boys' footprints left tracks in the snow, causing concern about being detected by the guards. After quick deliberation, they decided to walk backward to confuse the Germans into thinking they had stepped in the opposite direction. A few of the resistance workers were on bicycles, causing more of a problem. So as not to leave tracks in the snow, they had to carry their bikes on their backs.

The orders for the prison attack were explicit:

- Let nobody pass you
- Kill every German
- Do not retreat
- Blow up any automobiles helping the prison guards.

Despite the difficulty of the mission, not only did the liberation of Beinema depend on them, so did the safety of their comrades. The attack team consisted of six tough boys who marched in the dark of night to the prison gate where they pushed the doorbell. The wait felt like an eternity. At last, they heard the rattle of keys. A little porthole in the gate opened. The leader of the knock team, dressed in German uniform as a disguise, told the guard in a perfect Elzas accent that he was delivering five prisoners suspected of plotting sabotage. The guard told him to wait. To their surprise, the gate opened with the prison commandant in pajamas. As soon as the gate opened, the team leader yelled, "Attack!" In unison, they pointed their pistols at the German.

"Hände hoch!" (Hands up!) The rescuers killed him instantly. They found the keys to the cells on the guard's dead body. Quick as lightning, they opened the doors and gathered the freed prisoners in the street where they escaped on the waiting bicycles.

Arie had kept himself in the dark of night, allowing the team to do their rescue work. When everyone was safe, he took the keys to the prison cells and threw them in the nearest ditch, where no one could find them.

Later that night the wind was howling, and he heard a light knock on his front door.

He often stayed behind after work hours at the Census Bureau. He told the commandant that he needed overtime to clean up the files. He needed more time to search the town's archives.

That evening, he received a call from a trusted resistance worker, who urgently needed a hiding place for two individuals in imminent danger of arrest for blowing up the pumps at the water and sewage plant in Mill. Arie immediately set to work and contacted the Brecht family. Speaking from his office, he was cautious and spoke in duplicitous language.

"I have two packages for our Gestapo colleagues, which I must deliver tomorrow," he said. The message was clear: Arie was looking for underground housing. "Be ready to receive one colossal packet and one tiny one," he added. "Okay, then ... we will see you tomorrow." Brecht had never operated without passwords. The one chosen for tonight was "The Tulip is Yellow and Black." For two days, they waited for the delivery. About 6 o'clock in the evening, the doorbell at Brecht's home rang four times. A large man, Flab, filled the doorframe; he delivered the correct password. Brecht remained suspicious. There was only one "colossal package" at his door. Where was the tiny packet?

"We expected two packages. Where is the other one?" Flab looked confused, then confessed. "I lost him on the way over here ... my mate comes in a small packet; he is a dwarf named Troll. He never speaks much." Brecht was astounded that the resistance had members from all walks of life, but who came up with the idea of using a dwarf for their dangerous actions involving dynamite? Brecht organized a search party, and they backtracked to the place where Flab said he had his last contact with Troll. Cautiously, they knocked on the door.

"Are you looking for Troll?" asked Brecht, who opened the door. Flab answered affirmatively.

"He is in the back room with his wife ... she just gave birth to a baby boy. My spouse is a midwife," he explained.

"Is it a midget baby?" was the only thing Flab could think of asking. They snickered.

CHAPTER 14

Wewelsburg Castle

RUMORS BEGAN FLOATING THAT MANUS WAS SHEL-
tering a resistance worker. He wondered if his friend Jope was
the culprit. Perhaps he had picked up signs that Danya was
staying with him. As a result, Danya spent day and night in
the dungeon, hiding from the Gestapo. A fat candle sat on the
floor making a miniature volcano of wax. She made her bed on
an earthen bench, with a mattress made of straw, a pillow, and
blanket. Like a little girl with her rag doll, Danya firmly held
her only prized possession: the wooden box with the fragrance
flask.

It was late at night, and all was quiet in the castle. Danya
closed her eyes and rested, wrapped in her blanket on her make-
shift bed. It started slowly, but before she knew it, six inches of
water had pooled on the floor. With her meager possessions,
she climbed out of the hideout, stumbling over blocks of granite. When Manus saw her, he rushed to her side and reassured
her that she was safe. They agreed that she did not have to go
back into hiding. In case of another raid by the Gestapo, they
would find a better solution.

They were out of bread, butter, cheese, and anything to eat. Manus, looking sheepish, sipped ersatz coffee.

Dressed in her old woman disguise, Danya took the streetcar to the grocery store in the hope of exchanging coupons for whatever food the Nazis had not shipped to Germany. A half loaf of bread, a slice of cheese, and coffee would make her happy.

In town, people aimlessly walked along the sidewalks, pedaling down the streets with empty baskets or queued for food in lines that extended for blocks. With defeated looks on their faces, they hurried past the German soldiers without making eye contact. They watched them goose-stepping in the middle of the street, singing their favorite *Heimat* (country home) songs. It was the German way to win over people's hearts. After all, the Dutch were of the same Germanic origin. The truth was the German songs heaped nothing but scorn and anger upon the Dutch.

In the streetcar, on the seat next to her, someone had left a newspaper. She noticed a special news bulletin on the front page: "Political Enemies of the Reich Arrested in Holland and Belgium." She read the names of people who had been rounded up in citywide raids. In horror, she read her parents' name, Mandraskit, among those arrested and jailed in Brussels. Tears rolled down her cheeks, but she remained motionless. She must not show her emotion publicly. They might question the cause of her distress. Nobody must know her name was Mandraskit.

No, this cannot be true, she thought, looking through her tears at the parading troops stridently singing. Hitler's henchmen pretending to be country home boys filled her with disgust. She must take some risk to get even with the Germans for what they had done to her parents.

She returned home without exchanging any coupons.

It brought to mind memories of the time she had spent with Satanaya in her father's study. "I will be there with you in difficult times." She found some comfort in her mentor, Satanaya, who inspired her to be bold and courageous. She became resolute in her decision as she recognized the time had come. A strange voice gave her reassurance: "You are ready to fight, to take action." *Was it Satanaya?* She must have meant the resistance. Happiness sprang loose within her. She had dreamt of this day when the call to action would come.

When she saw Manus in the kitchen, she was still fuming over the news of her parents' imprisonment. Holding back on sharing her true feelings, she only told Manus that she must contact Arie.

She no longer trusted Manus, worried that he was still hanging around in the company of Jope and Joris, the Nazi sympathizers. In her mind, she created a world without Manus, the secret world of the Dutch Underground. That evening, unbeknownst to Manus, she pedaled to a secret meeting of the underground in Mill.

Arie met her at the back door to the hall where the meeting was scheduled. In a few words, she told him what had happened to her parents. However, he wanted to talk to her about an important assignment to help London with intelligence data. He needed her for himself to take charge of the newly created Madonna Courier Network.

Danya became a regular at the meetings; she felt like she belonged. Swallowtail clouds of cigarette smoke filled the air. Tarpaper nailed into the window frames made any light from inside the room invisible. The only light came from two oil lamps.

She seated herself on one of the wooden benches. Opposite her sat two young men wearing patched coats and ragged pants, with cigarettes dangling from their mouth. Between them sat a pencil-thin girl so shy she just stared at the overflowing ashtray.

Arie sat in a corner assembling a scrambler radio that had been air-dropped from England. He was the only one with the kind of expertise to handle such technical chores. The radio sender could transmit coded messages to the office of SOE (Strategic Planning for the Allied Forces) in London. The London top brass in charge of intelligence had complete confidence in Arie, because of his technical background in radio communications, encoded messages, and foreign languages. Only London knew of Arie's role as a double agent. The staff at SOE was the only one privy to his "nom de guerre: Schorseneel." The Germans would have great difficulty pronouncing his name.

As the resistance workers dribbled in, one by one, avoiding attention by the police, the crowd inside grew impatient. Kees Slooter, the team leader, grabbed a stick, banging it on the wooden table.

"I am Slooter, head of the Mill resistance. We are not Germans; we fight for freedom to our death. Today we are looking for a few courageous young women to become active in our Madonna Courier Network." He spotted Danya and nodded in her direction. She had been sitting in the meeting without speaking. She was first on his list for head courier. For this assignment, he needed to assure the group of her qualifications. His first question was directly aimed at her:

"Why did you mark that house on Porter Street with red ink?" Danya remembered the bottle of red ink she had tossed.

"It was the ideal way to alert the resistance workers to stay away."

"Meaning?" She exhaled evenly.

"Arie alerted me that an emergency situation had come up. He found out the Gestapo had set a trap to capture resistance workers delivering false food stamps at this residence. Time was of the essence, so I immediately devised a plan to splatter red ink on the house to alert resistance couriers to stay away." Everyone laughed at the cleverness of the idea.

Danya turned towards Arie. He winked at her, moving closer to her so he could whisper in her ear.

"You already know how to transport downed flyers. Are you ready to increase your responsibility?"

"How?" She was not that gullible and asked for clarification.

"We need a courier route organized for delivery of coded messages, transporting them in relay fashion from chapel to chapel. You know of these chapels through Manus. They are found along the roads, making them ideal drop sites, without causing suspicion." Danya wanted to know more. She remembered Manus had created many of the statues for these chapels.

"We need someone who can head up a group of young women, working like links in a chain," Slooter explained. "Yea, a human chain of couriers, moving swiftly and silently like the legs of a caterpillar, fast, ensuring that the encoded messages reach our point of transfer to London. From there, Arie will take care of the transmission over the scrambler radio."

Arie held up his hand and faced Danya. "We don't say more than we must, Slooter," he reminded. "Danya knows how to take risks. I am confident she has a knack for this type of work. She will be an excellent leader." He dared not mention anything more about her Circassian background and how her people were known for taking on risky tasks in warfare. Arie reached into his leather bag hanging on his chair and pulled out a large roll of paper. He showed it to the audience; it was the outline of the geographical locations of the Madonna Courier Network. It showed a map of the major roads in Holland, with an "X" next to the location of each chapel.

"Each of the chapels displays a statue of the Virgin Mary, created by Manus. Danya has intimate knowledge of their locations," Arie said.

"Well? Speak up." Arie whispered in her ear. With these words, Danya heard the call to arms which she had been anticipating. Slooter looked at her.

"Will you take the responsibility?"

Slooter planned for the women to operate as flower girls, taking fresh flowers to the chapel altar; what an excellent ruse to keep the Germans off track.

"It would be too dangerous for any of the regular resistance workers in this room. The Gestapo is already watching us. On the other hand, Danya is an outsider. Besides, a pretty girl like her would be less suspect of being a courier."

"I will serve as a courier in the Service of her Majesty's Resistance Force," Danya declared firmly. Arie had helped with this formality. A sense of destiny filled her. Finally, here she found something of importance in her life, something that mattered, sending military intelligence data to London. Through her clandestine work, she would play a role in hastening the liberation of Holland. Maybe, she thought, she would see her parents again soon, thanks to her covert work.

"Do not get caught," Slooter cautioned gravely. "How old are you?"

"Twenty-one."

"With your limited experience in resistance work, how will you manage to keep your assignment a secret from your family? It will not be easy."

"My parents are in prison." The underground workers around the table looked at each other and nodded their approval. Everyone in the room realized that her commitment meant revenge. Most of them were in the same predicament. They nodded their heads in unison: she will be a loyal and fierce fighter. Nobody knew that she was also a courageous Circassian.

Arie rose to add his endorsement. "She has already proven herself transporting downed British flyers to safe houses …"

To prove herself as a courier, she had to pay particular attention to her disguise. She dressed as an elderly woman in an ankle-length dark dress, black shawl, rimmed glasses, floppy hat, and wicker basket hanging from her handlebars.

Arie took the responsibility to inscribe military intelligence on the strips of silk cloth cut from the parachutes of downed British flyers.

Arie was in charge of encoding and inscribing the silk strips with German anti-aircraft installations, Wehrmacht barracks, Gestapo headquarters, railroad tracks, and names of Dutch officials collaborating with the Nazis. Arie had complete access to their names from the Census files, for which he was responsible.

The courier girls rolled the strips and bound them with a thread of orange ribbon to remind them that they were fighting for the "House of Orange," the dynastic order of the royal family of the Netherlands.

With the scrolls tucked in her brassiere, Danya began her mission. Under the bright hot sun, she climbed aboard her bicycle with its white stripe on the mudguard and pedaled to her first drop. While cycling, she rehearsed the steps to follow, making sure that she was safe in her mission. The flowers in her basket lent an authentic touch to her disguise. No German would suspect that the chapel had become a hiding place for hiding encrypted messages.

She parked her bicycle on the side of the chapel and furtively surveyed the surrounding area for any danger. When she opened the door with a squeaky noise, she entered the silence of the chapel, now alone with the Virgin Mary. She knelt in front of the altar, put her hand on Mary's mantle, and raised her head, looking up into the eyes of the Virgin. She felt an ethereal aura surrounding her as she reflected on the ancestral bond between herself and Mary.

In the stillness of the chapel, she experienced an inner peace. She prayed:

"Oh Madonna, shelter me

Down from Heaven shield my pathway

Kneeled in prayer, stay with me

I cannot live when you are gone."

It was late evening. Danya passed a farmhouse, where she dropped off a bundle of the pamphlet: "Free Holland." Suddenly, two Gestapo agents jumped from behind the bushes and ordered her to stop. She hit the brakes hard and came to a jolting stop, stepping off the pedal with one foot. The excitement of the new courier turned quickly into sweat collected on her palms. She took a deep, calming breath.

"Papiere!" They demanded that she opened her handbag and examined her ID card and ration coupons. Then, disaster struck. She had forgotten to hide the illegal pamphlets. One of the agents took a closer look.

"What do we have here? Distributing illegal pamphlets is punishable by execution." They shackled her and took her to the local police station. The silence of the night cast an unbearable fear on Danya. She wondered how many hours she had to live unless Arie came to the rescue. Danya was afraid she was the only one in jail. It frightened her.

In the middle of the night, a voice broke into song:

"My God, my God, why have you forsaken me?

Why are you so far from saving me?

O, my God, I cry by day, but you do not answer,

And by night, but I find no rest."

Were they singing for Danya to let her know she was not alone?

When morning came, she heard noises at the other end of the prison block. Gestapo guards led the prisoners to their execution on the prison common. They continued singing in crescendo as they exited the building. Through the little window in her cell, Danya heard the command by the executioners to line up against the wall underneath her window. Suddenly, machine guns broke the stillness of the early morning. Danya listened to the prisoners collapsing while continuing their song until the firearms snuffed out their last verse.

"Amazing Grace, how sweet the sound,
That saved a wretch like me."

The next morning Arie returned to his office at the Political Police Station where the prison was. He saw Danya's name on the prison list. Without speaking, he walked by her jail cell, made eye contact and winked at her. He must stay in his deep cover of double agent.

Danya was relieved to see him. He had already contacted van Lansfoort, who had spoken by telephone with Professor Habers in Wewelsburg. When a Circassian fell in grave danger, the Adyghe Intelligence Network sprang into action. With the knowledge that Danya's father held a high position in the Adygha Intelligence Network in Belgium, van Lansfoort, Habers, and Arie placed a top priority on her rescue.

The following day, two guards escorted her to a waiting car. No longer shackled, she held her satchel of personal belongings. She was no longer frightened, but anxious to know her destination.

"Where are we heading?"

"Wewelsburg Castle," the driver replied curtly.

Danya had never heard the name. For hours, she rode in silence. It was dark when they arrived. A guard opened the gate to the compound, and the car swung around to the back of the castle. An SS guard took her from the car to the prison basement, leading her through a dark hallway and locking her in a small cell with a loud bang and disappearing. Danya saw only empty cells, with no other prisoners present.

The SS had built Wewelsburg Castle as a fortress on a mountain in Westphalia, Germany. Only a few top echelons

SS were aware that it served as the SS indoctrination site under the direction of Heinrich Himmler, Reichsfuhrer – SS.

The castle had a dark history, based on an old legend that hundreds of accused witches had been tortured and executed there. Himmler billed the castle as the "Center of the World," which pleased Hitler. Fascinated by tales of King Arthur and his Knights, Wewelsburg Castle was his "Camelot."

In 1935, Himmler founded an elite Nazi research institute at Wewelsburg called the "Ahnenerbe." Its mission was to unearth new evidence of the accomplishments of Germanic ancestors using exact science, which could not have been farther from the truth. In reality, Ahnenerbe was in the business of mythmaking, distorting the truth, and churning out carefully tailored stories to support Hitler's ideas. He believed that only Aryans possessed the genes necessary to create civilization.

The primary modus operandi of Ahnenerbe was investigative experimenting on humans as well as excavations of gravesites throughout the world, including the Northern Caucasus Mountains. Habers, the professor of History of Human Ethics, was recruited to join Ahnenerbe to help determine the best philosophy for Germans to live by and identify which actions are right and wrong. As a Circassian, he believed he could secretly influence the SS by defining concepts such as good and evil. Sadly, he became convinced that he was a voice in the desert and failed in his endeavor. However, Himmler kept him on to define the moral value of the Aryan race. Since 1940, he rose to the rank of Special Advisor, which made him extremely vulnerable while also serving in secrecy as a member of the Adygha Intelligence Network and answering to Voroshilov in Circassia.

The results of excavations in Circassia yielded a trove of archaeological finds, including shards of pottery with swastika symbols. This find saved Habers' reputation. When presented with the information, Himmler became ecstatic, declaring that the archaeologists had found evidence of the "Germanic Font of Civilization" in the Northern Caucasus. Of course, the professor, functioning as an unwilling scientist to please Himmler, kept it a secret that this could not be further from the truth. For centuries, traders from India traveled to Circassia over the old Silk Road, often carrying goods inscribed with the swastika. To them, it was merely a symbol of good luck. To the German researchers, anxious to please Hitler, it was the "Germanic Grail."

On the second floor of the castle, the SS installed the SS Rasseamt (Race Office) where they made their decisions about which ethnic people to exterminate. Himmler arranged for the signet rings of the fallen SS officers to be on permanent display in an urn in the middle of the large round table in the room as their way of showing their loyalty even after death to Hitler.

At precisely 9 o'clock in the morning, two Gestapo guards shackled Danya and rushed her into an elevator. Something important was happening. With every click of the rickety wheels, the old elevator labored closer to the second floor, where it came to a screeching halt. Danya walked through a corridor lit by a row of single bulbs hanging from the ceiling. The guard stopped at an old oak door adorned with a large SS symbol. After banging three times with his truncheon, the guard threw the doors open, and all became suddenly quiet in the large room. She counted ten uniformed officers seated around an enormous round table, with one exception dressed in civilian clothing. Due to the vastness of the room, she could barely make out his name: Professor Gustav Habers III. She vaguely recollected the name but could not place it with certainty.

Sun rays pierced the tall windows, bringing the mosaic inlay in the floor into full view. In each window stood a pedestal with a strange-looking object. In the center of the object, Danya saw the SS Ahnenerbe symbol in vivid colors radiating in a burst of silver flares. It reminded her of the monstrance used in the Catholic Church to worship the Holy Bread. She felt nauseated that the Germans had borrowed this imagery.

Her eyes wandered around the room until they rested on the nameplates on each pedestal: Jews, Poles, Slavs, Gypsies; it did not take long before she realized that these people decided deportation to the concentration camps. She panicked. She frantically searched for the Circassians and didn't see their name.

With the Skull and Bones SS Standard in front of him, General Heinrich Tauber looked larger than life. With the loud thump of the gavel, he blasted the attendees to attention. In unison, all heads turned to the general.

Tauber nodded at Professor Habers. With a quick glance at Danya, he wondered if she had learned that he was a member of the Adyghe Intelligence Network, he started. "At the request of Reichsführer-SS Heinrich Himmler, I bring for special consideration before this council the case against Danya Mandraskit." Danya wondered what he meant by "special consideration." It soon became apparent to Danya that Habers was an essential figure in the SS. She did not know a lot about him, but something gave her a glimmer of hope.

He opened his file, emblazoned with the swastika.

"Danya Mandraskit is of a pure bloodline, with family roots deep in the Northern Caucasus Mountains. The Gestapo found her distributing illegal literature, punishable by execution. She belongs to the Circassian race, of which there are 500 living in Holland. They are an exceptional people known for their courage in battle." He paused to collect his thoughts explaining how the Circassians could be of great help to the Aryan cause.

"Before we get to her punishment, I must first report to you on the Lebensborn Project. Lebensborn is a state program sponsored by the SS with the goal to increase the birthrate of 'Aryan' children by coupling German women with Nazi soldiers." With a grim look on his face, he turned immediately to the conclusion on the last page of his report and announced: "Generals of the SS Supreme Command, I have to report that the Lebensborn Project is a catastrophic failure." They sat dumbstruck at his blunt statement. It was highly unusual to hear criticism of a project that had originated with Hitler himself. They considered the professor a courageous fool, almost suicidal.

"In my conversation yesterday with the Führer, Himmler told him that Lebensborn was a disaster," he continued, vehemently explaining that the children in Lebensborn were found to have an inferiority complex, lacking in motivation for combat duty. "This is now unacceptable to the Führer. He stated that by now we should have created legions of young Nazi warriors to compensate for the losses in Russia. The Fuhrer declared as nonsense the idea of blond hair and blue eyes as essential features of Aryan eugenics." The professor paused, looking around the table at the generals rolling their eyes. Hitler himself failed the test of Aryan genetics. Nobody dared to speak.

Enraged, he concluded. "The Fuhrer charged me to restart Lebensborn on a different footing. The new name for the project is 'Lebensborn II.' I presented my proposal of introducing Circassian genetics, whose ancestors originate from the land of the earliest Europeans. Our excavations in caves and gravesites have shown that they believed in the symbolism of the swastika. The progenitor of all Circassians is in the *Book of the Nart Sagas*. When I informed the Fuhrer of the god-woman Satanaya, he became quite excited. At this point, the Fuhrer stopped me and showed his knowledge about the German world of occultism, in which he emphatically believes. He introduced the famous Maria Orsitsch, head of the All German Society for Metaphysics. I informed him that she had been my student at Gottingen University, where she studied Ethics of Philosophy. I told the Fuhrer that I would make every attempt to locate a direct descendant from Satanaya to start the new Lebensborn Project. He was ecstatic at this prospect and instructed me to initiate Lebensborn II immediately in collaboration with Orsitsch, with her academic perspective on the Aryan without blue eyes and flaxen hair."

Danya sat quietly listening to Professor Habers' report. His revelations dumbfounded her. But then it started to become clear how Habers was playing his Circassian card, making a dangerous attempt to save her from execution.

He paused, closing his portfolio and turning to Danya. She was frightened to the bone.

"This brings me to Danya Mandraskit, caught with illegal pamphlets in Holland. It took raw courage to go on the road and distribute this literature, against the laws of the Nazi Regime. In some way, she committed a heroic deed, defying our policies. She is well-aware that she misdirected her efforts against the Nazi rule in Holland by distributing pamphlets hostile to our policies. However, she is a direct descendant of Satanaya, queen-progenitor. She is ideally suited to be at the pinnacle of the New Lebensborn Project. Her offspring will fill our ranks in the military with brave troops, ready to fight to the death in the spirit of their god-woman. They will lead us to heroic deeds, essential to building the 'Thousand Year Reich.'"

Danya was in shock. In exchange for her freedom, she would have to agree to become the progenitor of the modern Aryan fighting machine. Danya shuddered at the thought of what was to come, sleeping with SS and Gestapo soldiers. She must show her courage and resist the proposition of becoming the matriarch of a new race. She wanted to offer more to the world than just her Circassian beauty.

Tauber rose and looked at Habers.

"At this moment remand Danya Mandraskit to your guardianship to initiate the Lebensborn II project." Habers led her towards the elevator. Downstairs, his Mercedes was waiting to drive Danya to her destination. She had no clue where she was heading. After four hours, Danya could still not believe she was not in restraints.

She turned to Habers: "Who are you?" She finally mustered the courage to ask while she stole a quick glance to check how he reacted to her question. With a smile, he kept his eyes fixated on the road.

"What I am going to tell you must stay between us," he told her after a short pause. "Some time ago, researching populations in the Northern Caucasus, Himmler took note of my study of the Circassians. When asked whether they should be on the list for extermination, I was adamant that they could play a vital role in our destiny as a race." As they crossed into Holland, he told Danya about her father's whereabouts. At the time King Leopold III was deported to Germany, Danya's father had been picked up by the Gestapo and put in jail. He noticed the anguished look on Danya's face.

"The Adyghe Network is hard at work collaborating with the Belgian Resistance. When the Knock Team is together, it will attack the prison to set your father free. It may take a little time to prepare the team." Danya felt a ray of hope that she would see her father again soon.

"You must swear that you will not talk to anyone about my membership in the Adyghan Intelligence Network. If you violate the pledge, I will shoot you."

CHAPTER 15

Murder in London

ARIE KNEW IF HE DIDN'T ACT NOW AND MURDER THE mole at the Queen's mansion in London, the Germans would find out he was a double agent.

The big lights on the wheel fenders of the British Westland-Lysander aircraft were of no use. Turning on the headlights would make it too easy for the Germans, alerting them to the drop. All the pilot could do was watch for the infrared signal in the cockpit. When the message fell silent with a "ping," the pilot knew he had entered the right triangulated entry point. He would be flying at five hundred feet, in complete darkness, except for a circle of candlelit paper bags in the middle of a remote pasture. Barely visible from the air, these missions were always perilous, and too often, the Germans were waiting in ambush, looking at the same burning candles.

The hatch in the aircraft opened, excreting two Dutch Underground agents with black parachutes. Descending in the dark moonless night gave them the eerie feeling of falling into a bottomless hole. When their parachutes opened, they wafted down, collapsing on the wet grass. Some of the aviators ended up in trees. Three smaller parachutes also followed them in the landing zone, delivering automatic guns, pistols, bazookas, and grenades.

Suddenly, out of the pitch black night, Gestapo with pistols drawn rushed the parachutists as they struggled to disentangle from their lines. As an aviator pulled his handgun, the Gestapo immediately gunned him down. They forced the other downed parachutist into a radio communication vehicle, seating him in front of a transmission console. Holding a pistol to his temple, the soldier radioed under duress to London: "Mission accomplished." The intelligence analysts on the other end were immediately suspicious; the missing security code told the decoders at Bletchley Park in London that there was a problem. To test their suspicion, the British decided to send another aircraft the next morning delivering two new Dutch agents and more ammunition and food. Immediately after the drop, Section-N of the Dutch Intelligence sent another message to confirm the second drop. They needed to hear the security cipher: SCUFVER267 in the message confirming the parachutists' safe arrival. The missing cipher compromised the network in Holland. Had the Germans captured the downed parachutists and forced them to transmit a fake message?

Arie attended the briefings that morning at the Lants-Commandatur (headquarters of the German military) in Le Hague. The officer in charge reported the killing of two downed agents and the capture of a stock of ammunition and food supplies. He confirmed that one of the captured agents had refused to cooperate, and the German guard shot him in the head while operating the radio console.

Arie took it as a warning to heighten his vigilance when communicating with London. As a double agent, Arie used the S-phone, an exclusive issue to Special Operations agents like Arie working behind enemy lines. The S-phone was preset to a secure channel for coded conversations between staff officers based in London and agents in the field.

A daring character, Arie prided himself on outwitting the Gestapo. He installed his radio transmitter in the same building as the Gestapo Office was housed. He found a little cubbyhole in the attic of the old structure, with a nest of storks in the chimney. He made sure the Gestapo's mobile detection unit was away on patrol, allowing him to transmit for a few minutes every night. Of course, he risked the Gestapo patrols changing their surveillance schedule from night to daytime, but he was willing to take the gamble.

Tonight, his message was brief and concise. He never failed to follow protocol, routinely including the secret cipher. When London agents decoded and read Arie's note: "Dutch communication network compromised. Cease all transmission," their mood turned somber.

Moreover, Colonel Kuypers, head of Section-N in London, found something peculiar with the message. "Why had Arie failed to send a copy of this message to Klaus van der Zandt, first secretary to Queen Wilhelmina?" In 1941, shortly after the invasion of Holland, she and her family had fled to London. Kuypers continued: "You know how the queen is adamant about being in the loop, even on the most sensitive intelligence information." Kuypers paused, wrinkling his pockmarked face that resembled a cauliflower. "This must mean that Arie does not trust Klaus, without so stating in his message. We must interpret this to mean that Klaus is leaking information from the Queen's mansion to the Germans in Holland. For some time, I have had my suspicions about him. I will direct Section-N to install a listening device at the Queen's residence," Kuypers told his staff.

Within two hours of installing the counterintelligence device, they received proof that Klaus was a traitor. N-Section set Klaus on a bogus operation called "Plan Holland," consisting of details about plans by the Allied to help the resistance. Klaus dialed the telephone number of the top German Commandant,

Seys-Inquart, the renowned butcher of Holland, and informed him of the deception, thereby activating the counterintelligence listening device. Upon whom would fall the task of murdering the traitor?

In London, English and Dutch intelligence officers called a joint meeting in the presence of Prince Bernhard, head of the Dutch Military Forces. The decision was swift: Klaus van der Zandt was a traitor, responsible for the death of 40 Dutch resistance workers. The Prince sentenced him summarily to die for his heinous crimes. He demanded that the Dutch Army Intelligence Unit kill Klaus following the ritual for the death penalty for treason. The Ancient Rules of the House of Orange required that Klaus die with a white carnation in his left lapel. The prince also insisted that a Dutchman perform the execution.

"I will make immediate contact with Willem van Lansfoort in Holland, our liaison with the resistance." He telephoned Willem and briefed him on the mission.

"We have two options: an outright killing or a staged automobile accident. Given the urgency, I favor the first option," van Lansfoort opined, singling out Arie as best suited for the task. The prince agreed.

Arie was informed of the decision the next morning while visiting van Lansfoort in Holland. Van Lansfoort said, "First, we must transfer you to England without the Germans learning about your absence." Then an idea lit up his mind: "In 1938, you made a deal with the Germans to store their mini-submarine in the port of Scheveningen. Is that submarine still there and operational?" Arie recalled the caper. It would now come in handy if he could find a way to steal the mini-submarine from under their noses for about twenty-four hours.

"Do you think you could use this asset without being noticed?" van Lansfoort asked, smiling. "It would allow you to slip into England overnight and return the next day."

Arie was always eager to play the high-stakes game. However, he needed a technician to prepare the Biber submarine. He knew just the man. Two years ago, Arie had convinced the local commander of the Armed Forces to employ Dieter De Vries to maintain and safeguard their submarine. Dieter, a close friend of Arie, had received specialized training in marine engineering and Arie had recruited him into the resistance. That was not a problem as the Germans had killed his brother during a recent parachute drop, so Dieter was ripe for revenge.

Arie brought Dieter up to date with the details of "Project Kill Klaus." He needed the Biber in top shape by the next day. Still angry about the killing of his brother, Dieter did not agree to let Arie perform the execution; he was adamant about completing the mission himself.

"I must avenge my brother," Dieter said. Arie noticed his left eye twitching nervously and thought Dieter might go berserk at a missed opportunity to be the executioner. He put his arm on his shoulder to soothe his raw emotions.

"You are a major partner in the plot by preparing the submarine and helping me steal the submersible. Prince Bernhard gave me the specific order to kill Klaus. I have my good reason to get Klaus." Dieter shook his head and backed off.

Dieter met with Arie late Saturday afternoon. They counted on the Gestapo to be celebrating at the local tavern all weekend. The moonless night was ideal for crossing the North Sea without being seen. In an inflatable, they rowed to the entrance of the hangar where the submarine was anchored. Arie beamed with excitement at the sight of the submersible, painted black without markings, it was ideal for his top-secret trip across the channel. Dieter opened the hatch, making sure not to trip the alarm. He slid through the opening into the seat facing the operating system. He showed Arie the navigation controls. Arie had no problem following Dieter's directions. Once Dieter had finished, Arie took his seat.

Arie floated on a cloud of pride. He could never have imagined stealing an experimental submarine, hidden in a Dutch port under German control. He was already thinking about how the officers' party in England would react to his arrival.

As he turned the key, the entire control panel illuminated in green, red, and purple lights. Arie threw the throttle in reverse and submerged just enough to slip under the guardrail. Dieter had set his compass with the coordinates for Folkstone Harbor, England.

He listened carefully to the gentle engine droning, keeping his eyes on the blinking lights on the panel; all was going well. At 6'3" tall, Arie cleared the hatch ceiling by an inch.

Arie never hesitated to take on perilous tasks with exceptional courage. He had to ingratiate himself with the German military at all times, and he had become good at it. In his disguise as a double agent, he had no choice but to excel in his duty as Gestapo. Now he was on his way to England in the uniform of the Gestapo.

For ten hours, he had been navigating without incident, and he was getting excited about heading for the free world.

At the mid-point of his voyage, a rogue wave thrust Arie against the hatch handle and for a moment, he blacked out. Alone in the tiny capsule of the submarine, Arie felt overcome by claustrophobia. He experienced flashbacks of his life as a double agent in Holland, the roundups of Jews, beatings, pushing people into the open trucks in the cold of the night. The earsplitting screaming of mothers and children resonated.

Then, the disturbing question. "How will the Dutch people treat me when the war is over, and I'm called to account for the persecution of Jews?" he asked himself on his way to London. One incident left an indelible imprint upon Arie's conscience. He shook his head in remorse and idly groped for a thread of redeeming value in the atrocious act.

I should never have pursued the little girl through the backyard during a raid, he thought as he relived the scene. *The raid on the music hall was already over, and I noticed a ten-year-old girl escaping through a side door. "Come here little mousy!" I called, grabbing her by the scruff of her neck while she kicked and screamed. I hit her on the head with my weapon, and she fell limp. I dragged her by the collar and threw her into the lorry beside her parents.*

Oh, the horror, as I reminisce about what I have done. I deserve punishment for my actions. Perhaps, after I kill Klaus, the Dutch will understand that I did it as a double agent. If I execute Klaus, I will save the lives of numerous resistance workers and stop this traitor from carrying out his perfidious work. Oh Lord, help me through this agony.

Approaching the coast of England, Arie pushed his thoughts away and began to feel exhilarated at the thought of entering the world of Winston Churchill. In London, only a few intelligence officers knew of Arie's arrival, but they did not know in what class of submersibles he would arrive. They had never laid eyes on a Biber.

Arie navigated the mini just below the water's surface. When he peered through his periscope, he expected to see a beacon in the light tower, sweeping the harbor. However, all was dark. At night, England was under complete blackout, so as not to give away targets to the German bombers.

Once he approached the harbor, he flashed a tiny orange light, sending a brief message using his unique code, "SCUFVER 267." Daylight was breaking, and he remained submerged until he came within one hundred yards of the light tower. In one of the lower windows, he noticed someone flash a quick response code. A small tugboat appeared out of nowhere, hooking a heavy cable to the bow of the vessel. Arie felt a sudden lurch as the cable became taut. Three navy officers stood at attention to salute Arie, dressed in an angler's outfit, which they found odd. They had no idea of Arie's real mission in England. The Biber submarine captured their attention. The mystery submersible, invented by the German Navy, was in English territory. They must examine it while it was here.

An unmarked jeep waited to transport Arie to the British intelligence headquarters at Bletchley Park. Colonel Kuypers, head of N-Section (Intelligence in the Netherlands), was behind the wheel, and he acknowledged Arie by pointing to the seat next to him. Arie noticed his beak-like nose and bushy mustache. Without speaking, they coursed through the coastal landscape at high speed.

He started the conversation on a light note: "Shall I call you 'Schorseneel?'" He chuckled as he tried to enunciate the Dutch vegetable with the correct intonation. He failed. Now it was Arie's turn to smile.

"Not a bad try. If you were German, you would fail the test."

"How much do you know about the Enigma Coding Machine?"

Arie gave him a lesson in the secret world of German coding and decoding, using the enigma, an electro-mechanical rotor cipher system. Kuypers stopped his lecture.

"Enough! I am convinced that the real 'Schorseneel' has arrived."

On this warm day, Arie enjoyed the landscape, noting the deep furrows of the freshly plowed fields. He loosened his angler's vest. Kuypers saw how skinny he was.

"You look so scrawny ... no food in Holland?" His words offended Arie.

"People are starving to death. Have you not heard of the 'Hunger Winter?' The Germans came up with a cruel way to punish the Dutch people: famine as punishment for the railroad strike. They cut off all food and fuel shipments to the western provinces in Holland. As a result, 18,000 people starved to death. I promise you, once Holland is free, the Dutch will exact revenge for this and other atrocities." Kuypers pointed to a tin can in the back of the jeep. Inside were stale sea biscuits, hard as a rock. Arie reminded himself to be careful not to bite on the molar where the SS dentist had implanted the cyanide capsule when he became a Gestapo as his declaration of being a "Vollstandig Gestapo." Arie looked around for some water to soften the biscuit.

While speeding down the coast, Arie noticed a military compound stretching as far as the eye could see. As they rushed through the gate, Arie read the sign: "First U.S. Army Group (FUSAG)."

"At the intelligence briefings at the German command in Le Hague, there was always a question mark," Arie commented. "The Germans believed that FUSAG was a legitimate army. To them it was clear proof that the invasion of Europe would take place in Calais, and not in Normandy."

At this moment, Kuypers had an idea.

"You will set up Klaus to radio the Germans confirming the existence of this U.S. Army Group. If they believe him, it will throw off for General Rommel the entire defense plan of the European Continent. It will be a huge disinformation coup for us," Kuypers smiled at Arie.

"Confirming George Patton as the commanding general of this ghost army will give the German commanders in Holland something to worry about." Continuing on their trip, Arie looked through the side window of the jeep, where he saw a farmer with a prodding stick, poking at a bull. Kuypers slowed down and wanted to know what was going on.

"Look at the huge gashes on the side of that Sherman tank. That farmer is trying to coax the bull away from the military vehicles parked in his pasture." Arie sat in disbelief. It showed to Arie that the English had become masters of ingenuity and disguise in the war of deception.

"Let me be sure I understand what we are planning to do," Arie began. "We want him to confirm via radio that this entire military complex, although made from cardboard, is poised to invade Europe in Calais, France. It will represent one of the war's complete and unabashed fakes to throw German intelligence off kilter. The deception was textbook Churchill style."

In the distance, several wooden structures stood hidden in the woods. They had arrived at Bletchley Park. The trees along the road to the entrance formed a natural canopy, keeping the access to the mansion shielded from enemy aircraft. At the gate, a sentry with a machine gun at the ready ordered them out of the jeep. Arie wondered if his ID papers would be a problem. For double agents, identification papers were always tricky. Finally, Arie was cleared under the code name Schorseneel and arrived at the office of N-Section. The officers at the meeting had already set in motion the plans to assassinate Klaus.

Once they arrived at the London district where the Queen's mansion was, Kuypers steered his jeep onto an adjacent street. Arie disembarked, dressed as a fisherman. Throwing his travel bag and fishing rod over his shoulder, he strode nonchalantly to the residence of Queen Wilhelmina in exile. He was confident that Kuypers had briefed Klaus. Arie would start by announcing to Klaus that the resistance radio network in Holland could no longer be trusted; the Germans had infiltrated the web and were transmitting disinformation about German military positions via captured Dutch parachutists.

Klaus now believed more than before that he was in good standing with the English intelligence at Bletchley Park, and it strengthened his position as a German spy. The Queen's mansion was in a wooded area. Four guards protected the property with sten guns at the ready. When Arie approached the gate, he gave Kuypers' letter to the guards. The guard opened a side gate and waved Arie through. He walked for several hundred meters, until he reached a large pond with water lilies, reflecting the majesty of the mansion, a stunning piece of Victorian architecture.

Klaus greeted Arie with a cold handshake. He informed Arie that it would be best for the two German sympathizers—as he thought of Arie—to walk around the domain. It was a sunny day, and a lonely dog barked in a kennel.

Klaus knew that Arie worked with the Germans in Holland.

"The Queen left yesterday for Canada, visiting her family." Arie thought it would be best if she were absent while a crime was committed on her domain.

Three days earlier, Klaus had received an urgent request from the Germans in Holland to step up intelligence about Patton's First Army Group in England. Arie convinced Klaus to radiograph to the German military in Le Hague about the First U.S. Army.

"I just drove by the base of the First U.S. Army," Arie told Klaus. "They have an impressive military compound, with tanks, artillery field ambulances, ammunition depots, and more. There are at least a million military personnel on the premises. You must tell the Germans that radio traffic further substantiates the existence of this large base. Do not forget to tell them in Le Hague that the local vicars complained to the newspapers about the behavior of Americans on the base. Make sure that the military in Holland understands the enormity of this intelligence. The existence of this army at this latitude cannot mean anything else but an invasion of Europe in Calais, not Normandy," Arie told him.

Klaus walked Arie into the garden. "The radio is installed in the abandoned barn. We will go there first to send the message." Now Arie was on his way to achieving his goal. Klaus turned a few knobs and pushed a few switches, and without consulting any manual, he swiftly entered the security code on the German bandwidth. He spoke in the mouthpiece in perfect German. Arie had no trouble understanding the message. Klaus had just perpetrated his final act of betrayal.

About a hundred yards from the barn, they admired a patch of white carnations in full bloom, the flower of the House of Orange. Klaus stooped down to pick one carnation as proof of his allegiance to the House of Orange. He placed it in his right lapel. Arie grabbed his knife, hidden in a pocket in his angler's outfit. It was a rapid action switchblade.

Without a word, Arie jumped on Klaus from behind and thrust his knife deep into Klaus' chest. Klaus slumped into the flowerbed with a deep gurgling sound. "Oh, no!" It was over in three seconds. Satisfied that he had accomplished his mission swiftly and quietly, Arie wiped his knife on the grass before plucking his carnation. Smiling, he proudly showed the carnation as he saluted the guards.

Arie walked through the same side street from where he had come. Without speaking a word, he entered the waiting car. Arie kept the carnation in his pocket. He had an idea to whom he was going to give it as a souvenir.

He returned safely in his Biber to the hangar in Scheveningen, where Dieter was waiting. They did not talk much. Arie pulled the carnation from his pocket and gave it to Dieter.

CHAPTER 16

The Escape

Himmler's trusted advisor Professor Habers raced his big Mercedes with SS license plates through the town of Mill. It was a rarity for the townspeople to see a big shiny SS vehicle with a high-level dignitary from Germany. As he drove past the local church, Habers pointed out the missing windows, blown out during a recent bombardment. Last month a bomb had hit the church, blowing out the original stained-glass windows.

Arie had been patiently awaiting the Mercedes' arrival so he could escort Habers with his motorcycle to the castle. Danya, sitting next to Habers in the passenger seat, glanced at him with a quick wave of the hand. Habers wondered how well she knew Arie and what the townspeople were thinking of her, seeing her in an SS vehicle.

Everyone in Mill knew Arie worked with the Gestapo and was responsible for rounding up Jews destined for German concentration camps. Under normal circumstances, he would assign one of his agents to escort duty. This time around, he provided the escort as a special favor to Habers and because

Danya was in the car. He wanted to make sure Danya's return from Wewelsburg was without incident.

At the far end of the lane, leading to the drawbridge, Habers saw the castle where Manus stayed. He opened the gate.

Once they arrived, Arie rushed to open the door of the Mercedes on Danya's side, as if she were the dignitary. She immediately took off, flinging herself into Manus' arms, much to his surprise.

When Habers, Arie, and Manus came together on that day as Circassians, it was as if destiny had brought them there for a particular reason. They gathered to protect Danya from further harm. In unison, they experienced a sense of tribal pride. In times like these, when Circassians congregate, they followed their ancestors' tradition of secrecy and solidarity in purpose. Circassian males took an oath to protect their women to the death.

Together, they marched through the grand hall meandering through the maze of the Stations of the Cross. For the first time, Habers admired the life-size figures created by Manus. In the darkened room, the half-finished monuments loomed like tombstones in a cemetery. In reality, the rough granite blocks represented the work of a sculptor who had lost his zeal for the project as the result of the war.

Towards the back of the hall, a single beam of light from a broken window fell on Hitler's death mask. Habers grinned. With one eyebrow raised over his monocle, he chuckled and shook his head. He didn't need to use words to express his feelings.

Habers faced a difficult situation, having to pressure Danya to join the Lebensborn Project, to which the SS had sentenced her as a condition of her release from jail. If she refused, she would meet the execution squad. He wondered if he would have the courage to defy Himmler. With a gesture of his long-fingered professorial hands, he started. "I brought

Danya back to you, Manus, and rescued her from the clutches of Himmler. Her dossier showed that she committed an act of treason, distributing illegal propaganda hostile to the Nazi Regime in Holland, punishable by execution. In some odd way, I convinced the SS Council in Wewelsburg that her crime, although an act of treason, was, in fact, an act of courage. I convinced them that she had acted out of patriotism. The SS leaders are practical people. With the large hordes of German prisoners of war in Russia, the shortage of soldiers was becoming clear. For this reason, the officers in Wewelsburg decided to commute her death sentence on condition that she join Lebensborn and procreate Aryan soldiers. The officers gradually became convinced that the commutation of her death sentence was in the best interest of Germany."

Danya had already made up her mind that she would never agree to the deal Habers had made to save her life. She would rather sacrifice her life than submit to Nazi rule.

"Joining Lebensborn is worse than the death sentence!" she shouted at Habers. "Never. My dignity and pride as a Circassian mean too much to me. Pull your pistol and kill me here and now." Her eyes shot bullets at him.

His Circassian background compelled him to find a way to absolve her from the Lebensborn sentence. Not sure how he could handle this situation, he clearly understood the consequence of acquitting Danya from the obligation of joining Lebensborn; he would be signing his death warrant.

Arie stepped forward and spoke the magical words, invoking the Code of Ethics of Circassia. "As true Circassians, we must stand by Danya and save her. Remember the oath that every Circassian takes: 'To protect the Circassian woman to the death.' It is the code of every Circassian warrior of yesterday and today, as it has been for thousands of years. We shall fight for her and keep her out of the Lebensborn Project." Habers looked at Arie and Manus and nodded in consent. He decided to be a true Circassian, despite his Gestapo uniform.

"The Nazi Regime has instituted the 'Hunger Winter' in Holland," Arie continued. "They've been starving the Dutch into submission, requisitioning all means of transport and stopping all commerce from east to west. Severe food shortages will result in the death of thousands of innocents. The Germans decided on this cruel punishment meted out to innocent people for acts of sabotage which they never committed." Arie pulled out Danya's new ID card.

"This is your German ID, which will give you safe passage at checkpoints," Arie said, handing her the card with the letter "C" in large print. As a precaution, he had registered her in the census files as "Circassian," an ethnic group now exempt from deportation. Professor Habers had convinced the SS in Wewelsburg to exempt Circassians because of their relation to the original Aryans. After all, they had found archaeological evidence in Circassia that the swastika symbol was part of their culture.

Arie was proud to point out that Danya was the first individual in Holland officially assigned to this ethnic class.

"At checkpoints, just pretend to be a member of Lebensborn and they will give you full respect," Arie told her. Arie and Habers advised Danya and Manus to leave the castle.

Manus was not yet ready to leave his atelier. He feared the Germans would destroy it all. For months, Manus had been idle, unable to muster the energy to complete the Stations. He meandered between the rough granite blocks, holding his chisel and hammer. Resting his hands on the cold stone of Station VIII, Manus stood there beholding the figure of Jesus, dripping blood while wearing the crown of thorns. He tried to find comfort in the suffering of Jesus. The longer he searched, the higher the agony of despair. He despised the Gestapo and struggled to come to grips dealing with Danya's lot as a refugee from Lebensborn. Did he love her enough to give up his art-work in Holland and flee to Belgium?

A cup of coffee made from burned radicchio grind, commonly known as chicory, might stimulate his imagination, he thought. Danya, on the other hand, was ready to leave Holland and began gathering her belongings for the trip. She washed her clothes and hung them out to dry while she searched the cupboards for food. Whatever she could find, she stuffed into an easy-to-carry burlap handbag which she carried over her shoulder.

The next morning, they watched two rats fighting over a scrap of old Gouda cheese. In a lighthearted moment, Manus told Danya how he planned to deal with the Gestapo the next time they came looking for her, thinking it might change her mind and convince her to call off becoming a refugee. "The poet Goethe gave me the idea." He found his booklet of Goethe's poetry and read from the "Rat Attack":

> 'Once upon a time a rat
>
> Kitchen-bred on cheese and fat
>
> Till his paunch had swollen smoother
>
> Than his counterpart on Luther
>
> All about the house, he dashed
>
> Till the enemy was thrashed.'

"As improbable as it may sound to you, Goethe's poetry has inspired me to formulate my attack plan," Manus snickered. "Could he have foreseen what was going to take place in our kitchen? Wait and see; next time the Gestapo come, I will have a surprise for them."

Danya laughed until she cried.

They did not have to wait long to try out Manus' attack theory. On that same day, it was dark and raining. Danya

177

needed to take a break from packing. She turned to the back window, looking out at the woods behind the property and saw light beams bouncing around the trees. In the stealth of the night, another raid was underway; the Gestapo was looking for Danya again. She wasted no time rushing to her hideout. In minutes, they were inside. Manus made sure he hid her dishes and cups in the kitchen, leaving no trace of evidence that two people were living in the castle.

One of the Gestapo snarled at Manus as he held a pistol to his head.

"Last chance! Where is she?" He was getting used to the tactics, and he stiffened his resolve, holding firm, despite the feel of the cold steel of the revolver on his temple.

"If I knew where she was, I would never tell you," he stated boldly. The agent stared at him with his steel blue eyes and came close to pulling the trigger before finally throwing Manus against the side door in the kitchen. The action opened the door to the room where Manus gave the rats sanctuary. Three furry creatures emerged, scurrying along the wall, noses upturned in the air. Before long, they smelled the fresh leather of the Gestapo boots. The attack was on.

"This is it! Enough nonsense!" an agent cursed and snarled. He pulled his pistol, aiming to shoot when his colleague stopped him.

"Nein! You are an idiot! The bullets in your pistol are not for rats; you must reserve your bullets for the enemy of the state: Jews! Put your weapon away!" The Gestapo stormed out of the castle, snarling about the victory by the rats. The rats had won!

After they left, Manus could not wait to fetch Danya from her hideout to give her the good news. He regretted that Danya had not witnessed what had happened in the kitchen. When he told her, she raised her hand to her mouth and laughed loudly. She remembered the story of the Rats of Hamelin from school.

"A long time ago, I read about the Pied Piper of Hamelin. By the sound of the flute, he led the rats to their death. However, today their day of revenge arrived, by chasing the enemy from the castle." Returning to reality, she looked at Manus. "We still need to leave the castle. It is too dangerous to stay here."

They left in the middle of the night. Manus looked back one more time, fearing for his artwork. On foot, they walked over dirt roads and pasturelands, occasionally stirring a cow or bird. They hoped to find a meal with the underground family in Eindhoven.

It rained through the night and by the next morning, they were soaking wet. Gratefully, they arrived at the designated address in Eindhoven and knocked softly on the back door. Frans de Bolder peered through the porthole and recognized the refugees. He opened the door and warmly welcomed the wet visitors. After eating a tasty but meager meal, Manus asked Frans about his dogs.

"I do not see your friends around. Are they well?" Through his rimmed glasses, Manus saw Frans' eyes watering over. He shook his head.

"We had to put them down for lack of food. We hardly have enough to feed ourselves. We want to do what we can to help downed RAF flyers. Three weeks ago, several parachutists ended up in our cornfields." Manus felt guilty having sat around the table with people who were giving up their last crumbs of food.

The next day, in the early morning hours, while still dark, Germans arrived at the farmhouse and smashed in the front door with the butts of their rifles. While loudly screaming, "Raus!" they raced through the living quarters and dashed upstairs, barely giving Danya and Manus time to climb through the back window and flee into the fields behind the house.

The German patrols always started their searches upstairs in the bedrooms. The shepherd dogs that accompanied them ran straight to the warm bed where Manus and Danya had spent the night. The empty warm bed was enough proof the couple had harbored refugees.

Manus and Danya stayed quiet in the cornfield, where they hid. Then they heard the dreaded machine guns. In cold blood, the Gestapo had executed the family against the back wall of the farmhouse. They wept.

They waited until night to walk again, even though walking under the protection of the darkness made their journey even more treacherous. They had to remain extremely vigilant for landmines. Danya had already stepped on barbed wire, which caused severe lacerations on her legs.

Once out of Eindhoven, they were not far from the Belgian border. Manus stopped abruptly and pointed to a weathered sign lying in the grass: "België." As long as they moved towards the street lights in the distance, they knew they were traveling in the right direction.

Snow began falling, and cold enveloped them. A young couple pushed a stroller with a child against the strong westerly wind. The girl stopped and pointed skyward; just below the heavy cloud cover, she spotted the V-formations of Allied airplanes moving eastward towards Berlin. A shrieking noise suddenly pierced the air, not farther than a hundred meters from Manus. An errant shell fell on the young couple, instantly killing parents and child. Manus and Danya rushed to the scene. Their maimed bodies lay spread around the bomb crater. Danya broke down in tears and fell into Manus' arms, sobbing.

Exhausted and hungry, they arrived in a small town, looking for scraps of food. With the little cash they carried, they had to find someone willing to sell on the black market. On a side street, a brave soul dared to hang the Belgian national flag, which flapped in the wind as the first sign of a nation daring to show its national flag while liberation was imminent.

Clinging to the running boards of cars and trucks, on bicycles, and on foot, they walked in the direction of the Allied troops—an endless stream of refugees, dragging with them overloaded carts and wagons filled with everything they owned. A woman wearing a heavy overcoat and hat pushed a baby carriage holding a large grandfather clock. A young mother carried a squealing baby while pushing a cartful of cackling chickens. Farmers observed the crowd of refugees shuffling by in despair, unable to offer food. The fields were barren. For months, they had been under orders not to grow food on their farmlands.

A large black automobile sat in a ditch, perforated with bullet holes. Against a tree, a little boy cried. In the back seat, someone frantically tore strips of a handkerchief to stop the bleeding of a dying mother.

"It was a Stuka aircraft. Those damned Moffen!" someone cried. People gazed at the sky, watching the British Spitfires chasing the German Stukas as they prayed for an end to the war.

Their next stop was an old oak tree where they spent the night. The constant wail of air-raid sirens made it impossible to fall asleep. Three Stukas headed straight for them; they rushed into a ditch and watched a bomb hit the village church. The steeple teetered for a moment and then toppled over. Manus shook his head in disbelief.

Shivering in the morning cold, they moved deeper into the farmlands, still watching for landmines. They followed a lane of tall sycamore trees, their branches forming high arches that shielded them from the warplanes above. In the next town, they noticed people coming outside, talking in excited voices. "When are the Allied Forces coming to liberate us?"

A hundred meters from the road, they saw a roadside chapel. Danya opened the creaky door that looked ready to fall off its hinges. She immediately saw the statue of the Virgin Mary. They knelt on the little prayer bench, the only piece of furniture there. Danya read the inscription above the figure: "Welcome to the weary traveler. Kneel down to say a Hail Mary, and I will lift your burdens." Tears trickled down her cheek.

"This is the first statue of the Virgin I made several years ago," Manus whispered to Danya. The statue lifted their spirits. Despite the sanctity of the chapel, they decided to spend the night there. By now they were in Belgium.

The next day, they traveled on, walking toward the town of Merksplas, where heavy artillery broke out during the evening and lasted until early morning. When all fell silent, they gathered pine needles from the nearby woods and made a mattress in a bomb crater. They had heard that bombs never dropped twice in the same place. Exhausted, they fell asleep. Whether it was fear or the need to be together in danger, it was the first time that they had fallen asleep in each other's arms.

Later that morning, Manus woke and studied the hand-drawn map to his sister's home in Schoten, their destination. He realized it would take another three days of walking to get there. On the back of the map, he found a poem by Lord Byron from the *Anthology of Love Stories*. The rays of the morning sunrise stretched over the rim of the crater until they found Danya, still asleep in a cocoon of pine straw. The beams alighted upon her beauty. Manus sat next to her and in a whisper, he started to read:

> *"She walks in beauty, like the night*
> *Of cloudless climes and starry skies*
> *Meet in her aspect and her eyes ..."*

As he recited the poem, Danya stirred and opened her amber eyes to let the sun's warming rays caress her face. Manus noticed a flicker of gold sparkle in her eyes, as he had never seen before.

"Thus mellowed to that tender light

One shade the more, one ray the less,

Which waves in every raven tress."

He stopped and tenderly stroked her black raven curls that fell over her forehead and then returned to the poem:

"Or softly lightens o'er her face

Where thoughts serenely sweet express

How pure, how dear their dwelling place

So soft, so calm, the smile that wins, the tints that glow."

Now fully awake, Danya smiled at Manus. She did not reach out to him to gather him into the cocoon of her warmth and love. He had waited so long for that moment and wondered if he would ever win her over to be his true love. He finished reading the last line:

"A heart whose love is innocent!"

A dark cloud moved over the sun. Manus despaired, knowing that Danya's love for him would remain innocent forever.

"I know the love you have inspired in me belongs to someone else," Manus told her.

Exhausted after a long day's walk, they reached Campina Canal. The moonlight glistened on the rippling waves in the water. Manus pointed to the thick furrows carved by the Brabander horses while towing barges in the canal. They provided the cheap horsepower to transport grain and coal.

Following the road, sidestepping horse droppings, they heard, "Ack, ack," as rifle shots rang out. A pigeon fell from the sky a few meters in front of them. They dared not move for fear the Germans would lay claim to the kill. After a while, Manus moved towards the lifeless pigeon, happy to have found food. He quickly tucked it into his satchel and continued to walk along the canal. Cautiously, they approached a barge moored on their side of the canal.

On the bow of the barge, they read the sign: "Noah's Ark – River Zoo." They had no idea what it meant. Precariously balancing over the gangplank, they boarded the barge as a Schipperke dog alerted the owner. Skipper Woody sported a mustache with the ends turned into little question marks. In the middle of his friendly face, he clenched a meerschaum pipe.

"What are you two doing on my barge?"

"We are refugees from Holland heading for Antwerp," Danya spoke first. "We would like a place to sleep tonight. Can we stay on the barge?" Manus had learned that boat people were often willing to provide transportation for the resistance movement in Holland. Without hesitating, the skipper waved them inside to meet his wife. She was a lively and friendly woman, with that particular character trait of having a solution for every problem.

"We do not have much food. Yesterday we caught some eel in the canal, which I am cooking on the stove." Manus showed her the pigeon, and at the sight of the meat, she became ecstatic. The skipper examined the ring on the leg of the bird.

"This pigeon is special. It carries coded messages. These pigeons are war heroes; they fly along waterways to their destination. Let us open up the tiny canister attached to the ring and retrieve the coded message. Yes, the code is in English, destined for the resistance in Holland." Danya wanted to tell them that she had been a courier for the resistance and also carried these same canisters, delivering them to roadside chapels. She wanted to say more about her dangerous work as a courier with the resistance in Holland, but she remained cautious.

When Manus again brought up their need to spend the night, the skipper's wife looked at her husband and nodded in the direction of the zoo on board. Noah's Ark on the canal was a favorite attraction for children during the war years. For ten cents, they visited this little zoo of small animals: caged mice, rats, gerbils, snakes, beetles, and butterflies.

"The cage next to the cobra snake is empty. It is the cage where we kept the python. It is large enough for two people to spend the night," she said. The skipper took his pipe out of his mouth and pointed toward the stern.

"The Germans will never come here knowing we have cobras on board … they like everything in its cage, not being intimidated by animals." Manus chuckled, thinking of his rat story.

After spending a peaceful night on board, Danya awoke abruptly at daybreak, screaming. She pointed to a small hole in the boards where the tongue of the serpent in the next cage flickered through the narrow opening. Danya fled the cage they had slept in and ran off the barge, straight into the horses feeding at the trough. She left it up to Manus to thank the skipper for his hospitality.

When they found the street where Manus' sister lived, it was late afternoon. They could not have known how fortunate they were to arrive when the curfew was off. War was still in full swing. Twenty-six tanks lined up under the Linden trees; their turrets pointed at the city of Antwerp. The cannons still smoked from the shells they had rained an hour earlier on the city across the canal. A large tank nearly blocked the entrance to Uckle Avenue where Manus' sister and family lived.

CHAPTER 17

A Train to Nowhere

IT WAS A BEAUTIFUL SPRING MORNING IN BRASSCHAAT. Today, like every day, he kept his radio on the bookshelf in the study. His favorite place was behind the *Book of the Nart Sagas of Circassia*. During the war, it was illegal to own or listen to a radio. However, Kadir took his chances; to keep up with his duty as a spy with the Adyghe Intelligence Organization, he had to know what was going on in the world. Listening to the BBC gave him hope that the liberation of Europe was not far off.

On September 3, 1943, the Allied troops invaded Italy. In January 1944, more good news came when the BBC reported that the Russians had broken the 900-day siege of Leningrad. The Russians sent two hundred and fifty thousand German military to the gulags in Siberia. Despite the optimistic news, most of Western Europe was still under Hitler's iron grip.

The arrest of Kadir's neighbor for listening to the BBC did not deter him from tuning in to the news from London. In case of trouble, he could always count on John Ferrat, his close friend in the royal palace. But had he become too bold?

He glanced through a crack in the curtains before picking up the newspaper that was delivered to the front door every day. Just as he had feared for some time, he saw two Gestapo agents marching up the driveway, with machine guns drawn. With the butt of their weapons, they banged on the door. As Kadir opened the door, they marched in with machine guns drawn. The men threw Kadir to the ground.

"Stay facedown with your hands on your head!" Fatima heard the commotion from upstairs and came rushing downstairs to see Kadir on the ground. The agent held a pistol to his head.

"Oh my God! Oh my God!" she cried. They handcuffed her and shoved her against the wall. "Stop wailing!" Meanwhile, the other German yanked Kadir from the floor, dislocating his shoulder and causing him sharp pain.

At gunpoint, the Germans marched the Mandraskits to a waiting truck. One of the two Germans seated himself on the bench opposite them in the back of the truck. Fatima sobbed, and the German poked his machine gun at her chest. He wagged his finger and sternly ordered her again not to wail.

As the truck rolled over the Albert Canal Bridge, Kadir suspected that their destination was Central Prison in Antwerp where the Germans incarcerated the Jews. This prison was a stopover on the way to the concentration camps in Germany. "Where are we going?" Kadir asked the soldier. He shrugged his shoulders, lighting a cigarette and mumbled.

"Brussels." Fatima noticed the deep worry in Kadir's face.

When they arrived at the prison, the truck made a sharp turn and came to a jolting halt in front of a three-story building. The guards hurried them into a small office that reeked like mettwurst, a sausage made from pork and garlic. First, the guard demanded that they deposit their jewelry, watches, and money on the table. A body search followed. He handed their clothes back to get dressed and marched them to their cell. It measured 5 x 8 feet, with a two-tiered bunk bed, blanket, and a small table with two stools. A bucket in the corner served as a toilet.

Fatima sat down on a stool and buried her face in tears. Kadir needed to show her that he was strong under these adverse conditions. He paced up and down to think through how to best deal with the situation.

"We were forewarned. Our neighbors were already picked up for listening to the radio. Who gave our name to the Gestapo? Wait, we both have the same gardener; it must have been Walter who betrayed us."

Although he was a member of the Adyghe Intelligence Network, he had no training in how to handle torture. He was worried that he might crack under pressure. Somehow he had to get in contact with John Ferrat at the royal palace who would be able to secure his release.

Suddenly, a guard opened the door and pointed his pistol in the direction of the interrogation room. "Sit down!" he yelled. Sergeant Baumgartner opened his dossier and barked at the Mandraskits: "Where is Danya?"

Kadir had no idea the SS had issued an all-points bulletin for his daughter, who was now a fugitive from the Lebensborn Project. The sergeant's question hit Kadir like a thunderbolt. *Had they been arrested because of Danya?*

"I have no idea what Lebensborn means. She is in Holland studying and stays with my sister-in-law."

"Are you telling me that you have not spoken to her?"

"Due to the war, we are not able to stay in touch."

"Your sister-in-law died in a bombing raid. Danya's last address is Castle Lindendale in Mill; she's living with a sculptor. We know that the Germans arrested her for distributing illegal propaganda material which resulted in the death penalty. She has escaped, but we will find her soon. You must tell me now where we can pick her up." Baumgartner looked at Kadir, his eyes shooting arrows of frustration.

Kadir looked him in the eye. "I do not have any knowledge where she is, and *if* I knew, you would still not get it out of me," Kadir stated firmly. The sergeant jumped up holding his whip and lashed it across Kadir's face. His head fell sideways, and he felt a trickle of blood dripping from his eye. The sergeant moved to Fatima.

"Let me ask you."

"I am sorry; I do not know what you are talking about." Overcome by the terror that a mother feels when faced with news of her daughter's fate, Fatima sobbed uncontrollably.

Back in their cell, they saw cockroaches crawling over the walls and bunk beds. Kadir stood guard at the cell door to kill them one by one, but to no avail. The cell walls were made of brick and whitewashed. The only source of light during the daytime came from a small opening in the ceiling. It was the single view they had of the outside world, sometimes blue, more often grey, and rainy. Inmates left their marks on the walls, messages of sadness and despair: "Free Belgium – Down with Hitler – Execution tomorrow."

During that rainy evening, the lightbulb in the ceiling flickered, then extinguished for good, leaving them in total darkness. Puddles of water started to form on the floor. Would they be left to drown in their cell?

"We will find a way to contact Ferrat at the royal palace," Kadir affirmed, attempting to console his wife.

In the morning, the slamming of metal on metal signaled the opening of cell doors. Guards delivered breakfast through a little door to the prisoners' cell. It consisted of one cup of imitation coffee, made from chicory, and a slice of bread, showing teeth marks from rats. However, the inmates were too hungry to notice such detail. They made sure not to leave any crumbs on the floor. Rats came out at night scampering over their blankets, looking for food scraps.

Every Friday morning guards released the inmates to the exercise yard that amounted to an outside cage with barbed wire on top. As the sun came out, the prisoners rejoiced in a moment of singing the national anthem:

> *"But woe to you if, willfully pursuing dreadful plans*
> *You turn on us the bloody cannons fire*
> *Then all is over, and all is changing*
> *And you shall see the <u>Boches</u> fall from the tree of Liberty."*

Chanting in French helped disguise the changing of the words to "Boches," a contemptuous term used to refer to a German soldier. The guards never caught on. The secret lifted their spirits in hopes that liberation would come soon.

In prison, the drainpipe had been a reliable communication system to use by tapping on it in code. In the middle of the night, a mysterious voice sent this message: "Allied troops closing in on Brussels. Heavy artillery in the suburbs." The prison was located four kilometers from the center of the city. Kadir could hear the pounding of the heavy guns. Now it became a matter of surviving the bombing of the liberation forces. He took Fatima in his arms to protect her from the onslaught.

By the hour, the sounds of artillery changed to machine guns in the neighboring streets of the prison. The guards grew excited and worried, not knowing what to do with the prisoners. Some argued to set the inmates free; others opted to execute them.

Suddenly, the guards flung open the cell doors with a loud bang, without any explanation. All of a sudden, in a single file, the inmates marched along the empty streets to the Gare du Nord train station. A long line of cattle cars came into view as they entered the station. The guards crammed the prisoners into the filthy vehicles reeking of urine. Standing, they cried, holding hands, not knowing their destination. They feared the worst, being sent to Germany.

Kadir stood out in the car with his broad shoulders and long beard, grown in prison. He held Fatima. She recognized his expression of angry determination. With his loud voice, he addressed the crowd: "People, listen. Together we will be strong!" The group was too frightened to put any credence to his words.

Acrid smoke puffing from the locomotive engines in the station filled the air to the stained glass ceiling above. The whistle blared, deafening the wailing and crying in the cattle cars. With a sharp jolt on each connector mechanism in the train, the locomotive labored to pick up speed. Gert De Vries was no friend of the Germans, but they needed him to be the conductor of the train.

He was awakened early in the morning by two Gestapo agents banging on his door. They ordered him to the railway yard to ready his locomotive. He did not expect to be called up for duty since he planned to retire the following month. Many of his colleagues were in jail for having supported the Railroad Strike the previous month which crippled all transport of German war materiel. Gert was one of the few who had managed to stay out of trouble.

Once he arrived at the railway yard, he was ordered to load enough coal and water to travel 500 kilometers. There was no doubt in his mind that his destination was Germany. When he rolled the locomotive from the parking into the station, he heard the sobbing and moaning of the prisoners locked in the cattle wagons. Gert shook his head and mumbled to himself.

"I cannot do this. Another load of Jews to the gas chambers! With the Allied Forces close to liberating Brussels, I am going to save these poor souls," he said under his breath. There was not a lot of time to come up with a ruse to delay the departure of the train and allow the liberating forces to catch the train before escaping to Germany.

The train was at full steam power and ready to leave. Gert was still checking the gauges until three Gestapo agents boarded the engine compartment and ordered him at gunpoint to move the train.

"To Antwerp. Now!" As the train moved from the station, Kadir kept himself occupied listening to the click-clacking of the iron wheels over the track joints. Tension grew amongst the inmates. One hour into the trip, several had fallen unconscious from heat and exhaustion. They collapsed on the floor, in danger of being trampled in the close quarters.

The train approached Mechelen, the midpoint between Brussels and Antwerp. The train engineer had stoked the engine to an alarmingly high temperature. The gauge registered well over the red line, at which point it was no longer safe to operate. The locomotive could explode at any point, killing the crew and guards on the train. Gert knew all too well that he might end up dead on this journey, but he hoped at least he'd save the people in the cattle cars.

The alarm sounded, alerting the guards. The engine lost power, and the train slowed down. Gert told the guard he had to steer the train on a side spur to allow military transport to come through as they evacuated in advance of the Allied Forces. One of the Gestapo hit Gert in the face with his pistol.

"You get this train moving or else I will shoot you!" the Gestapo threatened. Gert said he needed to order a new gauge from the repair depot in Antwerp, knowing he would be unable to obtain a new gauge because the depot had been sabotaged by the White Brigade the week before.

"If you shoot me, you will have nobody to drive the train, and the Allied Forces will find you within hours. Your only chance to make it out alive will be with me at the controls," Gert bluffed.

In the distance, they heard machine gunfire. The Allied cautiously approached the train. The prisoners started to sing "Ave Maria."

On Wednesday, September 3, at 2:30 p.m., the German guards jumped from the train and ran into the cornfield where the train was parked. As soon as they had left, Gert and his engineer went to the cattle wagons and opened the doors. The sunlight startled the emerging prisoners. Several failed to make it into the field. For them, it was too late.

Cries of "Free at last!" rang through the air. The jubilant passengers had no idea what the engineer had accomplished, but they danced around him to say thanks to their hero. "Thank you for bringing the train to a halt and causing the guards to flee. You saved our lives!" After a while, a jeep belonging to the Canadian military rolled up to the locomotive. Gert quickly briefed them on what had transpired.

Soon afterward, Canadian military trucks arrived with water and supplies. They loaded the freed prisoners for transport to a nearby school. The Mandraskits ended up in the rectory where Van Roey, cardinal of the Catholic Church of Belgium, resided.

On the following day, for the first time in four years, the forty-nine bells of the carillon of Mechelen rang out over the city in all its glory. Three years later, the people of Belgium added the famous "Liberation Bell," commemorating those who fought for freedom in Belgium.

CHAPTER 18

Canadians in the Street

THIS MORNING, ON UCKLE AVENUE, THE SKY WAS A faded blue, with thin clouds stretched as far as the eye could see. A sharp whistle, a loud crackle, followed by a sharp jolt, and it was over. The bullet by the German sharpshooter thrust her violently backward onto the dirt road. With her eyes wide open, her vision blurred into streaks of light and darkness. As she lay in the dirt of the avenue dying, the last image she saw was the British bombers on their mission to Germany to free Europe from the tyranny of the Nazis, fighting for the freedom she would never live to enjoy.

As the big metal birds in the air disappeared, the silence of death descended upon the avenue, following the tragic death of a neighbor shot to death over a curfew violation. She succumbed without doctor or priest.

A German sentry, standing guard at the military compound at the end of the avenue, had fired a single bullet. The soldier obeyed orders and did his duty. To the people in the neighborhood, it was another execution of an innocent civilian. The women in the avenue pulled the curtain aside just enough to see who had fallen victim to the latest act of German brutality. Their eyes filled with tears as they wept in sorrow over another victim of the war.

After four years of occupation, they had no choice but to keep on with their lives until the end of the war. The war was going badly for the Germans. Their ranks depleted of Wehrmacht soldiers, Hitler had no choice but to send fifteen-year-old teenagers and old men in their sixties. They were poorly trained soldiers, indoctrinated by a zeal for a cause long lost. The young ones were obsessed with an enthusiasm for revenge, not seen in the professional soldier of the Third Reich. People looked upon the young soldiers and lamented, "So young, just boys trudging through life with their heads hanging down, scared, desperately trying to stay alive."

Overnight, Allied bombers hit houses in the avenue. The cellar walls vibrated down to the foundation, with dust falling from the ceiling. A baby cried all night.

"Shut that baby up! I am trying to sleep!" someone yelled.

"He is afraid!" the mother yelled back.

"So are we." Silence finally fell over the city, almost more deafening than the sounds of war. By early morning, the "all clear" sounded, but it had become meaningless. All night long, everyone was awake.

In the morning, one by one, people came outside to survey the carnage, talk with a neighbor, and share worries about what was to come. They pointed at the military compound at the end of the avenue, which was the primary reason for the frequent bombings. However, the people in the avenue were a stubborn kind and steadfastly refused to obey the orders from the Germans to leave their homes. "Nein" was the typical reaction when the Germans knocked on the door.

"When will it end?" was the question on everybody's mind. For only a few hours every day, the German military lifted the curfew to allow people to get food. Then it was back to the basement, where they did their best to survive by candlelight, oatmeal, cow udder, and a few drops of oil. Deprivation, hunger, and fear surrendered to despair as they spent yet another night holed up in the dank basement. At night, the Germans ordered a total blackout, to make sure the Allied bombers would fly over without noticing the well-camouflaged military command post at the end of the avenue. The tall Linden trees in the avenue offered the perfect cover for the fifty Panzer tanks pointed at Antwerp. The roar of the guns at night kept everyone sleepless.

Neighbors became alarmed at the numbers of war victims dying in the rubble of their homes as the result of bombardments. People trapped in the basement as the result of a cave-in needed to find a way to escape to the outside. Someone mentioned breaking through the wall, connecting with the neighbor's basement. This solution gave the trapped people a chance to survive. With the houses situated in rows, it created a safe passage to several adjacent homes. Within days, it became apparent that this solution saved lives. Moreover, there was the unintended consequence of building a social network. Neighbors shared news about the war efforts and gave each other a measure of hope that the liberation was coming soon. One of the neighbors was so brave to keep a radio receiver hidden from the Germans. At night, he listened to the latest news on the war efforts in Europe.

At night, Louis, Bertha's husband, risked it to climb to the attic, pushing the little roof window open to observe the spectacle of bombardments over Antwerp. Louis wanted to have a good view. He positioned himself on a wooden crate he had found in the far corner of the attic so he could look out over the landscape of the entire city. On orders of the Germans, the city lay under a mantle of darkness. The fall air in the streets shivered beneath a cold, dark sky. The wind tumbled through the trees, shaking loose the withering leaves. In a sudden flash, hundreds of phosphorous bombs were unleashed over the city, leaving a faint bluish light. It was a light spectacle reminiscent of Richard Wagner's operas of doom. For half an hour, the lights floated over the city, illuminating the desired targets for the Allied bombers. Louis could barely make out the airplanes against the darkness in the sky. They moved like slinky monsters, intent on mechanized doom. In unison, six bombers fell out of their V formation and swooped down over their targets. Within seconds, the city was ablaze with dozens of fires. Then suddenly, the bombers were gone. The sky was empty, still and dark again. The moon dared to show only half its face, reassuring the world that life would go on.

Every time the resistance committed another act of sabotage, the Germans reduced the curfew hours to punish the people. The new time would now run from 9 to 11 instead of 12 o'clock in the morning. With no food left on the shelves in the stores, mothers had nothing left to feed their children. Due to severe vitamin shortages, lice had become a scourge inflicted on young children. It was like a curse. Mothers hurried home sobbing as they returned from the doctor. They felt ashamed that their children were shaven bald. Doctors had no choice but to shave the children and apply a solution derived from petrol, which created an unpleasant odor. A little girl carried a bag of her cut curls as if to keep them for better times.

A mother in the avenue grew desperate. Her four-year-old girl showed signs of malnutrition. Day by day the girl lost energy and had collapsed the day before. The mother went to the German commander and asked permission to pick up an extra cup of milk. When the commander steadfastly refused, she did not back down and refused to leave his office. He pulled his pistol and killed the young mother on the spot.

When word got out about the murder of the mother, "Boomke" or "Little Tree," as he was known, made up his mind. He decided that he had enough of the Germans denying milk to the children. He put on his black trench coat and bowler hat, grabbed a large bucket, and took off for the farm, located a kilometer from his home. Every morning, he walked in the middle of the avenue, in defiance of the armed sentry positioned at the gate of the military compound. He waved his white handkerchief at the sentry and went to fetch his milk. Upon his return, he went from door to door, distributing a cup to each family with small children. Mothers wept in thankfulness for saving their children.

One day, the same German sentry had enough of his bravery and shot at him but missed. The bullet passed between his legs and pierced his raincoat, leaving a big hole. Every day, Boomke kept walking, despite the danger. Later on, nobody understood why the soldier did not shoot again. Had he intentionally misfired, as he remembered that he had children back home in Germany? Every morning, Boomke walked with his pail until liberation. After the war, he received the highest Medal of Honor bestowed upon a civilian for extreme bravery in the face of the enemy. Thirty years later, at his funeral, his raincoat with the bullet hole was spread over the casket, commemorating the heroism of this brave neighbor that had saved the children of Uckle Avenue.

Desperation pushed people into dangerous acts. Every time the Germans banged on the front door with their rifles, ordering a family to leave, it infuriated Louis. He stood firm and boldly refused. Then one morning, he went to the shed in the backyard and placed a pitchfork next to the front door. In the hallway near the front door, a stroller stood ready with provisions in case of an emergency. When Bertha, his wife, noticed the pitchfork, she immediately knew what Louis had in mind and went into a panic.

"Louis, please do not do this!" She fell to her knees and rested her tear-drenched cheek on his hand, begging him to remove the pitchfork. Louis was a fanatic anti-Nazi and, on many occasions, had declared he would have no problem taking care of the Germans.

"The first German who forces himself through my door will go on this pitchfork," he declared, as Bertha cried through her tears.

"They will kill all of us!" He pulled her toward him and gave in, putting the pitchfork back in the shed.

Every night, the family said the rosary, to be freed from the evil of the German occupation. Louis tossed his rosary on the table and shook his head when they continued their prayer: "To forgive those who trespass against us" in the "Our Father Prayer."

"No, I cannot say the words," declared Louis. "That is too much for me. Remember the twenty-two young men executed at the school last week. The Germans must go first before I speak these words. Let's skip that sentence and go to '*Lead us not into temptation and deliver us from evil*.'" He wiped a tear from his eye. Danya and Manus, Bertha and her father, Antonius Habers, fell silent when they heard Louis speak.

As he had done for months, at the end of the day, Antonius let the delicate notes of the "Ave Maria" song roll from the strings of his violin. Those who lived with him in the basement intently listened to the music of Schubert. Danya, seated on the wooden bench in the cramped quarters of the basement, noticed the face of the neighbor's six-year-old girl, Olivia. The beautiful black curls fell around her little face as she puckered a smile, listening to the music. She reminded her of her image in the mirror when she had prepared for her birthday party nine years ago.

With the waning notes of the "Ave Maria," Manus waxed reminiscent of the days when he wielded hammer and chisel, carving the details into the granite of the Stations of the Cross. He looked at Danya and put his arm around his Circassian beauty, who had so faithfully served as his model for the mother of Jesus. Would the carvings of the Stations of the Cross in Mill still be there, left untouched by the Germans? Would he find his atelier in the state he had left it?

The next day, a neighbor at the end of the street knocked on the door and told Antonius that every night they hear his music reverberating through the passages of the basements on Uckle Avenue. He continued to play that song until the Allied Forces arrived to liberate their avenue.

Day after day, Danya spent her time helping Bertha with the household chores. After several weeks, she still felt like a stranger in this family. At night, Danya wanted to be alone, close to the passageway in the wall to the neighbor's as if to signal her readiness to break out of the confinement of the basement. She preferred to seat herself on a wooden bench in the shadows of the flickering candlelight. No longer sixteen, she had become a woman of the Circassian realm, with her smooth olive skin and beautiful eyes defining her. The courage that was so much part of the amber in her eyes burned hotter than ever before.

Manus adored his model for the sculptures of Maria and realized how little she had physically changed from the girl he had first met. Manus did not want to tell Danya, "I am worried about you ..." To Danya, they were the wrong words.

"Worry not about me," she paused, well-aware that the resistance movement in Holland had become extremely precarious. German sympathizers had infiltrated the organization and caused the death of hundreds of resistance workers. The need to replace the fallen resistance workers reached Danya in Belgium through a secret radio channel arranged by Arie. It aroused in her the spirit of the Circassian warrior woman.

After a long silence, she answered. "Yes, soon I shall return to the resistance in Holland. That is where my destiny lies. Satanaya told me last night in my dream."

Danya's words galvanized the family. Ravished by hunger and despair, they stared at each other upon hearing Danya's words. They knew Satanaya had spoken to her. Danya looked at Manus to see if he still stood with her in her mission.

"As a courier, I must be there to drive out the last German from Holland," she added.

It did not matter that she had been jailed, followed by the Wewelsburg ordeal. That night, Danya set an example of raw courage for the family hiding in the basement, anxiously awaiting liberation. She spoke with a tinge of hope.

"Every evening, we hear the music in the streets of Antwerp, celebrating the liberation of the city of Antwerp. Soon, the marching band of the City of Schoten will be in our avenue."

Bertha cried. "When will it all end? We are running out of food!" she lamented. She had been a creative cook with the provisions at hand. Oatmeal pancakes with onion slices and a little bit of remaining sugar served with a slice of pumpernickel bread became daily fare.

The hardest part of living in the basement was the lack of fresh air. The potatoes in a wooden box in the coal cellar started to sprout, despite the darkness, and the combined smell of coal and potatoes was nauseating.

Through it all, neighbors found joy in exchanging whatever food was available for the day. A few kind words from a trusted neighbor did a lot in keeping their spirits up. One of the avenue people found the courage to rebel against German regulations and listened to the BBC Station in London—their only link to the free world. The news bulletins left the impression that the war was nearly over. However, Danya knew the end of the war was still several months away.

"In my dream last night, Satanaya told me that difficult times lie ahead of us," she told the family gravely.

The bloodstains on the wall of the schoolhouse left a vivid reminder of the brutality of the last days of the Nazi Regime: a memorial to the twenty-two young men executed for acts of sabotage. They were punished for blowing up the central electrical switching station, thereby knocking out power for the entire city. The tension between the occupying forces and the local population was escalating into open hostility. No less than fourteen times, the Germans ordered the people to leave their homes, declaring the avenue a dangerous war zone. Every time, Louis had one short answer: "Nein."

During the first days of October in 1944, the sun barely broke through the cloud layer. This morning was different. The sun rose bright and cheerful. Manus remarked to Danya how quiet it was on the avenue. The guns in the tanks had fallen silent. Soldiers smoked cigarettes, in an ostensibly cheerful mood. Were they talking about going back home to Germany? Around 10 o'clock, as if on command, the tanks turned on their engines, revved up on high and turned eastward. As he had done before, Manus went upstairs to peer through a crack in the blind. He ran downstairs and saw Bertha.

"They are leaving the avenue! Going east to Germany!" Manus wanted to see more of this spectacle of retreat by the Germans.

"Wait! It is too dangerous! The White Brigade needs to do its work first," Danya told him. When she was a courier, she had heard of the White Brigade in Belgium. They had connections with various intelligence networks, which included the Adyghe Intelligence Organization and the Dutch Intelligence Services in London. She had learned from Arie about the tactical moves the underground had planned for the arrival of the Allied Forces. In charge of clearing the street of automatic weapons nests, they took it upon themselves to jail collaborators. After four years of betraying their people to the Germans, revenge came down hard on them.

The avenue had to be cleared of any residual resistance by the Germans, in their futile fight to hang on to a lost cause. Heavy hand-to-hand combat broke out in the avenue between the White Brigade and German soldiers, who had been ordered to defend the military compound at the end of the avenue at all cost. The partisans were well-equipped with machine guns and hand grenades, and they did not hesitate to use their weapons on the Germans. German soldiers in the avenue ran out of ammunition and were hunted down with hand grenades and machine guns. The White Brigade showed no mercy. Soldiers of the German Third Reich died amidst the tall weeds and bushes of the empty lot across the street, where once stood houses, now bombed and laying waste. It was a gruesome scene.

Fifteen minutes later, a civilian truck slowly crawled through the avenue, with three partisans, machine guns at the ready. Louis, seated in the front, held the list of collaborators and German sympathizers in the street. He pointed at several houses. The truck carried heated tar pots and brushes, ready to mark those houses identified on the White Brigade list as collaborators. Louis led the way with his broad brush dripping with hot tar and painted a couple of houses with swastikas. Shortly after that, a large truck showed up and rounded up the inhabitants living in the swastika-marked properties. The White Brigade incarcerated the males at the Central Jail in Antwerp, and their spouses were dispatched to the zoo and locked in cages designated for the gorillas.

While Louis' family remained sequestered in the basement, fearful of the hand-to-hand combat, Manus stationed himself upstairs, where he kept watching through a slit in the blind. Then he saw the unbelievable, like a ghost from another world, a jeep belonging to the Allied Forces crept slowly forward. With a machine gun mounted in the back, it crawled through the street, checking each house for enemy machine gun nests. They were Canadians dressed in leather jackets with heavy fur collars, sten machine guns at the ready, and a belt with hand grenades.

"They have arrived! The Canadians are on the avenue! We're free at last!" he yelled, hugging Danya. Bertha was left standing by herself without Louis; there was no one to hug her to rejoice in this moment of liberation. *Where was Louis?*

Manus went to the passageway in the basement wall to shout to the neighbors: "They are in the avenue!"

"Where is Louis?" Bertha asked all day. Louis had gone missing. He had disappeared without a word, and nobody knew when he would come back. He had taken his place with the White Brigade.

Bertha knew where Louis kept a particular bottle of liqueur for this occasion: Elixir d'Anvers. She went to the coal cellar and retrieved it from a cubbyhole in the wall.

"Should we not wait until Louis has returned? He will be here soon."

Louis never came home. The same sharpshooter who had allowed Boomke to live had killed Louis. He was the last war victim in the city of Schoten.

CHAPTER 19

Reprisals

DURING THE FIRST WEEKS OF LIBERATION, SENTI-
ments toward the German collaborators and black marketers
boiled over into a frenzy of retaliation. Less than three days
after the liberating forces entered the avenue, people were
anxious to emerge from their basements. The acts of naked
revenge committed by the White Brigade did not come as a
surprise after the Nazi atrocities endured during four years of
their occupation. The hour of retribution for the years of Nazi
terror had arrived with full vengeance, and the Belgians were
going to make it count.

A brigade truck stormed through the street proudly flying
a giant flag with the letter "V" for victory. The truck screeched
to a halt and agents brandishing machine guns raided the residence of the Van Berkel family. The Van Berkels had collabo-
rated with the German authorities for their financial gain. They
were guilty of having provided fabricated information. Their
victims perished from typhoid at the Bergen-Belsen concentration camp in Germany.

The unsuspecting owner opened the door, and brigade
agents immediately put the shackles on, made from German

copper shell casings, a special touch by the White Brigade, reminding the Berkels of their ties to the Germans. They picked up three more collaborators. They looked at each other—they were fellow collaborators from the same secret "cell" of traitors. A few neighbors came outside, shook their fists, and spat on them.

"Deutscher Schweine!" they yelled. Many of them had lost a husband or son in Bergen-Belsen.

Fueled by the anger of the bystanders, one of the resistance soldiers pointed his machine gun at Van Berkel. "I will make sure you are going away for a long time for the murder of the seven families!" he shouted. One of the agents pressed his pistol to Van Berkel's forehead. "I'd like to shoot you seven times until every drop of blood has oozed from your body!" he shouted as he came face to face, shooting sparks of raw hatred from his eyes.

The Canadians had received permission to set up a first aid/emergency clinic for the neighborhood in number 26 of the avenue, where the Habers family lived. The landmines hidden throughout town continued to cause many casualties. The injuries were often so severe that the Red Cross staff was not able to save the victims. Too often people in the avenue saw the wooden boxes with the remains of the landmine victims going to the morgue. It lay a shroud of sadness over number 26.

It was late fall, and the wind blew the last leaves from the Linden trees lining the avenue. They were getting ready for spring foliage. On this warm day, trucks with the brigade flags sped through the avenue looking for specific addresses. The underground had planned for this operation three years ago. They picked up the girls who had dated German soldiers. For them, they had an unusual punishment in mind, making it clear how disgusted they were about their sexual behavior with the enemy soldiers.

Using a loudspeaker mounted on the truck that transported the girls, a brigade man called on the townspeople to come outside and express their feelings of disgust. The people came by the dozens, throwing eggs and rotten tomatoes and spitting on the girls. The brigade had arranged twelve chairs in the middle of the avenue, where they tied the girls with ropes that bit into their flesh as they wrestled to free themselves. A local barber cut the girls' blonde curls. It was his punishment. He had been a secret investigator for the SS. Some of the neighbors collected the hair and put it in a paper bag. A member of the brigade instructed the barber to coat the girls' scalps and faces with black shoeshine. The warm weather caused the shoeshine to melt in streaks, running down their face like a striped clown mask. The girls showed no remorse, screaming and laughing at the onlookers as if it was nothing more than a charade.

Few neighbors knew Danya. She was the mystery girl who lived at number 26. When Danya came outside, she saw Gerda, a neighbor's daughter, amongst the girls. Danya wondered what had happened to her blonde curls, and why the black shoeshine?

"These are the girls who went out with German soldiers," a neighbor whispered. Stirred by her feelings of aversion, Danya rushed ahead of the crowd of people to confront them. She stepped on a chair and asked for quietness. She looked at each girl.

"While you were laying with the enemy, enjoying yourself in bed with them, these same Nazis executed your fathers and brothers as they fought for your freedom! How could you bring yourself to such acts of debauchery? A year ago, the SS Supreme Court in Wewelsburg convicted me, sentencing me to lay with the Nazis as part of their Aryan Breeding Program. I said 'no' and risked my life by escaping to Belgium. Never would I have allowed a German to touch my body! Never! I have lived in hiding ever since. People are still dying in Holland, where I shall return as a courier with the underground. Now, you must face your punishment by the White Brigade, under their Code of Retribution for War Crimes."

Canadian soldiers came by on patrol and ordered the girls released. Their order did not sit well with the people.

"We will come after you to tar your home!" they shouted. Members of the brigade followed the girls with a bucket of hot tar and plastered the swastika symbol on the façade of their homes, branding the girls as "Nazi prostitutes" for life.

One of the girls approached Danya. Through the dripping shoe wax on her face, Danya saw a tear rolling down her cheek. It was Gerda.

"Danya, I regret what I have done. I did not dare to say 'no' to the Nazis who came at me. It is true that these same Germans executed my brother. I'd like to go with you to Holland and fight beside you as a courier." Danya paused, looking her over.

"Before you make that decision, you must remember that you will put yourself in great danger. The work as a courier puts you deep in enemy territory. If caught, they will kill you," Danya warned.

"I must go with you to liberate myself from my past mistakes. The time is here to face my deepest fears. I am ready to give my life in the fight against the Germans, in retribution for what they did to my brother." Danya thought she sounded sincere and agreed to let her make the trip with her.

"You can come with me."

Two weeks earlier, Arie had found a way to contact Danya and alert her that the Allied Forces desperately needed experienced couriers to transport coded messages in the German-held territory. The Allied Forces had great difficulty recruiting girls with Danya's experience. What made the courier girls' task even more difficult was the fluid situation of German military movements over dikes and canals, which required reconnaissance on foot and inventiveness to stay in hiding.

The Dutch Resistance was in close communication with the Belgian Brigade. As soon as the war was over in Schoten, Arie notified the Dutch Underground where they could find Danya. The Dutch intelligence unit of the resistance needed her to return to her former position as head courier in the Moerdijk Region, with its famous bridge over the Rhine River in Holland. Her familiarity with the relay system of dropping coded messages in the roadside chapels made her the top-ranked courier for the region. It was no coincidence that she knew the details of each drop site. Each chapel housed a statue of the Virgin Mary, carved by Manus. They were located at ten-kilometer intervals along the main road, running through Danya's assigned area.

Delivering the coded messages without arousing suspicion by the German military was routine for Danya. Before her capture and imprisonment in Wewelsburg, she had already deposited hundreds of silk scrolls in these same chapels. Each scroll contained vital data about German positions, troops, tanks, and artillery deployed by the Germans as a last desperate defense before the Allied would breach the border with Germany. The bridge over the Rhine River in Moerdijk was a key strategic objective for the Allied, to secure this main road for the invasion of Germany.

Danya knew the danger she faced by re-entering German-occupied territory. If they discovered that she was on the list of "Most Wanted Criminals" and an escapee from Himmler's Lebensborn Program, they would summarily execute her, but Danya felt it was her mission to help drive the Germans out of Holland and was willing to risk her life. Had Satanaya not spoken of the dangers in her father's study?

The war had caused severe food shortages throughout Belgium. One day, the parish pastor invited them for supper.

They entered the rectory and smelled the stew cooking in the kitchen, made with bay leaves and allspice and little chunks of pork belly fat drifting atop the broth. It was the family's first meat dish in months. Word around the dinner table was that they ate a rabbit, but not long after their dinner visit, word leaked out that the pastor's cat was missing. The pastor never raised rabbits!

Each morning, everyone listened to the news on Radio Belgique, which broadcasted from London. Despite the success of the Allied Forces, Hitler planned a massive counterattack into Belgium, known as the "Battle of the Bulge." On the morning of December 16, 1944, the German Army launched a surprise attack in the Ardennes Mountains of Belgium. Opening the main road to Antwerp and occupying the port was Hitler's final strategy to stop the Allied invasion of Germany. General Eisenhower had designated Antwerp as a significant point to disembark troops and equipment for the Allied.

After fierce fighting around Bastogne, the Allied denied the Germans access to the vital road to the port city of Antwerp, three hundred kilometers to the North. By January 25, 1945, the battle was over. The end of the hostilities in the Ardennes Mountains came at a considerable cost of lives on both sides, making the Battle of the Bulge the costliest military battle in Western Europe.

Hitler became so infuriated at the German loss that he ordered immediate attacks on London and Antwerp with the V-1 and V-2 rockets, his "Miracle Weapons." The photographic evidence, collected as early as May 1943, showed how far the Germans had come in developing the V-1 and a rocket known as the V-2. However, the British believed that Hitler did not have the fuel nor launching pads to fly his V-weapons to London.

Four years of Nazi terror had robbed the population of any form of entertainment. In an ironic twist, the shooting down of German V-1s became the entertainment of the day. It was after dark when Manus joined a small group of people on a hill above town from where they could see the anti-aircraft guns firing at the rockets in the sky. In the distance, a few cows grazed around the cement pillboxes, a legacy of the German occupation. Broken-down trucks, jeeps, burned-out tanks, and munitions boxes littered the grasslands. Seated on the grass, huddled under blankets, the crowd kept an eye on the night sky, gazing towards Germany. It was like a festival atmosphere, with Belgian beer flowing freely.

"Let's see how many V-1s the Americans can hit tonight!" shouted a spectator. "I heard the Americans are getting good at stopping these killing machines from reaching Antwerp and London. I like to see the action with my own eyes."

Three dark objects ominously buzzed over the horizon, crossing the border, sounding like loud lumbering trucks.

"Look how many are going up to their target aiming at the slow lumbering V-1! How can they miss?" someone yelled, as people pointed to the sky, following the fiery balls of the anti-aircraft batteries. One of the shells hit the steering mechanism, causing the V-1 to turn 180 degrees, back to Germany. Shouting hoorays and locking arms, they danced as if they were celebrating the winning goal at a soccer game.

"Gooooo…al! I hope it kills Adolf in Germany!" someone yelled.

An hour later, the Americans downed a V-1, which crashed three hundred meters from the spectators. They approached the hot smoldering wreckage cautiously.

"What are these strange-looking handles on the outside of the V-1?" someone asked.

"I know what these are … they are the handles of water buckets," another bystander proclaimed, running closer to the bomb and poking it with a stick.

"Because iron ore had become scarce, the Germans had to resort to the use of household buckets to manufacture their V-1 bombs. They knocked the bottom out of the water buckets and flattened the sides, not bothering to remove the handles. I bet it takes a hundred buckets to make one bomb ... pity on the German housewife, doing her housekeeping without her water bucket." They laughed.

By day or night, V-1 and V-2 rockets rained down on Antwerp. The civilian authorities ordered a general evacuation into the countryside, where no V-1s were falling. After packing a stroller and an old bicycle, the Habers set out on foot to make the trip into the Campina Region.

Danya was surprised to see Gerda waiting for them. At first, they did not speak to each other as Gerda followed Danya in the hope of becoming a courier.

"Are you ready to lay down your life for your brother?" Danya finally asked. "Remember that courage is resistance to fear. Your courage will demand that you go to dangerous enemy places." Not sure that she could live up to Danya's expectations, Gerda listened carefully to her words of encouragement, remaining silent.

It was winter, and a light coating of snow made the walking difficult. The refugees pushed and shoved in their desperate search for a place to stay overnight. Several of the elderly were too exhausted to continue walking and sat down on the cold, wet ground, staring into the distance, refugees in their homeland. They held their rosaries, silently reciting their Ave Marias. They had hoped the war would be over by now.

Suddenly a sharp sound over the horizon signaled a V-2 rocket.

"V-2 incoming! Down in the ditch!" someone yelled. Before anyone could find cover, the ballistic rocket landed, killing and injuring dozens of refugees. People wailed and trembled in fear. Danya set out to help the victims. She worked furiously, ripping strips of cloth from her dress to stop the bleeding. She ordered Gerda to do the same.

It was almost dark when Manus pointed at a chicken farm. Martha, the widow who lived there with her four sons, received them with open arms and a smile. A pot of chicken stew bubbled on the stove. The Habers had not eaten all day. They enjoyed their supper while Martha apologized for the simple meal. She showed them a newly built chicken house, a low-slung small structure, barely big enough for six people. She brought hay from the barn for bedding. It had a faint smell of chicken droppings.

On this windy evening, everyone worried that Hubert, Bertha's little boy, had not come home before dark. Pa Habers suggested they start the evening prayer without Hubert. While they were reciting the rosary, Hubert rushed in, holding a little cat in his arms.

"Mommy, look what I found! Can I keep it?" He put the animal on the floor, where it fell, unable to stand. Danya inspected the animal.

"How did it survive? It only has three legs, and one ear and an eye are missing." Pa Habers jumped in. "It must have been another victim of a landmine." The family decided to share their food with the unfortunate creature. A week later, they were not only looking for the pussycat, but Gerda had also disappeared without a trace. Danya wondered where she had gone.

In the spring of 1945, the Allied successfully drove the Germans deeper into Holland. The battlefield stretched along the Rhine River into the Dutch Delta Waterway System. The Germans held onto this tract of land as a last resort, securing for themselves an escape route to the homeland. They put a high priority on the last major bridge over the Rhine River to keep the road open to Germany.

Danya and Manus left the family to enter Holland. Danya pondered whether to take up her position as a courier or to stay on with Manus for a while longer. On the other hand, Manus was just as anxious to return to Lindendale Castle to resume his sculpting on the Stations of the Cross. Plus, he was not letting Danya leave on her own into the embattled areas.

The old bicycle without rubber tires made for a bumpy ride. Danya had to hold on, sitting on the crossbar. Finally, after an absence of one year, they were heading home to their castle in Mill. Broken military equipment, jeeps, trucks, tanks, ammunition boxes, jerry cans still leaking gasoline lay strewn about, reminders of war waged in Holland. The white crosses along the road with handwritten names of the fallen soldiers left a deep impression on the couple. They continued along on their bicycle when Danya pointed at a metal object in the grass.

"I wonder what the little metal plate is doing in the pasture." They stopped to investigate. It was a "dog tag" military issue inscribed with the name, "Mark McGuffey Pfc. – First Canadian Army." Manus remembered the cross without a name a few hundred meters back.

"There is a chance that this name tag belongs to the soldier in the unnamed grave. Let's go back and leave it on his cross." They paused at the gravesite and Danya swept away a tear.

The demarcation lines between the retreating German Armies and the advances of the Allied Forces were often blurred. Traveling along the rural roads made it difficult to know whether they were in German or Allied territory. In the distance, they saw a sign with a couple of bullet holes: "The Netherlands." Manus noticed it first.

"At last, we are back in Holland." Danya gave him a quizzical look as if this was a significant event. Finding a place to spend the night was more on her mind.

The moon was out and in the windows of the faraway farmhouses, candlelight flickered. The first town across the border in Holland was Reusel. In the dark, they spotted a structure that resembled an old abbey. Manus looked at Danya.

"Let's find out if the Friars have room for us." Friar Dominique opened the gate.

"How can we help?"

"We are on our way home to Mill and have not slept for several nights. May we call on your hospitality?" Friar Dominique waved them in.

"You must be hungry. We have food left from the evening dinner." When bedtime came, Dominique announced the convent rule: "Separate sleeping quarters for males and females." Manus looked at Danya. He asked if they would consider an exception to their rule.

"We arrived here together and would like to stay together." After a brief consult with the father abbot, Dominique returned with a smile.

"Good news! You can stay together." Two days later, Manus was back on his rickety bicycle. The chain repeatedly derailed and needed grease to keep it from jumping off the track again. In his travel bag was the sandwich with butter and cheese that Dominique had provided for the road. He smeared the butter on the chain, which made the clickety sound disappear. They ate the other half of the sandwich, less the butter. By evening, Manus walked up a hill and raised his arms, pointing at a familiar sight.

"Our first windmill! We are close to home!" he announced hopefully. After a long day on the road, Manus spread their blanket on the grass and fell asleep with Danya in his arms. Danya woke during the night when she heard Manus murmuring in his dream.

"Oh, Dulcinea! Dear Dulcinea!" He cried out in a soft voice that gave away how much he was in love with Don

Quixote's girl; sweetheart of the "Man of La Mancha." Danya wondered whether Manus was dreaming about their aimless wanderings during the war years. Did he see himself as the "Errant Knight" of La Mancha in search of his imaginary love? Had he read Don Quixote's story?

> *"O Dulcinea, my princess!*
> *Sovereign of this captive heart!*
> *Grievous wrong hast thou done me by dismissing me*
> *And by cruelly forbidding me by decree to appear in thy beaute-*
> *ous presence*
> *I pray thee, sweet lady, to remember this poor enslaved heart,*
> *Which for love of thee suffers so many pangs."*

Danya wept for a while. She looked deep into her soul and was not sure whether she had betrayed Manus. During their time together, she had never given her full love to him. For sure, he was her faithful protector, just like Don Quixote. Then she remembered the words spoken by her mother to "wait until you meet your prince for life." She looked into her handbag and pulled out the box with the fragrance bottle. With this heirloom came the promise to her mother not to open it until her prince embraced her.

When Manus awoke, he was in a joyful mood, looking forward to the trip to the castle. Manus mounted his bicycle and waited for Danya to get on.

"Up you go, Rozinante." Rozinante was the old hack of a horse mounted by Don Quixote. The Errant Knight shepherded his love into the realm of imaginary chivalry.

CHAPTER 20

A Sculptor's Dream in Ruins

At last, they were on their way to the castle they had not seen in over a year when they had fled for their lives. Holland was in the midst of the Hunger Winter instituted by the Nazis in retaliation for the Dutch Resistance.

So far, they saw no signs of German forces lingering to defend their lost cause.

Danya walked along, feeling restless, knowing she had to tell Manus soon that she must make her move to the frontlines of the war. Reflecting on Manus' "Dulcinea Dream," Danya realized she was merely a figment of his imagination. She must find time to be on her own.

Manus and Danya decided to spend their last night on the road in an abandoned windmill. In the bright light of the full moon, they saw two of the four blades were no longer there. Chaff left over from the last grain threshing was piled up in the corner. It would make for good bedding. Danya could not put aside her restlessness and find the peace to fall asleep. Clutching her fragrance box, she went outside into the night. The light of the moon struck the image of Satanaya on the flask as if to seduce Danya with the fragrance of enchantment.

She vividly remembered Satanaya's words: "Trust me. I will stand by your side, giving you strength and courage. Have no fear; you will overcome your obstacles. In the end, you will toss your tulips in the Rhine River, which will run red with blood. On that day, you will cherish your victory; the liberating troops will honor you for your heroic deeds. Go forth on your mission. I bless you as a child of the Nation of Circassia."

When she replaced the flask inside the wooden box, she discovered a tiny silk scroll bound with an orange ribbon. In the bluish light of the moon, she could barely make out the words written in black ink:

"My Dear Danya:

I see the stars twinkle in the beauty of your eyes, amber in color with a gold fleck.

Your angelic face draped with black curl bespeaks of mystic charms not yet revealed

You are a wonderland of Circassian magic, the enchantment of love

As I engage in battle and encounter my enemy, your magical powers will save me from mortality

To embrace you under Satanaya's veil of magic, wait for me, my darling."

It was signed, "Schorseneel," Arie's nom de guerre. She remembered that moment when he told her to keep it in the wooden box, not to read the scroll until the time had arrived.

"It's Arie's poem!" she exclaimed. Danya knew that he had practiced the art of poetry. In the early days of the Dutch resistance, verses were the language used for encrypting messages, a cryptographic method developed by the Special Operations Executive in London. This unusual method of exchanging messages in poetry aided the local resistance movement in communicating with agents in Nazi-occupied Europe. In London, at their secret intelligence meeting, they had expressed the belief that the enemy did not have it in their Germanic nature to suspect the use of poetry in cryptology. Poem coding was safely used during the war years and was easy to decipher.

Danya wondered if Arie was practicing poetry writing in his role as a double agent or whether he was creating a love story for her. She remembered that glint in his eyes during that first encounter in the castle, the look of determination. But was it just a short strand of love by a man she did not know? Tormented by her feelings for Manus, who had stood by her during the long periods of hiding from the enemy, she had to decide whether she would abandon Manus.

At last, they reached the village of Mill. They were now close to the castle. It was late spring, and the rosewoods showed their early blossoms. With the sun setting, Manus hurried on his bicycle with Danya, avoiding another night sleeping under the stars. A few cows mooed as if welcoming them home.

The last rays of the sun cast a unique glow on Danya, highlighting her features as a Circassian beauty. What made her so special were her eyes, her raven black hair, and her regal look; she was a true descendant of Queen Satanaya.

His pipe in his mouth dipped up and down with every pedal push on his bike; not a single puff of smoke had come from the old pipe; for months he had run out of tobacco. With his French beret askance on his head and his long hair flowing in the breeze, he was in full sculptor regalia, ready to arrive at his domain.

They arrived on Castle Lane when Manus started to have difficulty keeping his bicycle between the deep tracks left by the tanks. The tall trees still lined the dirt road, giving the entrance to the castle its aura of aristocracy. One more sharp turn to the left and then they should see the castle. Finally, there it was. They could make out the outline of the old structure against the starlit sky, but they saw that something was missing. Manus fell to his knees and raised his eyes to the heavens.

"Merciful Lord, is this the castle I left a year ago? Where is the water in the moat? Did the swans become war victims?" As he walked through the gate entering the courtyard, he was shocked by the devastation. He hurried through the opening where the oak doors had been. The Hall of the Knights was lit by the moon, casting an eerie glow of death over the interior. He raised his eyes and looked up into the sky with its million stars. A gaping hole replaced the roof over the Hall. Manus had to steady himself before asking the question he feared the most.

What had happened to the Stations of the Cross? He saw broken pieces of carved granite, lit by the bluish moonlight as a ghostly field of ruin. In vain, he tried to remember which part belonged to what station. The old paintings on the walls depicting the ancestors were strewn about, dislodged from their ornamental frames, like ghostlike figures staring to the heavens. The further he stumbled through the debris, the more dejected he became.

The crater in the middle of the hall told the story of this massive destruction, an errant V-1 rocket had slammed into the castle through the roof and demolished the entire back wall. After the long day travel and surveying the disastrous situation, they fell asleep in the old kitchen, amidst utensils, dishes, and broken chairs.

The next day, amongst the rubble in the Grand Hall, Danya found a metal cigar box bearing the name "Schimmelpennincks." She opened the box and showed it to Manus.

"Look what I found," she said. "A picture of Anna Maria Petrovsky, a common Circassian name. Do you know who she is?" He hesitated for a moment. To the best of his knowledge, no picture existed of Anna Maria. He never thought to find a picture of his grandmother. His father told him that no photographs existed of his mother. He reached into the box where he found a letter. They seated themselves on a block of granite and Danya studied the picture as Manus read.

"It's a love letter from Professor von Ewers, my grandfather!

'To Anna Maria, my Darling,

Whom I silently visit wherever you are

Your eyes radiating with wonder, joy, and longing

With heaving bosom, you kissed me with passion

You gave yourself to me and took me in your arms

Striving to find the words - Sheer bliss remembered forever."

Manus removed his pipe without taking his eyes from the poem. The photograph of Anna Maria captivated Danya, who was thrilled to find the image of a Circassian woman. She turned to Manus.

"If her last name is 'Petrovsky', it is one of the most recognized names in Sochi, capital of Circassia. You should feel honored having her as your grandmother," she told him. Danya's words left a deep impression on Manus. He felt a sense of pride and had never felt so close to Danya. His memory transported him back to the day he had visited Clara at Lindendale Castle when she revealed that Anna Maria was his grandmother. Back then, his heritage did not mean much to him. At that time, he could only focus on his art. Since that time, he had learned much from Danya about the origin of the Circassian people, their traditions, and culture. He never saw the connection with his family as true Circassian descendants from an aristocratic lineage. He now realized that he would be the end of the family pedigree if he had no offspring.

Desperately, he rummaged through the debris in the hall to find the early sketches he had made of Danya. Overjoyed, he rushed to Danya to show her his old drawings from ten years ago when she had first became his model.

"I looked all over for these sketches!" Manus smiled. To his surprise, the words dropped from his mouth. "The wonder of your beauty has not changed since the early days." At last, he found words to express his true feelings by listening to his inner spirit. The blue in his eyes gave away the fire of love that had been burning in him for so long.

"Every day when I see the rays of the sun light your face, they bring out the splendor of your exquisite beauty. When I look at you, my heart rejoices to be with you. Then darkness falls over me to realize that without you, I would be a miserable wretch. I have to accept that you are under the spell of Satanaya, touched by her veil of enchantment. Without you, my dear Danya, I only have the celestial night, the moon, and stars, which we shared for so many months when we were forced to sleep in the open. They will always be there as a remembrance of the time we spent together."

Danya knew she could not delay any longer telling Manus about her final mission as a war courier. She had to take care of unfinished business in the resistance. Her determination to succeed showed in her eyes, burning darker than ever before. When she saw Manus in the kitchen with his long flowing locks and bushy, unruly beard, she realized that he was no longer the sculptor she had met years ago. She had to let go of her feelings and tell Manus that she had decided to leave him and rejoin the resistance.

"I want you to know that last night was my last night here at Castle Lindendale," she began. "I am called back to my duty to serve in the Dutch Resistance to help my comrades in battle.

As soon as possible, we must end the Hunger Strike imposed by the Nazi Regime. I know that the resistance needs me urgently on the battle lines along the Rhine River."

In a trembling voice, he feebly managed a few words.

"Going into battle now, you are risking your life." Danya raised her hand as if taking the oath to her Circassian womanhood.

"It is in me to be a woman of courage to face the enemy. I must fight to the death for the freedom of Holland. I must help the resistance drive the enemy out of our land; this is how I was born and raised. We fight to the death for our beliefs. That is my pledge to Satanaya," she stated firmly. Her determination closed a chapter in Manus' life best described as "Love Unremitted." Never before had his admiration for Danya ran so deep.

She packed her travel bag with her most prized possession, including the wooden box.

Manus had forgotten about the dozen tulip bulbs in the brown bag he had set on a windowsill in the Grand Hall. He was surprised to see the Rembrandt tulips that morning as he strolled around the castle to survey the damage. He was astounded to find the forbidden tulips blooming outside the castle wall. They were not supposed to be in existence any longer. The rocket that had hit the castle had sent the bag of seven-year-old bulbs flying outside, landing amidst a pile of debris and dirt. Manus chuckled at the thought that he had rebelled against the government's order to destroy all the Rembrandt tulips in 1937 when the Agricultural Commission had placed these tulips on the list of banned products

He cut half a dozen to give to Danya on her trip to the frontline of the war. He could not find any appropriate wrapping paper, except an old newspaper.

"I do not have anything to offer as a farewell gift. Please take these first tulips of the season on your journey. When you arrive at the Moerdijk Bridge, please deposit them in the vase on the altar of the chapel by the side of the road. You will remember the statue of the Virgin Mary in the Moerdijk Chapel. We both traveled there to attend the inauguration ceremony. It was the last statue of Mary and Jesus I made for the roadway chapels program. Meanwhile, I will pray to Mary that you will be safe. I hope we will see each other again soon." A single tear rolled down into his scraggly beard. Gently, he kissed her on the cheek, searching for a final word.

"Tomorrow, we will merely be friends, but every day, I will see your eyes, bright and dark, burning with the fire of bravery. I will keep the sketches I made of you as the model for Mary of Jesus; I will treasure them forever," Manus pledged.

Danya sadly watched Manus breaking down in front of her, unable to soothe his pain. Manus sighed deeply and continued. "Now that it is over, the truth sits bitterly. I wish I could hold your hand forever."

Danya packed her satchel with food leftovers. Her role as a courier would require her to deposit silk scrolls with coded messages as close as possible to the Moerdijk Bridge. She would have to time the delivery of critical intelligence data to the Allied to coincide with the crossing of the Rhine River of the Allied tank formation. Her instructions stated that she must deliver the secret messages to the tank commander of the Royal Canadian Armored Corps, assigned to capture the Moerdijk Bridge.

The bridge was still in the hands of the German Army. The Germans were desperate to hold this strategic target. They had reinforced the command post with cement blocks and emplacements of automatic machine guns. They were confident in blocking the Canadians from crossing the Rhine by blowing up the bridge. On the German side, engineers worked all day on a ship, anchored under the bridge, placing six large explosive charges.

Living in the ruined castle by himself, Manus became a ghost figure, stumbling daily through the rubble of the demolished Stations of the Cross, still hoping to recover his carving tools. On this rainy morning, he tripped over Hitler's face-mask, lying against the wall. The piano wire still dangled from a single beam. He lifted a massive piece of granite and smashed the mask into a thousand pieces, mumbling, "So much for the Thousand Year Reich."

CHAPTER 21

Blood & Tulips

DRESSED IN GESTAPO UNIFORM, ARIE LEFT ON HIS motorcycle for Groenlo, located one hundred and forty kilometers east of the Moerdijk Bridge that connects North and South Holland over the Rhine River. The corpses in the street left a deep impression of revulsion on Arie. He knew that the German occupiers had gone too far. For four years, he had served the Germans in the disguise of a double agent. He could not continue in his dual role, now that he was face to face with the truth of the Nazi regime.

Arie, still in Gestapo uniform, had not had any food for two days. Finally, he found a place where he hoped to eat called the "Tavern Princess Irene." Packed with German officers, it smelled of sausage and cabbage. Cigarette smoke hung heavy over a table where a Wehrmacht colonel and two of his captains argued over the importance of defending the Moerdijk Bridge at all cost. It was right that the bridge served as a vital river crossing for the retreating Germans. If the bridge were to fall into Allied hands, thousands of German troops would be trapped.

No one wanted to sit with Arie in his Gestapo uniform. He sat alone in a corner, where he saw an underground paper, *The Parool*, on the table. The headline left no doubt about what had happened: "Slaughter on Texel Isle." The subtitle stunned him even more: "Circassians Kill Hundreds of Germans." He felt a lot of pride that his people had taken it upon themselves to rebel against the Germans on the island. Two years earlier, these Circassians were part of a battalion of eight hundred so-called Red Army (Russian) soldiers from the Caucasus Mountains. The German Army had captured them on the battlefields around Stalingrad and had given them a choice: become prisoners of war in Siberia or go to Holland to defend Texel Isle. They made a secret pact amongst themselves to go to Texel with the promise to rebel against the Germans and join the Allied Forces. It was a daring proposition. In February 1945, they transferred to Texel Isle. After a stay of one month, preparations started for their transfer to the Dutch mainland to oppose Allied advances.

They were still in the clutches of the Germans, but the time had come for the Circassians' rebellion. They had been waiting for this moment to take their revenge, and they were going to show it in the stealth of night, just like their forefathers had done when they mounted their defenses against their invaders in the Caucasus. Just after midnight under the leadership of Commander Shalva Loladze, they had a lot of success. The Circassians gained swift control of the entire isle. During the operation, which they had baptized "Murder in Silence," they slashed the Germans' throats with knives and bayonets while they were asleep. It was the most massive slaughter of Germans in a single night without firing a single shot. Members of the Dutch Resistance participated in the massacre. The ultimate success of the rebellion hinged on their rescue by the Allied Forces, before the Germans could send in the

Gestapo to implement their reprisal, the execution of the entire Circassian battalion. Sadly, the Allied never came to the rescue.

Because of the difficulty in traveling over land, von Habers had ordered a small aircraft, a Fokker VIII, to fly in secrecy from Wewelsburg to Texel Isle to join the Circassian rebellion. During the war, he had maneuvered to keep it a secret that he was a member of the Adyghe Intelligence Network. Once he left, he made it clear to Himmler that he would not return to the SS. He decided to put his life on the line to rescue the survivors on Texel Isle. Once he landed at Texel Isle Airport, a Circassian soldier took him by motorcycle to meet with his commander. When they turned into the township of Nieuweschild, a German sharpshooter who had survived the slaughter aimed at von Habers, killing him instantly.

Two days earlier, Arie had received a top-secret cable with orders to do everything in his power to rescue the prisoners on the ship Batavia IV moored under the Moerdijk Bridge. The Canadian tanks were closing in on the Moerdijk Bridge, and the SS had not yet made firm plans on how best to defend the bridge.

One hundred and fifty captured resistance workers were on the ship Batavia IV anchored underneath the Moerdijk Bridge. They belonged to the Knock Squads ready to use brute force to rescue downed pilots. Condemned as an archenemy of the Nazi Regime, the Germans sentenced them to the death penalty for the killing of high-level German officers.

Arie had received a coded message from the high command of the Dutch Resistance, leaving no doubt about the urgency: "All resistance workers in Rotterdam were rounded up before being liberated. Urgent Request: We must find a way to release all prisoners by any means from the ship Batavia IV." Because of Arie's high position in the underground, this rescue mission was in his hands.

He rushed towards the Moerdijk District. In the fields along the highway, he noticed the bodies of high-ranking officers lying face down. He wondered if their officers had executed them. He also had heard rumors of mass suicides among the German officers now that they were losing the war. As a display of ultimate loyalty to the tenets of the Nazi Party, they preferred to kill themselves by biting the cyanide pill rather than become prisoners of war.

However, not all German officers wanted to end their lives, and they searched for a way to get leniency after the war during a post-war trial. They turned coward, worrying about their post-war treatment as war criminals. Some German officers boldly contacted the Dutch Underground trying to cut a deal to save their lives.

Arie hoped to find the German commander in charge of the bridge so he could negotiate for his post-war leniency. The release of the detainees on board the vessel anchored under the bridge was at stake. Arie had to convince the commander to set the prisoners free immediately. As a high-ranking officer in the Gestapo himself, he felt encouraged to succeed. However, it would not be easy. SS officers had control over the bridge control post. They had no respect for Gestapo and Arie knew it.

He was driving at breakneck speed on his motorcycle to arrive before dusk. It started to rain, which slowed him down. In Gestapo uniform, he managed to breeze through the checkpoints with nothing more than a salute by the sentries. As he approached the five-kilometer marker to the bridge, he heard heavy artillery coming from the West. Undeterred, he continued on his motorcycle in the opposite direction from the retreating German troops.

Inside the block hut on the bridge, the German commander was busy preparing the heavy explosives for the ship under the bridge.

"Look over there, Lieutenant Weissler," he said, pointing to a wooden box in the corner. The words, "Schwere Sprengstoff! Nur Brücke Demolierung Gebrauch" (heavy explosives only for use on bridges) were on the box. "There is no time to waste!" said the commander. "Lower the engineers immediately to the ship to install the explosives. Make sure they connect the wiring to the detonator box in our office. We must destroy the entire ship and kill all the prisoners at once, so the Allied will never find out who was on board."

The famous Moerdijk Chapel with the statue of the Virgin Mary came into Arie's view. He saw an old bicycle leaning against the sidewall and wondered who was inside.

As he approached the bridge, he realized the life or death situation he was in, running his tongue over his tooth implanted with the cyanide capsule. Two hundred meters up the bridge, Arie noticed the sentinels silhouetted against the evening sky, marching across the road, holding their automatic weapons at the ready. Shells fell closer and closer to the river, not far from where the control post was. When they saw Arie approaching, they suddenly directed their automatic weapons at his motorcycle. Once he was upon them, they led him to park on the side of the control block. Inside, Arie noticed SS Commander Rudenskranz, an old guard military man from the early days of the SS and Himmler. He wore a monocle and smoked a thin cigarillo. They exchanged the usual "Heil Hitlers" unenthusiastically. It was clear to Arie that he was still in the fight for the Third Reich, but just barely. For Arie to encounter such a hardened old school SS officer spelled nothing but trouble. He thought that most officers with a brain had given up on winning the war.

For years, internal strife between the SS and Gestapo had been mounting. With the defeat in Russia and the invasion of the Allied, their antipathy had only sharpened. The Wehrmacht soldiers of the German Army avoided both as deadly enemies. Arie was shocked to find himself become a prisoner of the Germans.

They took his pistol and tied his wrists and ankles tightly with thick rope. His fingers turned blue and numb. Of the two lightbulbs hanging from the ceiling, only one was working. The room smelled of cheap cigarette smoke. The SS commander removed his cigarillo and leaned into Arie's face.

"What is your mission?" he growled. "You have no business being here on the bridge." Arie noticed that he had one front tooth missing, which made him look like a Hun of centuries back. Arie refused to reply. His training taught him not to show any fear. He looked straight into the eyes of the commander. The commander walked to a file cabinet. The SS was responsible for running the labor and death camps for citizens from foreign nations, giving them the authority to override the Gestapo. The SS also kept a close watch over all intelligence operations. Arie wondered if they had learned about his affiliation with the secret Adyghe Intelligence Network.

He placed Arie's file on the table next to a black box. The red button on top of the box glared at Arie like the eye of a dangerous monster. Suddenly, a couple of shells fell close to the control block. The commander looked outside and turned to face Arie. He leaned into his face again, and in a throaty voice, questioned Arie about his nom de guerre. It came as a surprise.

"For sure, you must know the word 'Schorseneel.'" The German stuttered with the pronunciation. As he tried to pronounce the letters, he was embarrassed, as spit flew between the gap in his teeth. Arie chuckled as the German struggled with this typically Dutch word.

"Where did you learn to pronounce 'Schorseneel?'" Arie taunted. "You have not learned yet to pronounce it correctly. Why do you bother? You already have my name on file."

Now in the clutches of the SS, Arie's military status became rapidly mute. Following his training in the Dutch Resistance, he remembered the tactics to use during interrogation while being tortured. He had developed the ability to block from his memory any information about the Dutch Resistance, the Allied, and Adyghe.

When Arie clammed up and remained motionless, the commander became infuriated. Matters got worse when they found *The Parool* resistance newsletter in his pocket. Arie decided not to wait any longer and made it clear what he wanted to accomplish.

"I came here to negotiate the release of the detainees on the Batavia IV. I demand that you release them immediately!" Arie commanded.

"What makes you think that you have the authority to demand anything?" the commander sneered in a biting tone.

Arie knew he had to play his trump card and not show any weakness. "I speak to you as an officer of the Gestapo. I command your respect. The Allied know that the Batavia IV holds 150 top-ranked resistance workers from Rotterdam, destined to Bergen-Belsen in Germany. Your ship cannot outrun the advances of the Canadians. You better make a deal now to release them, to save your neck." At Wewelsburg Castle, as an SS officer, he had taken the oath of allegiance to Hitler and Himmler, swearing to serve the fatherland to the death. He jumped on Arie, ripping the military medals from his uniform and throwing them across the room. Arie became even more obstinate.

"If you do not agree with my demand, I have requested of the Allies that you be sentenced to die by hanging from the Moerdijk Bridge!" Arie threatened.

"There will be no release for these Rotterdam tugs and renegades on board the Batavia IV. They must suffer severe punishment!" declared the commander. "We have prepared a special method of execution for these prisoners." He signaled his lieutenants to start the SS torture, landing blow after blow on Arie's back and head with their truncheons.

"We will not kill you before we have caused maximum pain in retaliation for the suffering you have brought to the German Armed Forces in Holland!" the commander yelled over the sounds of Arie's groans. The blows came faster and faster until one of them hit him in the eye, which fell shut. Blood dripped from the corner of his mouth. The agent sneaked up behind Arie and forced a dirty rag over both eyes. He tied it around his head, causing excruciating pain. Blood trickled from his nose and ears as he fell unconscious. He no longer felt pain. He couldn't hear or see what was going on. The commander ordered the detonator placed in front of Arie.

"Why are you waiting? Slam his head into the red button! Fire!" In a flash, the lieutenant smashed Arie's head into the red button. In a split second, the explosion rocked the bridge on its pilings, causing an inferno of obliteration and destruction in the water. Body parts started to float, creating a bloodstained river. The shock from the blasts lifted the block hut from its foundation and broke the glass in the windows.

The commander looked at Arie's motionless body slumped on the wooden table, his face turned towards one side, one eye closed.

"Throw this despicable agent on the bridge … we will give the Canadian tanks the opportunity to crush him to death. Killing a Gestapo agent violates our military code." He paused, and then continued, "On the other hand, delivering this double agent may help us in case we are captured and tried for war crimes."

Two SS guards dragged the lifeless body outside and dumped him in the middle of the road to the bridge. When his head hit the pavement, the suicide capsule popped out of his mouth and rolled down the bridge.

Just then, an artillery shell made a direct hit on the block hut, killing the commander and everyone inside. The two guards on the bridge fled in their vehicle, undamaged in the explosion. In the little chapel on the bridge, Danya hunkered down behind the statue of the Virgin Mary, praying for protection from mayhem. The explosion underneath the bridge shook the little chapel. Miraculously, the statue of the Virgin was not damaged. She retrieved the silk scroll with critical military data from her satchel and readied herself to hand deliver it to the Canadians. She listened for a lull in the shelling. Suddenly, it was quiet when she peeked through the chapel door to see where the Germans had gone. She saw that there was nothing left of the control post. When she approached the structure in ruin, she noticed four SS lying motionless in the rubble. She ran to the roadway in the bridge where she saw a human figure lying in a crumpled position. She had no idea who this person might be.

Noticing the tattered Gestapo uniform and not knowing who the officer was, she approached him cautiously. She knelt beside him and turned toward his bloodied face. With the orange-colored cloth she had found in the chapel, she wiped his face clean. Abruptly, she backed off, startled. "Arie!" Unsure whether he was alive, she whispered in his bloody ear. "It is me, Danya." He failed to react.

The shelling from the Canadian tanks overhead resumed in full fury, chasing the German Army in the direction of Germany. She must stop the Canadian tanks trundling over the bridge, four abreast. The tanks spewed fire from all guns, sending shell after shell over Danya's head. The massive whooshing noise was like a firestorm killing an enemy that could no longer resist.

In the chaos, Danya mustered the courage to jump up and run straight into the on-rushing tank phalanx. She must stop them from rolling over Arie. Above her head, she frantically waved the bloodied strip of orange cloth. As if by miracle, the tanks stopped the shelling and came to a halt. Through his binoculars, the tank commander saw this diminutive figure energetically brandishing her banner. Not sure what to make of the situation, he climbed out of the tank with his pistol at the ready. Danya held her position in the middle of the bridge while signaling for them to stop. He looked at his lieutenant.

"You want to see real courage? Look at that girl. Who is she? Who would have the courage to stop our tanks? Does she not have any regard for her life? Or is her cause so great she is willing to sacrifice her life?"

"Stop! Stop the tanks! Help him!" Danya screamed at the approaching Canadian officers, desperately pointing to the body in the road. "You must help him! Save his life!" With his pistol at the ready, the officer demanded to know who he was.

"He is Gestapo. Who is he?" Together, they walked up to Arie.

"Please hurry! We must help him!" Danya said in a worried voice. "If I tell you his war name, you will understand."

"Do tell us right now," he urged.

"Schorseneel is his nom de guerre in the Dutch Resistance. In London, they will recognize him right away at MI-6. The reason for his Gestapo uniform is he is a Dutch Resistance double agent. An hour ago, the SS in the block hut on the bridge tried to kill him. They threw him on the bridge. Hurry! He is bleeding to death!" Her words were enough for the commander to signal a field ambulance to transport Arie to a hospital. Danya watched the ambulance disappear to the rear of the tank formation.

The tank commander thanked her for the rescue, and when she handed him the silk scroll with the encrypted message containing vital information about the German troops' movements, he saluted her. A cold rain started to fall. Danya sought refuge in the chapel. She knelt at the little bench in front of the statue of Mary and said a prayer of thanks. Raindrops falling from cracks in the ceiling of the small chapel mingled with her tears.

With a thunderous noise, the tanks rattled down the bridge towards Germany. When they came closer, the commander raised his arm to halt the tank phalanx one more time. He opened the hatchet in the gun turret and faced the girl who stood on the steps watching the tanks parade by her.

"I salute you as a true war hero of the highest order," the commander addressed Danya. "You have fulfilled your mission of delivering important information to rid Holland of the Nazis. We needed this intelligence to organize our strategies and defeat the enemy, liberating Holland from the curse of famine."

As the tanks rolled by, Danya waved the blood-stained banner in one hand and held the tulips in the other. Her tears mingled with the raindrops, as she murmured, "Free at last at such a high price." She took one last look at the beautiful flowers and walked towards the bridge. She looked down over the railing into the blood-stained waters of the Rhine River, where an hour earlier, 150 prisoners had perished in the explosions. She saw the bodies of her resistance comrades floating down the river as she wept and tossed the tulips in the Rhine.

"These are the last Rembrandt tulips the world will ever see," she said. "It only fits that they join the remains of these true heroes who sacrificed their lives for the Dutch Resistance."

EPILOGUE

The End of the War

THE TOWNSPEOPLE RAISED THEIR EYES TO THE church tower, waiting for the church bells to toll, celebrating the surrender of the German Army in Holland. The familiar ringing of church bells on Sunday mornings never came. Years ago, the Germans had removed the bells and shipped them to Germany where they melted them into cannons. The bronze from the bells in their churches had killed so many. Now the survivors looked up to the heavens for their ringing once more. The silence was deafening, a reminder of the five years of war under the repressive regime of the Nazis.

The war in Europe had finally ended, but in the little towns, the effects of the war were still evident. In Holland, the surrender came five days after Hitler committed suicide in his Berlin bunker. Despite his demise, hundreds perished during this five-day period. The Dutch wondered why it took five more days of killing before General Blaskowitz signed the surrender agreement on May 5, 1945, at a meeting in Wageningen. Holland was the last nation where Germany officially surrendered.

The Hunger Winter had weakened the Dutch people to such a degree that there was no energy left for celebrations. With coupons in hand, they stood in line with the hope of getting a scrap of food. The shelves in the food stores were mostly empty. A Canadian military truck entered the town with dried food provisions, dropped from the air in a field outside of town. Finally, word reached London about the desperate food shortages, so severe that people were collapsing in the streets. So far, the Hunger Winter had claimed 300,000 lives.

Danya had become anxious to find out what had happened to her parents. She returned to Belgium, her homeland, to search for them. On the train to Antwerp, Danya felt lonely, exhausted, and empty, awash with self-doubt about her future. She knew she must let go of bygones, unburdening herself of the weight of the past. It was difficult to convince herself that something new and beautiful was on the horizon. Returning to her birthplace, she prepared herself for a new chapter in her young life.

In Antwerp, trams to the suburbs started to run again in November, soon after the liberation of the city. Victoria Place was now the new name for Central Square. Music streamed from the restaurants, where the menus resembled again what they had offered before the war: Pommes Frites and Mussels, Trout a la Meunière, Riz de Veau and Belgian Waffles, Coupe Glacée for dessert. Danya had no money to spend on food. At Victoria Place, she found tram #63 to Brasschaat.

The closer the tram arrived to her birthplace, the more frightened she became. Overwhelmed by fear, not knowing whether her parents had survived the war, she struggled to find inner peace. They had been out of touch since she had joined the resistance three years ago.

What would await her in Brasschaat? She had another half hour to go before she would reach her destination. She reached into her satchel and found the weathered copy of the poem her father had composed ten years earlier. She started to read: "The moment I laid eyes on you and crowned you with your name, I knew my life would never be the same."

Her father could not have known how much the circumstances of war would change their lives. She re-read the last line in the poem: "But the end was just a beginning."

Had she arrived at the threshold of a new beginning? The thought of her parents' mansion in Brasschaat brought back memories of yesterday. It was here in her father's study that she had listened to the sacred words of Satanaya, Queen of Circassia. Her words of wisdom that foretold the end of the war: "I will be by your side to give you strength; you will witness war and famine, maiming and killing. You will be victorious; you will be hailed for your heroic deeds by the liberating forces. In the end, your prince for life will arrive. Remember, as a child of the Nation of Circassia; you will have the strength to reach your destiny." Satanaya's words had always given her a ray of hope.

Arriving in her hometown, Danya immediately went to the Rubens Restaurant, where she hoped to find someone who might know the whereabouts of her parents. Years ago, she had joined her father at this restaurant to meet the representative of the King of Belgium to discuss the diamonds for Queen Astrid's necklace. The restaurateur had aged during the war. His hair was now shoulder length, and his eyes glazed over; he looked famished. He held the daily menu card in his trembling hand. He could no longer get the special foods that made the elite in town come to his establishment.

"How can I be of help?" he asked Danya in a broken voice.

"You may not remember me," she began. "I came here with my father for an important meeting. I am Danya, daughter of Kadir Mandraskit." His eyes lit up as he reconnected with the past.

"Mandraskit? You are Danya?" he asked.

"I am looking for news about my parents."

"Two months ago, they were here asking about you. The last time they heard of your whereabouts, you were living in Holland. After that, they lost track of you."

"Where are they staying now?" she asked eagerly.

"Go to the Winkel Straat, where the Red Cross has set up the Refugee and Recovery Center." Danya's eyes widened with joy. She thanked him and rushed to the Red Cross center a few blocks away. At one time, Brasschaat was one of the most beautiful suburbs of Antwerp, where the rich and famous lived in their mansions. Heavily damaged as the result of bombardments, the homes now lay in ruin. Military equipment of all sorts was left abandoned in the front yards, what used to be landscaped lawns and flowerbeds. It was all so different from what she remembered.

She had feared this moment. Finally, she turned into the avenue where her parents had lived. With trepidation, she glanced through the lane of trees to catch a quick glimpse of their mansion. At the entrance to their domain, the wrought iron sign with the old Circassian name: "Adyghe" lay rusting in the tall grass. When she reached the mansion, horror struck her; their property had not escaped the ransacking by the fleeing Germans. She recognized a broken chair in the pond and saw their antique grandfather clock stuck upside down in the murky water. Where there had been a manicured lawn, weeds grew waist deep. At first, she did not dare enter the mansion. When she entered the opening where the front door had been, she saw the familiar birdcage. With the cage door wide open, she wondered what had happened to her beloved canary. *Had someone let it fly away to be free? Did it die from starvation?*

When she arrived at the Red Cross, large crowds stood around, some silently weeping, some rejoicing. Here, one would find out about relatives. Feeling alone and frightened, she entered the large hall, where she noticed all four walls covered with handwritten names. Unsure where to start, one list caught her attention: "Returnees from Concentration Camps." She panicked, wondering if she would find her parents' names here. Her family name was not there. She checked another list. Nothing. In the corner, she noticed a list of "Missing in War." Horror struck her when she saw her name: Danya Mandraskit. She was not sure how to react to this announcement. *Had her parents listed her as missing?* In anguish, she ran to the desk where volunteer workers were busy helping others. She had to wait in line like everyone else. Then her turn came.

"I saw my name on the list in the corner. Can you tell me who asked for me?" she asked. The worker took the dossier of Missing Persons, and when she found Danya Mandraskit, she pointed to her father's name: Kadir Mandraskit.

"Your father was here two weeks ago to register you as missing," the worker said. "It says in the register that they are staying at Calixberg Castle." Danya knew this property well, located seven blocks from where her parents used to live.

When she opened the heavy oak door to the castle, Gerda immediately recognized Danya. She was a former schoolmate. They embraced and looked at each other, as if to say, "We made it through this horrible time!"

"Come in! I am so happy to see you! You will make someone even happier. I have a surprise for you!" she smiled. Danya heard shuffling footsteps coming from the darkened hallway. He walked slightly stooping with a limp. He stretched his arms to embrace his girl. Danya wondered if this man was her father. The once proud Circassian patriarch of the Mandraskit family had turned into a ghost-like figure. He turned his head to see if his wife had followed him; she was not there. She was unaware of the goings on upfront; she had lost her hearing. Gerda went to gather her from the foyer where she spent her days recovering from prison life. She led her by the arm and moved her to where Danya was standing. A single tear rolled down her cheek as she laid her daughter's hands in hers, her face radiating the joy of a mother meeting her daughter, missed for such a long time. She was lost for words, gently stroking her cheek and touching Danya's raven black curls. She took a second look at her, pausing to admire her, unblemished by the war, still a Circassian beauty.

"I am so relieved that we are together." Her father looked Danya in the eyes. "Our Circassian spirit gave us the courage we needed to survive. The Germans tried to destroy us but to no avail. Our determination made us survive, and now we are together to rebuild our family tradition, in the spirit of our ancestors."

He was short of breath. Little by little, they did their best to share war stories. Danya decided to leave out the time she spent in jail in Wewelsburg and the verdict of the Lebensborn Program in exchange for her death sentence. During a pause in recounting their war stories, Kadir got up from his chair and shuffled to another room, leaving Danya with her mother. He needed time alone, reflecting on his role as a Circassian patriarch.

"I prayed for this moment for the longest time," her mother told her in this solitary moment. "We worried so much about you."

"I will be fine. I look forward to my future." Her mother slowly raised her eyes and smiled. With a wink, she inquired, "Did the fragrance bottle I gave you on your birthday survive the war?" Danya grabbed her satchel that she had kept with her during the war. She reached inside for the wooden box and opened it to show the perfume flask. A glow of happiness came over her mother's face. They looked at each other in silence. Proud of her daughter that she had kept her promise not to open it until the time had arrived, her mother reached for the flask. She still found the energy to uncork it and place a dab of the sweet-smelling cologne on her fingertip. She let Danya take a whiff, like a rite of passage. They took pleasure in the exquisite essence, known in Circassian circles as the "Fragrance of the Temptress."

"My girl, I feel that your time has come to meet your prince for life," her mother said.

It was early afternoon when Danya retired to her room. She placed a few dabs of the perfume behind her ears, relishing the bouquet of the mixture of three exotic scents. She recalled the words in the *Nart Sagas*: "The Circassian women were not only beautiful, but they applied the fragrance of the temptress as an aphrodisiac." For centuries, it was a secret kept strictly within the sorority of Circassian beauties.

She looked out the window where she saw the house cat stalking a field mouse in the rose bushes. Before leaving on her walk in the forest, she followed the Circassian tradition to light a candle in the candleholder. A yearning spread in her. It made her relaxed and playful.

As long as she stayed on the narrow path meandering through the trees, the forest was safe from landmines. She could hear the new leaves unfurl from their winter buds. Wildflowers abounded in a display of rainbow colors. She followed the path to an opening in the rhododendrons in full bloom with their red, pink, and white flowers. There, as if she opened a curtain to the atrocities of the war, she laid her eyes on acres of disabled war vehicles and equipment collected from the region. German and Canadian cannons, tanks, and burned out jeeps sat side by side; she wondered if they had finally made peace. The sound of the loud booms of shells exploding around the Moerdijk Bridge resounded in her mind. Images of soldiers dying in the broken tanks before her lingered in her thoughts. In this same field, a landmine had killed the parish priest as he returned from his priestly duty of administering the last rites to a German soldier.

In the distance, she saw young boys playing war games, jumping on artillery guns, climbing in and out of tanks. They played the dangerous game of detonating bullets found in the fields with hammer and nail. She had a difficult time watching the youth of this nation playing with the toys of a war that had ended only a month ago.

As she readied herself to return to the castle, she spotted a motorcycle missing a front wheel. The license plate was still hanging from the handlebar: SIPO 241, Arie's dog-tag number in the Gestapo. She wondered how his motorcycle had ended up in this field. *What had happened to him? Had he survived?* How could she forget the horrific condition she had found him in on the road?

A light fog fell over the wrecks of broken vehicles, pulling a curtain over the atrocities of war. The sun sank rapidly behind the big rhododendrons. When she turned away from the scene of carnage, a streak of sadness spread through her like dark fire. The baseness of the war overwhelmed her.

She heard a single hoot from an owl sitting on a low-hanging branch, eyes fixated on her. The same owl, who had spoken to her father in the woods a long time ago, was now with her. *Was it a call from her little brother who had died before she was born?* He would have been the only Mandraskit son, destined to be the patriarch of the family. Did he know what happened on the bridge? Was he trying to find out if she had lived up to the tradition of Circassia, delivering heroic feats? She stared back into the eyes of the owl.

"I did my best as a courier in the resistance," she murmured. "I tried to live up to the expectations as a Circassian. Satanaya gave me the courage to follow my path of destiny." The owl flew to the next tree and perched on the highest branch, curious to find out what was to come next.

It was eerily silent as dusk fell deeper over the woods. On the side of the path, she walked where young ferns were unfurling their fronds in light patterns. The temptation of the lilies-of-the-valley in full bloom was too much not to pluck a few. She rejoiced in the shape of each little bell-shaped flower dangling from the stem. The sweetly scented aroma comingled with the bouquet of fragrance from the Bottle of Enchantment. The stillness of the forest accentuated her feelings of loneliness.

Then she saw the shadow of a tall, lanky figure searching, feeling his way through a cloud of mist, hanging close to the forest floor. *He spotted the figure of a beautiful young woman.* He hastened his step. As he approached her, Danya saw the scar on his forehead. She remembered the wound over his eye. For sure, it was Arie.

He gently pulled her towards him. The shreds of doubt about how Danya would react to his tenderness started to unravel. The sky turned dark with long threads of mauves deepening the pink background. As he enveloped her in his arms, her head spun light and throbbing. The forest trees seemed to shake unsteadily around her. In the space of one day, her life's saga had changed for good. She had waited this long to be in the arms of her prince. She was calm now and rested her head against his shoulder, as she shook off the remembrance of the baseness of war. She felt his fingers interlocking with hers.

Dazed by the beauty of her exotic looks, he admired her eyes, reminiscent of Cleopatra. His emotions let loose as he gently pulled her closer. She trembled as he kissed her gently on the lips. She lifted her eyes and locked in with his blue eyes shining ever so vibrantly and vigorously. The memories of the war slowly drained from their spirit.

The air cooled into a thick layer of fog, engulfing the young couple in a cocoon of intimacy. Arie took her hand, kissing her and breathing in the fragrance of her secret perfume. She rested against a tree and looked at him in admiration. Her hero had arrived.

"You are the one I have been waiting for," she said, tilting her head and closing her eyes. He held her in his embrace, as thoughts of war atrocities slowly faded, making room for the ecstasy of love. Arie decided to unburden himself from a flashback to the days when she belonged to his brother.

"While you were with my brother, I held back my true feelings for you." She unlocked her eyes and looked over his shoulder.

"I only married Manus to protect myself from deportation by the Nazis," she told him.

"I remember all too well," Arie answered. "I was the one who told you to marry him. I did not want to give you up, but you were his model. You belonged to him. At that time, I saw in his eyes how much he loved you." He touched her cheek as she gazed in admiration at her hero, the double agent who had survived against all odds.

"When I was left to die on the bridge, you brought me back to life," Arie told her. "When you touched me with your banner, I could breathe again. I saw the love in your eyes. The inner strength of the Circassian spirit is with us now forever." He looked at the lilies-of-the-valley she had plucked earlier. "You are more beautiful than all the flowers in the world," Arie said, kissing her lips. "Our love will last forever," he whispered.

"Satanaya semper fiat!"

When (Professor) Habers, Arie, and Manus came together as Circassians, it was as if destiny had brought them there for a particular reason. They gathered to protect Danya from further harm. In unison, they experienced a sense of tribal pride. In times like these, when Circassians congregate, they followed their ancestors' tradition of secrecy and solidarity in purpose. Circassian males took an oath to protect their women to the death.

Together, they marched through the grand hall meandering through the maze of the Stations of the Cross. For the first time, Habers admired the life-size figures created by Manus. In the darkened room, the half-finished monuments loomed like tombstones in a cemetery. In reality, the rough granite blocks represented the work of a sculptor who had lost his zeal for the project as the result of the war.

Towards the back of the hall, a single beam of light from a broken window fell on Hitler's death mask. Habers grinned. With one eyebrow raised over his monocle, he chuckled and shook his head. He didn't need to use words to express his feelings.

Habers faced a difficult situation, having to pressure Danya to join the Lebensborn Project, to which the SS had sentenced her as a condition of her release from jail. If she refused, she would meet the execution squad. He wondered if he would have the courage to defy Himmler. With a gesture of his long-fingered professorial hands, he started. "I brought Danya back to you, Manus, and rescued her from the clutches of Himmler. Her dossier showed that she committed an act of treason, distributing illegal propaganda hostile to the Nazi Regime in Holland, punishable by execution. In some odd way, I convinced the SS Council in Wewelsburg that her crime, although an act of treason, was, in fact, an act of courage. I convinced them that she had acted out of patriotism. The SS leaders are practical people. With the large hordes of German prisoners of war in Russia, the shortage of soldiers was becoming clear. For this reason, the officers in Wewelsburg decided to commute her death sentence on condition that she join Lebensborn and procreate Aryan soldiers. The officers gradually became convinced that the commutation of her death sentence was in the best interest of Germany."

Danya had already made up her mind that she would never agree to the deal Habers had made to save her life. She would rather sacrifice her life than submit to Nazi rule.

"Joining Lebensborn is worse than the death sentence!" she shouted at Habers. "Never. My dignity and pride as a Circassian mean too much to me. Pull your pistol and kill me here and now." Her eyes shot bullets at him.

His Circassian background compelled him to find a way to absolve her from the Lebensborn sentence. Not sure how he could handle this situation, he clearly understood the consequence of acquitting Danya from the obligation of joining Lebensborn; he would be signing his death warrant.

Arie stepped forward and spoke the magical words, invoking the Code of Ethics of Circassia. "As true Circassians, we must stand by Danya and save her. Remember the oath that every Circassian takes: 'To protect the Circassian woman to the death.' It is the code of every Circassian warrior of yesterday and today, as it has been for thousands of years. We shall fight for her and keep her out of the Lebensborn Project." Habers looked at Arie and Manus and nodded in consent. He decided to be a true Circassian, despite his Gestapo uniform.